The Sign of the Stranger

by

William Le Queux

The Sign of the Stranger
by William Le Queux

ISBN: 978-93-59955-99-5

Published by

DOUBLE 9 BOOKS
2/13-B, Ansari Road
Daryaganj, New Delhi – 110002
info@double9books.com
www.double9books.com
Tel. 011-40042856

ABOUT THE AUTHOR

Anglo-French journalist and author William Tufnell Le Queux was born on July 2, 1864, and died on October 13, 1927. He was also a diplomat (honorary consul for San Marino), a traveler (in Europe, the Balkans, and North Africa), a fan of flying (he presided over the first British air meeting at Doncaster in 1909), and a wireless pioneer who played music on his own station long before radio was widely available. However, he often exaggerated his own skills and accomplishments. The Great War in England in 1897 (1894), a fantasy about an invasion by France and Russia, and The Invasion of 1910 (1906), a fantasy about an invasion by Germany, are his best-known works. Le Queux was born in the city. The man who raised him was English, and his father was French. He went to school in Europe and learned art in Paris from Ignazio (or Ignace) Spiridon. As a young man, he walked across Europe and then made a living by writing for French newspapers. He moved back to London in the late 1880s and managed the magazines Gossip and Piccadilly. In 1891, he became a parliamentary reporter for The Globe. He stopped working as a reporter in 1893 to focus on writing and traveling.

CONTENTS

Chapter One
The Advent of the Stranger

The shabby stranger seated himself familiarly in a nook beside the wide-open chimney of the tap-room, and stretched out his long thin legs with a sigh.

"I want something to eat; a bit of cold meat, or bread and cheese— anything you have handy—and a glass of beer. I'm very tired."

The village publican, scanning the stranger's features keenly, moved slowly to execute the command and lingered over the cutting of the meat. The other seemed to read the signs like a flash, for he roughly drew out a handful of money, saying in his bluff outspoken way—

"Be quick, mister! Here's money to pay for it." The meal was very nimbly and swiftly placed before him; and then the landlord, with a glance back at me seated in his own little den beyond, turned off the suspicion with a remark about the warmth of the weather.

"Yes, it is a bit hot," said the stranger, a tall, thin, weary-looking man of about forty, from whose frayed clothes and peaked hat I put down to be a seafarer. "Phew! I've felt it to-day—and I'm not so strong, either."

"Have you come far, sir?" deferentially inquired the innkeeper who, having taken down his long clay, had also taken measure of his customer and decided that he was no ordinary tramp.

The other stopped his eating, looked Warr, the publican, full in the face in a curious, dreamy fashion, and then sighed—

"Yes, a fair distance—a matter of ten or eleven thousand miles."

The landlord caught his breath, and I noticed that he looked still more earnestly into the stranger's weather-beaten face.

"Ah! maybe you've been abroad—to America?" he remarked, striking a match and holding it in his fingers before lighting his pipe.

"I have, and a good many other places as well," answered the tramp thoughtfully, resting and trying the point of the knife on the hard deal table before him. "I'm a wanderer—I am, but, by Jove!" he added, "it is real good

The Sign of the Stranger | 9

to see these green English fields once again. When I was out yonder I never thought I'd see them any more—these old thatched houses, the old church, and the windmill that generally wants a sail."

"You speak as though you know Sibberton—" the landlord said, and then he stopped uneasily.

The customer, who saw in an instant that his slip of the tongue had nearly betrayed him, answered—

"No, unfortunately I don't. I—well, I've never been in these parts before." And from where I stood I detected by the man's keen, dark eyes that he was not speaking the truth. The innkeeper, too, was puzzled.

"This place seems a pretty spot," the shabby wayfarer went on. "How far is it to Northampton?"

"Twelve miles."

The stranger sighed, glanced across at the old grandfather clock, and went on eating. There was silence after this, broken only by the buzzing of the flies against the window close to him, and the placing or adjusting of the tumblers which Warr had gravely begun to polish.

"Let's see," remarked the stranger reflectively at last, "if this is Sibberton, the old Earl of Stanchester lives here, I suppose?"

"He did live here, but he died a year ago."

"And young Lord Sibberton has come into the property—eh? Why, he must be one of the richest men in England," the fellow remarked with something of a sneer.

"They say he is," was Warr's reply.

Mention of the name of Stanchester caused me to prick my ears, for I had been private secretary to the old Earl and was now acting in that same capacity to the young man who had recently succeeded to the estates.

"And his sister, the fair one—Lady Lolita they call her—is she married yet?" inquired the half-famished man.

"No. She still lives with her brother and his wife up at the Hall."

The stranger grunted, and I noticed that he smiled faintly for the first time, but just at that moment he turned and catching sight of my back through the half-opened door, started slightly and appeared to be somewhat embarrassed.

Why did he make that inquiry regarding Lolita, I wondered? My father, Sir George Woodhouse, having been an intimate friend of the old Earl's, and his aide-de-camp when he was Viceroy of India, I had been taken into the latter's confidential service as soon as I came down from Cambridge, and for the past ten years had lived as a careless bachelor in a pleasant old ivy-covered house at the end of the village, being treated more as one of the Stanchester family than as the millionaire landowner's confidential secretary. The present Earl had been at Cambridge with me, and there was a strong bond of friendship between us.

"Yours has been a strange life," said the publican at last, in order to obtain more details of the stranger and his motive for inquiring after the people at the Hall.

"It has; I've drifted half over the world, but the passion for wandering is now pretty well worn out of me," wearily responded the other, taking a sip at his beer. "They say there's no place like home. I used to think so when the ship was steaming over the blue sea at nights with all asleep below and the clear stars shining over me. I don't think I shall live long; that's why I'm back again once more in England. But," he added, "we were talking of Lol—er, I mean Lady Lolita. Isn't she even engaged?"

"Not that I know of," answered the innkeeper. "If she were, some of the servants would be sure to chatter. There ain't much as goes on up at the Hall without me knowing it."

The estimable Warr was right. The tap-room of the *Stanchester Arms* was the village forum where the footmen, stablemen, kennel-hands and others employed in the Earl's great establishment assembled nightly to drink beer and discuss the gossip of the day.

"Ah! I suppose she's just as beautiful as ever?" remarked the stranger reflectively. His voice quivered oddly, and he rose wearily, brushing the knees of his frayed and shiny trousers. "She's one of the prettiest women in all England," added the ragged wayfarer, whose inquiries seemed to me to be made with some distinct purpose.

"She's lovely," declared Warr. "The papers often have portraits of her. Perhaps you've seen them?"

"Yes, I have," he answered, and the words came out with something like a groan.

At that instant there reached our ears the familiar jingle of harness bells, and Warr, turning quickly, cried —

"Why, she's just coming along! You'll see her in a moment!" And they both dashed to the small diamond-paned window which looked out upon the village street.

The stranger stood with his dark eyes peering out, his body drawn back as though fearing recognition, until a few moments later, when a smart victoria and pair of chestnuts dashed passed, and lolling within, beneath a pale blue sunshade, was the sweet-faced woman in white returning to the Hall after making afternoon calls.

"Ah!" he gasped as the marvellous beauty of that countenance burst upon him, and was next instant lost to view as the jingling bells receded. "You're right!" he said, turning from the window sadly, his face blanched. "She's more beautiful than ever—she's absolutely lovely!"

The man was a mystery. He attracted me.

The publican remained gravely silent, utterly at a loss to understand the stranger's meaning, while at that moment the latter apparently recollected my proximity, for he looked across towards where I, having had business with the innkeeper, still stood awaiting his return.

Suddenly turning to Warr, he said—

"I notice you have a gentleman in the parlour, there. I wonder whether you would give me just a couple of minutes alone? I want to ask you a question."

The landlord again glanced suspiciously at the mysterious stranger, but seeing the earnest, determined look upon his grizzled face, rather reluctantly consented, and conducted his customer across the low entrance-hall to a room on the opposite side, the door of which he closed behind them.

What transpired therein was in secret, but about five minutes later I heard the door open again, and the stranger, with heavy tread, walk firmly to the door.

"You won't forget the name," he called back to Warr in a strange hard voice just before he went forth. "Richard Keene—K-e-e-n-e."

"I've promised. Trust me," was the innkeeper's response, while a moment later the shabby stranger's form cast a long shadow across the sanded tap-room and vanished.

"That's a queer customer?" I remarked to Warr when he returned to me, for I had come down to pay him an account. "I don't like the look of him somehow."

"Neither do I," the landlord answered. "At first I took him for a burglar spying around to ascertain who was at home up at the Hall, but I've formed a very different conclusion during the past five minutes. He isn't a burglar, but he's somebody who evidently knows Lady Lolita."

"Knows her?" I exclaimed, surprised. "What do you mean? What did he tell you in private?"

"Nothing. He asked me to render him a service by giving a letter in secret to her ladyship, and as recompense gave me this." And opening his hand, Warr showed me a sovereign. "Something fresh, this!" he added. "A tramp who gives sovereign tips;" and he laughed very heartily to himself.

I did not join in his laughter, for on being handed the letter I saw it was inscribed to her ladyship and marked "Private" in a neat educated hand, and sealed with black wax with an unfamiliar coat-of-arms bearing a coronet and many quarterings.

"He told me also to tell her that Richard Keene has returned, and said that she would understand. Strange, ain't it?" observed the landlord, with a long pull at his clay.

"Very. If you wish, I'll undertake the responsibility of giving Lady Lolita this letter and delivering the message," I said.

"No. I'll have to come up to the Hall myself," was the innkeeper's reply. "The chap actually compelled me to take a solemn oath to deliver it into no other hands but her own!"

"Then it must contain something of supreme importance, otherwise it might surely have been sent by post," I remarked suspiciously.

"Yes, I feel sure it does. Did you notice how the fellow's face changed when he saw her drive past? He went as white as a ghost. He's a mystery— that he is."

"He is, without a doubt," I said. His announcement that Richard Keene had returned seemed to convey some covert threat. I recollected the tone in which he had uttered the name as he had crossed the threshold, and it caused me to ponder deeply—very deeply.

Little, however, did I dream of the terrible significance of that name; little did I at that moment anticipate the strange events that were to follow—that remarkable mystery of real life which proved so tantalising, so bewildering and so inscrutable.

Chapter Two
Concerns Lady Lolita

I strolled back up the long beech avenue to the Hall, apprehensive and puzzled. The stranger's manner, his curious expression when he had spoken of Lolita, and the bold way in which he had sent her the announcement of the return of Richard Keene were ominous. What, I wondered, did the letter contain, sealed as it was with the arms of some noble house?

I scented mystery in it all; mystery that somehow concerned myself. Why? Well, I will confess to you now—at the very outset. I, although but a paid servant of the Stanchesters, like any of that army of footmen and grooms, loved Lady Lolita in secret, and although no word of affection had ever passed between us, I nevertheless felt that her interests were my own.

My position was, I admit, a unique one. Lolita and I had been friends ever since our childhood days in India, when her father held the highest official position in the East and mine was his confidential assistant, and now, her brother having succeeded, she seemed to regard me as a harmless and necessary director of things in general. Very frequently I was invited to luncheon or to dinner, and treated always as one of the family, even though I was but a paid dependant. Yes, both the young Earl and his sister were extremely kind and considerate, and surely I had no cause for complaint, either in matter of salary, which was a handsome one, or in that of social standing.

So thoroughly had I mastered all the details of the great estate during the haughty old Earl's lifetime that I suppose my existence was necessary for the well-being of my college friend who had so suddenly found himself a millionaire. Indeed, he had admitted to me that he had never met several of his estate agents in various parts of the country, therefore I had the absolute control of them and generally superintended the revenue and expenditure, an office which entailed considerable work, inasmuch as besides Sibberton, the family possessed Stanchester House, that big white mansion in Park

Lane, Stanchester Castle in Warwickshire, Dildawn and its great deer-forest in Argyllshire, Chelmorton Towers in Sussex, and the Villa Aurora on the olive-clad hill above San Remo.

Sibberton Hall was, however, the seat which the young Earl preferred, and where he usually spent the few weeks of summer between the season at Cowes and that of the moors. As I came up the straight shady avenue of ancient beeches which met overhead for more than a mile, the magnificent façade of the splendid old place with its countless windows, its towers and high twisted chimneys stood in the soft crimson haze of the brilliant afterglow, its delicate traceries and marvellous architecture giving it almost the appearance of an illustration from some fairy tale. Built in the early days of Elizabeth by the first Earl of Stanchester, her celebrated minister, it was in the form of a quadrangle with wings abutting from the sides and ending at the extremities in towers, while its princely proportions were such as to place it among the largest and most notable family mansions in the country.

The last rays of sunset flashed upon its many windows as I emerged from the avenue, and then passing across the level lawns and ancient bowling-green, I entered the great hall with its wonderful ornamental fireplace and stands of armour, and proceeded along one corridor after another to the cosy room in the west wing which served me as study.

From the window where I stood for a moment in deep reflection I commanded a view for several miles across the great level park which was some ten miles in extent, and where, in the distance, rose another low, old-fashioned Jacobean building with clock-tower, the kennels of the Earl's famous foxhounds. My room was an old-fashioned one, like everything else in that fine mansion. Lined from floor to ceiling with books and in the centre a big writing-table, it had been given over to me by the old Earl when I had first entered upon my duties ten years before. The floor was of oak, polished like a mirror, and over the arched chimney was carved in stone the greyhound courant of the Stanchesters, with the date 1571.

I glanced at severed notes that had been dropped into the rack in my absence, and then casting myself into an easy chair lit a cigarette and continued my apprehensive reflections.

"Casting myself into an easy chair, lit a cigarette and continued my
apprehensive reflections."

The summer dusk darkened into night, and having a quantity of
correspondence to attend to, I went to the room I sometimes occupied,
changed, dined alone, and then about nine o'clock returned to my study to
finish my work.

Not a sound penetrated there. That wing was but little used, for above
was the long picture-gallery with the dark old family portraits by Vandyke,
Sir Joshua Reynolds, Kneller, and others, as well as priceless examples of
Gainsborough, Turner, Hobbema, and the world-famous Madonna of
Raphael. The room had been given to me so that I should not be disturbed
by visitors who, owing to the enormous proportions of the place, usually
wandered about hopelessly lost in their attempt to reach their rooms
without a servant as guide.

The name of Keene was puzzling me. Somehow I had a distinct and
vivid recollection of having heard it before, but in what connexion I could
not recollect, although I had been racking my brains ever since I had left
the village inn. I took down the old address-book used by my predecessor,
but there was no entry there. No, I felt somehow that I had heard the name
outside my connexion with the family, but where, or in what circumstances,
I could not for the life of me remember.

My hands were clasped behind my head, and with my work cast aside,
I was smoking vigorously, when there came a low tap at the door, and in
response to my permission to enter, Lady Lolita came forward gaily, a sweet
almost girlish figure in her cream dinner-gown girdled with turquoise blue,
exclaiming—

"Mr Woodhouse, I do wish you would do me a favour, would you?"

"Most certainly," I exclaimed, springing quickly to my feet. "What is it?"

"I want you to copy out something for me, will you?" And seating herself at my writing-table, she took up a pen and scribbled some lines.

Her gown suited her to perfection, the low-cut bodice revealing her white throat, around which sparkled a splendid necklet of diamonds that flashed beneath my lamp with a thousand fires. Upon her white wrist was a quaint Chinese bracelet cut from a solid piece of bright green stone.

Her face was perfect in its symmetry, and her finely-chiselled features were almost an exact reproduction of those of Lady Mary Sibberton in Sir Joshua's picture in the gallery above. The loveliness of the Sibberton women had been proverbial back in the Jacobean and Georgian days, and assuredly Lady Lolita inherited the distinctive beauty of the female members of the family. The delicately-moulded cheeks, the pointed chin, the sweet, well-formed mouth, the even set of pearly teeth, the wealth of auburn hair and the laughing blue eyes so full of mischief and merriment rendered her peerless among women, while her wit and easy-going good-humour endeared her to all, rich and poor alike.

As I stood by, watching her bent head beneath the lamplight, I saw that although she tried to write, her small white hand trembled so that the attempt was by no means successful. She seemed nervous and upset, for I now noticed for the first time that her breast rose and fell quickly beneath her laces, and that she was trying in vain to repress a wild tumult of agitation that raged within her.

"No," she cried, throwing down the pen and looking up at me, "I can't write. I—" And she stopped without concluding her sentence, fixing her beautiful eyes upon me. She was magnificent. That look of hers was surely sufficient to make any man's head reel.

"Do you know," she exclaimed suddenly, bursting into a nervous laugh, "I didn't really want you to write a letter at all! I only wanted an excuse to come into this den of yours—to speak to you."

Her laugh somehow sounded unnatural. With her woman's subtle tact she was, I knew, trying to conceal her agitation.

"To speak to me? What about?"

She grew grave again in an instant, and rising, crossed towards me. I saw that all the colour had died from her face and that she grasped the edge of the table to steady herself.

"I wanted to ask you—I wanted to see if you would do something for me," she said in a low tremulous voice, very harsh and intense.

Was it possible that Warr had already seen her and delivered the note and message from that mysterious stranger?

"What do you wish me to do?" I inquired eagerly.

"I want you to help me, Willoughby," she said. "I am in peril—deadly peril. You can save me if you will."

"Peril? Peril of what?"

"Ah! That I cannot tell you," she answered; then suddenly losing all control of herself she exclaimed wildly, "The past has risen against me, to torment me, to hound me down to the very depths of hell. Ah! Willoughby, save me—you will, won't you? You are my friend. Say you are—say you will help me," she implored with clasped hands.

"But what do you fear, Lady Lolita?" I asked in the hope of learning her secret.

"I fear death," she cried hoarsely. "The blow has fallen, and I am lost—lost."

"No, no," I said, taking her soft hand gently in mine and finding it cold, trembling in fear. "Do not anticipate the worst, whatever may be your danger."

"Ah! if I could tell you all—if I only dared to tell you," she sighed. "But even then you wouldn't believe it—you couldn't."

"But may I not know something of this peril of yours?" I urged. "If you tell me, I shall then know how to deal with it."

"You can only serve me at great risk to yourself," was her quick reply.

"In any way I can serve you, Lolita, do not hesitate to command me," I said, deeply in earnest and still holding her trembling hand in mine. By that wild look in her beautiful eyes I saw that her heart was gripped by some nameless terror, and that she was in desperation. Then, in a moment of deep sympathy, recollecting the stranger's ominous words, I added: "I love you now, Lolita, with the deepest devotion with which any man has loved."

And before she was aware of it, I had raised those thin white fingers reverently to my lips and imprinted upon them a tender lingering kiss.

Chapter Three
Which is a Mystery

In my hot passionate declaration I repeated my readiness to serve her, at the same time acknowledging the difference in our stations and the fear that my dream of happiness must be a vain one.

She smiled very sweetly upon me, and I saw her eyes were dimmed with tears. Her lips moved, but in the first moments no sound escaped them. I had taken her by surprise, I think, for she had always regarded me as friend, and not as lover.

"I thank you for your kind promise to assist me in this hour of my need," she answered at last in a voice that seemed to have strangely altered. "I know now that I enjoy your regard, although I—well, I must confess that I had no idea that, good friends that we have been all these years, you would end by really falling in love with me. You have, however, told me the truth, and a woman always respects a man for that. I know now that I have at least one firm and devoted friend." And as she spoke her fingers closed upon my hand.

As I feared, I had presumed too far. I had no right to love her, I, a mere paid servant of the family, yet she had treated my confession with sweet dignity and womanly tact that so well became her, and cleverly turned my declaration of love into one of friendship.

"To serve me in this matter would be to imperil yourself," she went on in deep seriousness after a moment's pause. "My enemies hold my future in their hands. To me it is a matter of life or death."

"I am prepared to undertake any risk for your sake," I declared. "Only suggest a course, and I will adopt it instantly."

"Ah, you are very good!" she cried. "How can I sufficiently thank you? In all the world you are the only friend I can really trust. Well, what I want you to do is this. Take the first train to London to-morrow and go to 98, Britten Street, Chelsea, where you will find a certain Frenchwoman named Lejeune. Tell her that I have sent you to implore her to tell me the truth; that if she fears to approach me direct you will act as intermediary; that if she withholds the secret it must result in my death—my death—you understand."

"In your death!" I gasped, puzzled.

"Yes. I cannot face exposure. I would prefer death!" was her hoarse reply. "Tell that woman that Richard Keene has returned! She will know." I watched her face and recognised how desperate she was. I had never before seen such a look in any woman's eyes.

"And what else?" I asked mechanically.

"Nothing. All you have to do in order to save me is to get a written confession from that woman. If she refuses, as I fear she will, then my fate is sealed. The blow I have been dreading these past years will fall. I shall be crushed, and Lolita Sibberton will be but the memory of an unhappy woman who fell the victim of as foul and ingenious a plot as was ever conceived by the mind of man." Her hands were clasped before her, and she shivered from head to foot. I saw that she was cold, and without a word wound about her bare neck my scarf that lay upon a chair.

"I will do my utmost in your interests," I assured her. "This woman—is she one of the conspirators?"

"Beware of her. She is treacherous, unscrupulous, and possessed of a cunning that is almost beyond comprehension. Act with discretion, and exercise every care of your own personal safety."

"Why? I have no fear in London in broad daylight," I smiled.

"Ah! You don't know," she cried. "In dealing with her, you are dealing with a person who would hesitate at nothing in order to attain her own ends. Until now, although a word from her could give me my freedom from this imminent danger that threatens to overtake me, she has kept silence and watched for my downfall."

"I will compel her to confess," I cried fiercely. "If it is within human power to save you, Lolita, I will do so. Trust me, because I love you."

She sighed, and again her eyes were dimmed by tears.

"And if you hear strange tales about me, certain allegations of—shameful stories, I mean—you will believe none of them till you have proof—will you?" she urged breathlessly, with a deep anxiety in her voice.

"No," I promised. "I will not. To me, Lolita, you are innocent, pure and good, just as when we were boy and girl together." And again I placed her finger-tips to my lips as seal of my allegiance to the one woman who was all the world to me.

At that instant there came a tap at the door, and I was compelled to drop her hand instantly.

Slater, the aged, white-whiskered butler, opened the door, saying in his squeaky voice—

"His lordship would like to see you, m'lady, in the library before sending a telegram—at once, if convenient."

"I'll be there in a moment," she answered, without turning towards the man to reveal her face. Then, when Slater had gone, she rushed to the small mirror and with her handkerchief quickly removed all traces of her tears.

"George is worrying about Marigold being alone at Aix-les-Bains," she remarked. "I'm rather surprised he let her go. If I were a man with a young and pretty wife, I shouldn't let her far out of my sight. But Marigold, I suppose, isn't an ordinary woman."

Her last sentence was indeed correct. All the world knew that the young Countess of Stanchester was the gayest and giddiest of the ultra-smart set in which she moved, and that after two years of marriage she had developed into one of the most popular and unconventional Society hostesses. The young Earl was not exactly happy—that I knew—and Lolita was usually his adviser regarding his purely domestic affairs.

Therefore, as she hurriedly put the finishing-touches to her countenance with that dexterity which a woman only possesses, she turned to me and again grasped my hand, saying—

"What I have said to-night, Willoughby, you will regard as strictly confidential. Act as I have suggested, and," she added with a catch in her voice, "remember that you alone stand between myself—and death?"

"I promise," I said. And opening the door, I bowed before her as she swept out, her silks swishing down the long corridor.

I closed the door again and flung myself back into my chair, utterly mystified by those fateful words. She had a secret, one that she was prepared to keep even at cost of her own life. To me, although she had not admitted that she reciprocated my love, she had entrusted her life.

Yes. I would force the mysterious Frenchwoman into confession, whoever she was. The thought of my love's peril roused me to action, and I seated myself at my table and set to work clearing off those letters that lay heaped up unanswered.

The clock on the stables had chimed midnight before I threw down my pen, locked my drawers, and slipping on my overcoat strolled through the silent house along to the great hall, where a footman in the bright blue and gold Stanchester livery let me out into the still, balmy night.

After the warmth of my room, the air was refreshing, and as I walked on down the dark avenue towards the village, the silence was complete save for the cry of an owl and the distant barking of the hounds in the Earl's celebrated kennels situated about a mile away. Where the trees met overhead the darkness was intense, but so often did I return home after nightfall that I knew every inch of the way.

Still pondering deeply upon my strange conversation with Lolita, I strode forward without any thought of time or place, and utterly oblivious to everything, until of a sudden I was aroused by hearing a woman's loud, piercing shriek.

I halted on the instant and listened. I judged the sound to be about a hundred yards to the left, in the darkness. After a few seconds it was repeated.

The cry was Lolita's! Of that I felt absolutely convinced.

Without a moment's hesitation I rushed forward, but in the cavernous blackness could discern nothing. I halted and listened, but beyond the hooting of the owl could discern no sound of any movement among that treble row of giant beeches.

At first I tried to convince myself that those cries of distress were merely heard in my imagination, yet they were, alas! too tangible and distinct. For a full quarter of an hour I lingered there, straining eyes and ears, but all in vain.

Then, with a resolve to take the man Warr into my confidence and invoke his aid to make a search, I rushed forward to the village, awakened him, and we both returned with lanterns as quickly as we could, and began to make a methodical examination of the spot whence I had believed the sounds emanated.

I learned from Warr one very curious fact, namely, that he had been unable to go up to the Hall to deliver the letter, and it was still in his possession. It therefore seemed as though Lolita had caught sight of the stranger's face as he peered forth from the tap-room window, and by that means knew of his unwelcome return.

For an hour we searched diligently both within the avenue and outside it, until of a sudden a cry from Warr caused my heart to leap.

"Good Heavens! Mr Woodhouse!" he gasped, bending to a clump of long grass in a deep hollow behind the huge gnarled trunk of one of the great oaks. "Come and look here!"

I dashed forward to the spot over which he held his hurricane lantern, saw what he had discovered, and stood appalled, dumbfounded, absolutely rooted to the spot.

The sight presented there rendered the mystery of that evening even more bewildering and inscrutable.

Chapter Four
Wherein a Strange Story is Told

For the moment we were both too aghast to speak.

The clump of rank high grass in the hollow had been beaten down, and in the centre, revealed by the uncertain light of our lanterns, lay a young man, whose white face and wide-open, sightless eyes told us both the terrible truth.

He had been murdered!

As I bent to examine him as he lay slightly on his side, I saw that from an ugly knife-wound in his back blood was still oozing, and had soaked into the ground around him. Both hands were tightly clenched, as though the unfortunate fellow had died in a spasm of agony, while upon one finger something shone, which I discovered to be a gold ring of curious, foreign workmanship, shaped like a large scarab, or sacred beetle, about half an inch long, and nearly as broad—an unusual ring which attracted my curiosity.

The grass around bore distinct marks of a desperate struggle, and from the position in which the young man was lying, it seemed as though, being struck suddenly, he had stumbled, fallen forward, and expired.

"He's been murdered, sir, without a doubt," exclaimed Warr, at last breaking the silence. "I thought you said you heard a woman's voice?"

"So I did," I replied, much puzzled at the discovery, for, to tell the truth, I had half-expected to find Lolita herself. Even at that moment I could have sworn that the cry was hers. "It seems, however, that I must have been mistaken."

"But who can he be?" exclaimed the innkeeper. "He's an utter stranger to me. I've certainly never seen him in Sibberton."

"Neither have I," was my response. "There's some deep mystery here, depend upon it," I added, recollecting all that Lolita had so strangely told me earlier in the evening.

"And my own opinion is that the fellow who called at my house this evening—Mr Richard Keene, as he said his name was—has had a hand in it," Warr declared as he looked across at me, still kneeling by the young man's body.

"Well, it certainly seems suspiciously like it. Both men are entire strangers, that's evident."

In order to ascertain whether there was not a spark of life still left, I undid the poor fellow's vest and placed my hand upon his heart. There was, however, no movement. The blow had been struck with an unerring hand, while the weapon had been withdrawn and carried away by the assassin.

He was well-dressed, dark-haired, with an aquiline and somewhat refined countenance. He wore a slight, dark moustache, and I judged his age to be about twenty-three. His blue serge suit was of fine quality, but was evidently of foreign cut, and his boots were also of foreign shape and make. His hands, I felt, were soft, as though unused to work, yet where he lay, in that damp hollow, I was unable to search his clothes properly to discover a clue to his identity.

The spot where he had been attacked had certainly been chosen by some one well acquainted with the park. The hollow, once an old gravel-pit, but now overgrown with grass, was screened by the trees of the avenue, so that any one in it would be entirely hidden from view, even in broad daylight. Therefore it struck me that the unfortunate victim had been enticed there by the assassin, and foully done to death.

Yet after hearing those cries I had certainly detected no movement. The murderer must have crept silently out of the grassy hollow, and struck straight across the park to the woods half a mile away. Had any other direction been taken, I must certainly have heard his footsteps.

But the woman who had screamed. What of her?

I had, at the moment, little time for reflection. Acting upon the innkeeper's suggestion I went off to fetch Knight, the constable, and my friend Pink, the doctor, while he remained with his lantern beside the victim of the tragedy.

As soon as the doctor saw him he shook his head, declaring that the wound had proved fatal a few minutes after he had been struck, while the constable, alive to the importance of the occasion, commenced suggesting all sorts of wild theories regarding the dead stranger. Disregarding them all, however, we obtained a hurdle, and Warr and Knight carried the body down the dark avenue, a strange and weird procession, our way lit uncertainly by the swing lanterns, our voices awed and hushed in the presence of the unknown dead.

The men deposited their inanimate burden in an outhouse at the back of the village inn to await the inquest which Pink declared would be necessary, and then, with a better light and the door closed against any prying intruder, we examined the dead man's pockets to see whether they contained anything that might throw light on the tragic affair or lead to his identification.

The constable, with the officiousness of his class, took out a ponderous note-book and with a stubby piece of pencil commenced to make an inventory of what we found—a pocket-knife, about three pounds ten in money, a gold French piece of twenty francs, a gun-metal watch and plated chain, a few loose cigarettes a box of matches, a pawn-ticket shewing that a lady's necklet had been pledged in the name of Bond, with a pawnbroker in the Westminster Bridge Road, about a year ago. Beyond that there was no clue to the dead man's name. We were all disappointed, for the mystery surrounding him was heightened by the absence of any letter in his pocket or name upon his underclothing. Men who go to a pawnshop do not usually give their real names, hence we knew that Bond was assumed. Indeed, in pawnbroking the name of the person offering the pledge is never even asked, the assistant filling up the voucher in any name that comes to him.

While the others were making careful examination of the maker's name and number of the dead man's watch, I chanced to hold his waistcoat in my hand, when between my fingers I felt something like a letter. In an instant I was prompted to take possession of it secretly, and this I managed to do, first crushing it into the palm of my hand, then transferring it to my pocket.

Was it possible that the crisp paper so cunningly concealed in the lining of the waistcoat contained a clue? My heart beat quickly, and I longed to escape from the place and examine it in secret. If Lolita had actually been present at the tragedy and had any connection with it, my duty was surely to conceal the fact. She had admitted that she was in deadly peril, and I had promised to assist her; therefore, by securing any clue and hiding it from the police, I was assuredly acting in her interest.

I had already managed to secure the ring surreptitiously from the dead man's finger before the body had been removed from the spot where we had discovered it, and as neither Warr nor the others had noticed it, I held it as a probable clue which I intended should be my secret alone.

"He was evidently struck with a long thin knife," remarked Pink, a muscular, clean-shaven man who was extremely popular in the district, a keen sportsman and something of an epicure. He had probed the wound and ascertained that its direction had been only too accurate. "Whoever did it," he declared, "knew exactly where to strike. I daresay he fell without a cry. The knife was very sharp, too," he went on, examining one of the black horn buttons of the young man's jacket-cuff. "You see it grazed this as he raised his arm to ward off the blow and shaved off a tiny piece, just as a razor might. The coroner will want to see this. I'll get Newman over, and we'll make a proper post-mortem in the morning."

Pink was a clever surgeon who masked his capabilities behind an easy-going good-humour. His poor patients were often convulsed by his amusing remarks, while at the houses of the county people he was always a welcome guest on account of his inexhaustible fund of droll stories, his shrewd wit, and his outspoken appreciation of a good dinner. His odd ways were the idiosyncrasies of genius, for without doubt he was as expert a surgeon as there was outside Harley Street, and I myself had heard praise of him from the mouths of certain London men with big "names."

The manner in which he examined the unfortunate young man who had so suddenly fallen a victim of an assassin showed that he was intensely interested. He grunted once or twice and sniffed suspiciously, and with some gusto took a pinch of snuff from his heavy silver box. Then, having carefully examined the man's right hand, he turned to me again, saying, as he pointed to it—

"That's strange, Woodhouse, isn't it?"

"What?" I inquired, detecting nothing.

"Can't you see. His hand is clenched. He grasped something just at the moment when he was struck."

"Well?"

He held the lantern closer to the cold stiff hand, and pointing to the thumb that was closely clenched upon the fingers, said—

"Can't you see anything there?"

I looked, and then for the first time detected that beneath the thumb was something white—a tiny piece of white fur!

"That's out of a woman's jacket, or boa, or something," he declared, gradually disengaging it, and placing it in the hollow of his hand for closer inspection. "There are one or two black hairs with it, showing it, I believe, to be ermine fur—a woman who wore some garment of ermine."

"Are you certain?" I gasped.

"Almost—but not quite until I put it beneath the microscope. Then I'll be able to tell for certain. But surely it couldn't have been a woman who killed him?"

"It looks very much like it, sir," remarked Knight, who had been gazing eagerly over the doctor's shoulder.

"Then what woman?" asked Warr, glancing across at me.

I held my breath. A silence fell between us. The mystery was of such a character that neither of us dare advance any further theory.

For my own part, however, the discovery of this tiny piece of fur was directly suspicious, and went much to confirm my belief that Lolita had been at the spot where the tragedy had been enacted, for I now recollected that sometimes when she went out after dinner she put on a wide ermine boa with long ends to cover her shoulders, a very handsome piece of fur that had been brought for her from Petersburg when the young Countess of Stanchester went to visit the Grand-Duchess Paul in the previous winter.

Was it possible that the poor young fellow had clutched at it in his dying grasp? Or had he seized the fur garment of some other woman?

Yet, I recollected, furs are not usually worn in mid-August save just to throw over a dinner-gown as protection from chills when the damp is rising after the heat of the day.

On the other hand, I tried to convince myself that the cry was not that of the sweet-eyed woman I loved; nevertheless, such thought was in vain. I knew that voice far too well to have been mistaken.

For quite an hour Pink continued his investigations as keenly and methodically as any practised detective, for he rather prided himself upon the manner in which he made discoveries about persons, and frequently astounded his patients by his knowledge of their actions and movements, which they believed only known to themselves. At last, however, he exhausted all the points possible to investigate without a post-mortem, and just as the church clock struck three we came forth, Warr locking the door of the outhouse, while Knight left us to ride on his bicycle into Northampton to report to the headquarters of the constabulary.

Pink's way lay past my house, for he lived in a big, square, comfortable house about a quarter of a mile out of the village, on the London road, and as we walked together up the silent street, he suddenly said—

"Do you know, Woodhouse, I have a firm belief that the young fellow has been murdered by some woman! We must search the spot early in the morning and see if we can't find some footprints, or other traces. Fortunately, it's damp in that hollow, and a woman's heel would leave a well-defined mark. Will you be ready at seven to go back there with me?"

The Sign of the Stranger | 27

The suggestion had never occurred to me, and my heart stood still when I reflected what tell-tale traces might there be left. But I strove to show no dismay, merely answering—

"Certainly. I'll be ready. We may discover something to give the police a clue."

"Police!" he cried. "They're useless. We shall have a swarm of thick-headed bunglers over here to-morrow. If they sent one smart man down from Scotland Yard they might do some good. But the plain-clothes men of the local constabulary haven't sufficient practice in serious crime to pursue any clever methods of investigation."

"Well, then, at seven," I exclaimed, for we had just reached my gate, and I was anxious to get to my own room and ascertain the nature of the paper I had managed to secure from the lining of the dead man's waistcoat.

"That's an appointment," he said, and as I turned and entered my old-fashioned, ivy-covered house with my latch-key, he pursued his way up the short steep hill towards his home.

Within my own cosy sitting-room the green-shaded reading-lamp was still burning, and Mrs Dawson, my attentive housekeeper, had placed my slippers ready in their accustomed corner. But throwing off my light overcoat I cast myself instantly into my favourite grandfather chair, and drew from my pocket the clue I had surreptitiously stolen.

The piece of paper was pale blue, and as I opened it a cry of dismay involuntarily escaped me.

What was inscribed upon it was so strange!

Chapter Five
Reveals Three Curious Facts

There was no writing on the carefully-concealed scrap of paper. Only five rows of numerals, written in a fine feminine hand and arranged in the following manner:—

63 26 59 69 65 56 65 33 59 35 65 44
49 55 22 59 57 46 78 63 23 98 59 39
46 67 82 45 58 35 54 45 46 26 78 75
68 75 49 64 22 86 48 73 78 45 62 45
76 47 64 66 85 44 78 48 73 78 58 62

I turned the paper over, utterly puzzled. It was certainly some cipher, but of a kind of which I knew nothing. Ciphers may of course be very easily constructed and yet defy solution. This appeared to be one of those. What hidden message it contained, I had no idea, save that it was certain to be something of importance and that some other person was in possession of the secret of the decipher, or its recipient would not have concealed it where he did.

If I could only read it, a clue to the dead man's identity would no doubt be revealed. But as I glanced at those puzzling rows of numerals I felt that to endeavour to learn their secret was but a vain hope. I had expected to find upon that scrap of paper some intelligible letter, and was sorely disappointed at what I had discovered.

The further I pushed my inquiries, the more mysterious the affair seemed to become. A dozen times I tried by ordinary methods to turn the numbers into writing, but my calculations only resulted in an unmeaning array of letters of the alphabet, a chaos quite unintelligible, therefore I was at length compelled to abandon my efforts, and after examining the ring and deciding that it was a copy of one of those old Etruscan rings that I had seen in the British Museum, I reluctantly went upstairs to snatch an hour's sleep before the dawn.

My brain was awhirl. Following so quickly the strange declarations of Lolita had come this startling tragedy with all its mysterious and suspicious features. As I lay awake, listening to the solemn striking of the hour from the old church tower which told me that daylight was not far off, I recollected that Lolita had probably recognised the shabby stranger in the tap-room of the *Stanchester Arms* as she drove past. I remembered how he had held back, as though fearing recognition, and also that, as the carriage went by, her head had been half-turned in our direction. If she had detected his presence she had certainly made no sign, yet it must have been that discovery that had caused her to speak so strangely and to seek my aid in the manner she had done.

Warr still had the sealed letter in his possession, therefore the only way she could have known of the return of the bluff fellow who called himself Richard Keene was by the discovery made by herself.

I remembered her fierce desperation and her trembling fear; how cold her hands had been, and how wild that look in her beautiful eyes — a hunted look such as I had never before seen in the eyes of either man or woman. Then suddenly I recollected what damning evidence might remain on that soft clay in the hollow where the body had been found. The detectives would certainly be able to establish her presence there! I felt that at all risks I must prevent that. I had promised to help her, and although there were dark suspicions within my heart I intended to act loyally as a man should towards the woman he honestly loves. I therefore set my alarm to awaken me in an hour, and just as the grey light was breaking through the clouds eastward over Monk's Wood, I rose, dressed myself, and concealing a small garden trowel in my pocket set forth for the spot before any of the villagers were astir.

The morning air was keen and fresh as I hurried up the avenue and with some trepidation descended into the hollow, fearing lest the report had already been spread in the village and that any of the curious yokels might notice my presence there.

But I was alone, and therefore breathed more freely.

Over an area of fifteen yards or so the grass was beaten down here and there, and in the cold grey light became revealed the dark stain where the victim had fallen — the stain of his life blood.

I searched around among the grass and over the soft boggy places bare of herbage, but found no footmarks nor any trace except that of the downtrodden grass where the struggle had evidently taken place and where the unknown man had apparently fought desperately for his life. After twenty minutes or so, fearing lest some labourers early astir might come to the spot before going to work, I was about to leave when, of a sudden, in a place where no grass grew upon the clay, I saw something that held me rigid.

In the soft earth was the plain imprint of the small sole of a woman's shoe, with a Louis XV heel!

Lolita wore high heels of exactly that character, and took three's in shoes. Was it possible that the footprint was hers?

As I looked I saw others, both of a person advancing and receding. One was ill-defined, where she had apparently slipped upon the clay. But all of them I stamped out—all, indeed, that I could find. Yet was it possible, I wondered, to efface every one?

If one single one remained, it might be sufficient to throw suspicion upon her.

While engaged in this, something white caught my eye lying upon the grass about ten yards distant. I picked it up and found it to be a piece of white fur about an inch square that had evidently been torn bodily out of a boa or cape—the same fur that had been found between the dead man's fingers.

This I placed carefully in my cigarette-case and continued my work of effacing the damning footprints. There were other marks, of men's boots, but whether those of the dead man or of our own I could not decide, so I left them as evidence for the police to investigate.

My eyes were everywhere to try and discover the weapon with which the foul deed had been committed, for the assassin, I thought, might have cast it away, but my search was in vain. It had disappeared.

Fully twenty distinct marks of those small well-shod feet I effaced by stamping upon them or scraping the surface with the trowel, and was preparing to return and keep the appointment with the doctor when of a sudden I saw, lying close behind the trunk of the giant oak, a half-smoked cigarette, which on taking up I found to be of the same brand as those found in the dead man's pocket. He had therefore kept a tryst at that spot, and had smoked calmly and unsuspiciously in order to while away the time.

Of men's footprints in the soft ground there were a quantity, but then I remembered how all four of us had tramped about there, in addition to the victim himself, and I was not sufficiently expert in tracking to be able to distinguish one man's tread from another's.

It was already daylight and in the distance I could hear the sound of a reaping machine in one of the fields beyond the park, therefore I was compelled to escape in order that my premature examination should remain secret. So I struck straight across the level sward to the London road, which ran beyond the park boundary, in preference to passing straight down the avenue at risk of meeting any of the labourers.

News of the tragedy I knew had not yet reached the Hall, otherwise the servants would have been out to see the spot, therefore I believed myself quite safe from detection until, just as I scaled the old stone wall and dropped into the broad white high road with its long line of telegraph lines, I encountered the innkeeper Warr who, mounted on his bicycle, was riding towards me.

He had approached noiselessly and we were mutually surprised to meet each other in such circumstances.

"Halloa!" he cried, dismounting. "You've been out again very early—eh?"

"I've been back to the spot to see if I could find any traces of the dead man's assailant," was my reply. "I thought I'd go back early, before the crowd trod over the place. Don't say anything, or Knight may consider that I've taken his duty out of his hands."

"Ah, a very good idea, sir," was the man's approving response. "I thought of doing so myself, only they're beginning to cut my bit o' wheat in the mill-field this morning and I have to go into Thrapston about the machine. I'll be back in an hour."

He was preparing to re-mount, when I stopped him, saying—

"Look here, Warr. You recollect that stranger who called and left the note for Lady Lolita last evening? Well, there seems considerable mystery about the affair, and somehow I feel there's connexion with the fellow's visit with this poor young man's death. If so, her ladyship's name must be rigorously kept out of it, you understand. There's to be an inquest to-morrow, and we shall both be called to give evidence. Recollect that not a word is said about the man Keene, the note, or the message."

"If you wish it, sir, I'll keep a still tongue," was his reply. "I've told nobody up to now—not even the missus."

"Very well. Remember only you and I know of this man's return, and the knowledge must go no further. There's a mystery, but it must have no connexion with her ladyship."

"You may trust me, sir. The family have been too good to me all these years for me not to try and render them a service. I quite agree with you that the stranger was suspicious, and from what he said to me in private it is certain that he must know her ladyship very well indeed."

"You're sure you've never seen that young man before?" I asked, watching his face narrowly.

"Him? No, I don't know him from Adam!" was the landlord's reply, yet uttered in a manner and tone that aroused my distinct suspicions. His assurance was just a trifle too emphatic, I thought.

I paused a moment, half inclined to express my doubt openly, then said at last—

"That letter—what shall you do with it?"

"Give it to her, of course. I'll come up to the Hall when I come back. I ought to have given it to her last night."

"Had you done so that man's life might perhaps have been saved—who knows?"

"Ah!" he sighed in regret. "I never thought of that. I didn't know it was of such importance. You see the missus is in bed with a cold, and I couldn't leave the house in charge o' the girl. They were a bit merry last night after Jim Cook's weddin'."

I was anxious to obtain possession of the mysterious letter, but I already knew that he would only deliver it to Lolita personally. Yet I had no wish that the man Warr should come to the Hall just at the moment when the startling news of the tragedy would create a sensation throughout the whole household. If he were to deliver the letter, it should not be before the first horror of the affair had died down. Therefore I made excuse to him that her ladyship was going over very early to Lady Sudborough's to join a picnic and would not be back before evening.

"Very well," he answered. "I'll come up then." And mounting his machine he spun away down the hill.

Next moment, from where I stood, I distinguished a trap approaching along a bend in the road. Three men were in it, two of them being in uniform—the police from Northampton.

Having no desire that they should know that I had returned to the spot to efface those tell-tale marks, the only way to avoid them was to spring over the wall again into the park, which I did without a moment's hesitation, crouching down until they had passed, and then crossed the corner of the park and entered the Monk's Wood, a thick belt of forest through which ran a footpath which joined the road about a mile further down. The way I had taken to Sibberton was a circuitous one, it was true, but at any rate I should avoid being seen in the vicinity of the spot where the tragedy was enacted.

Walking forward along the dim forest path covered with moss and wild flowers, where the rising sun glinted upon the grey trunks of the trees and the foliage above rustled softly in the wind, I was sorely puzzled over the innkeeper's manner when I had put that direct question to him.

Notwithstanding his denial, I felt convinced that he had recognised the dead man.

I had almost gained the outer edge of the wood, walking noiselessly over the carpet of moss, when of a sudden the sound of voices caused me to start and halt.

At first I saw nothing, but next moment through the tree trunks twenty yards away I caught sight of two persons strolling slowly in company—a man and a woman.

The man's face I could not see, but the woman, whose hair, beneath her navy blue Tam o' Shanter cap showed dishevelled as a ray of sunlight struck it, and whose white silk dress showed muddy and bedraggled beneath her dark cloak, I recognised in an instant—although her back was turned towards me.

It was Lady Lolita, the goddess of my admiration. Lolita—my queen—my love.

Chapter Six
For Love of Lolita

I held my breath, open-mouthed, utterly dumbfounded.

Lolita's appearance showed too plainly that she had been out all the night. Her cloak was torn at the shoulder, evidently by a bramble, and the weary manner in which she walked was as though she were exhausted.

The man, bearded, broad-shouldered and athletic, seemed, as far as I could judge from his back, to be of middle age. He wore a rough tweed suit and a golf cap, and as he strode by her side he spoke with her earnestly, emphasising his words with gesture, as though giving her certain directions, which she heard resignedly and in silence.

I noticed that when he stretched out his hand to add force to his utterance that she shrank from him and shuddered. She was probably very cold, for the early morning air was chilly, and the dew was heavy on the ground.

Without betraying my presence, I crept on noiselessly after them, hoping that I might overhear the words the fellow uttered, but in this I was doomed to disappointment, for at the edge of the wood, before I realised the man's intention, he suddenly raised his hat, and turning, left her, disappearing by the narrow path that led through a small spinney to Lowick village. Thus I was prevented from obtaining a glance at his features and blamed myself for not acting with more foresight and ingenuity.

After he had left her, she stood alone, gazing after him. No word, however, escaped her. By his attitude I knew that he had threatened her, and that she had no defence. She was inert and helpless.

In a few moments, with a wild gesture, she sank upon her knees in the grass, and throwing up her two half-bare arms to heaven cried aloud for help, her wild beseeching words reaching me where I stood.

My adored was in desperation. I heard the words of her fervent prayer and stood with head uncovered. Long and earnestly she besought help, forgiveness and protection; then with a strange, determined calm she rose again, and stood in hesitation which way to proceed.

For the first time she seemed to realise that the sun was already shining, and that it was open day, for she glanced at her clothes, and with feminine dexterity shook out her bedraggled skirts and glanced at them dismayed.

I recognised her utter loneliness: therefore I walked forward to her.

Slowly she recognised me, as through a veil, and starting, she fell back, glaring at me as though she were witness of some appalling apparition.

"You!" she gasped. "How did you find me here?"

"No matter how I found you, Lady Lolita," I responded. "You are in want of a friend, and I am here to give you help, as I promised you last night. This is no time for words; we must act, and act quickly. You must let me take you back to the Hall."

"But look at me!" she cried in dismay. "I can't go back like this! They would—they would suspect!"

"There must be no suspicion," I said, thoroughly aroused to the importance of secrecy now that the police were already in the park making their investigations. "You cannot return to the Hall like this, for the servants would see you and know that you've been absent all night."

"I'm afraid of Weston," she said. "She is so very inquisitive." Weston was her maid.

"Then you must come with me to my house," I suggested. "We could reach it across the fields and enter by the back way unobserved. I can send Mrs Dawson out on some pretext, and you can remain locked in my sitting-room while I go up to the Hall and fetch one of your walking-dresses. I can slip up to your wardrobe and manage to steal something without Weston suspecting. Then, when you return, you can explain that you've merely been out for an early walk."

The suggestion, although a desperate one, commended itself to her, and with a few words of heartfelt thanks she announced her readiness to accompany me.

I longed to inquire the name of the male companion, but feared to do so, seeing how pale and agitated she was. Her face had changed sadly since the previous night, for she was now white, wan and haggard, presenting a strange, terrified appearance, dishevelled and bedraggled as she was. She must certainly have been out in the park for fully seven hours. Was she aware of the tragedy, I wondered?

I told her nothing of the discovery. How could I in those circumstances? True, she was not wearing the ermine collar, as I had suspected, yet the prints made by her shoes as she now walked with me were assuredly the same as those I had effaced.

We spoke but little as we hurried along, creeping always beneath walls and behind trees, and often compelled to make long détours in order to obtain cover and avoid recognition by any of those working in the fields.

Compelled to scale the high wall of the park at last, I assisted her over without much difficulty, for although she preserved all her natural beauty, she was athletic, fond of all games and a splendid rider to hounds.

"If I can only conceal the fact that I've been absent all night, it will be of such very material assistance," she said after we had crossed the high road and gained the shelter of a long narrow spinney. "I shall never be able to sufficiently repay you for this," she added.

"Remember the confession of my heart to you last night, Lolita," was my answer. "We will discuss it all later on—when you are safe." And we pushed forward, our eyes and ears on the alert as we approached the village.

At last, by good fortune, I managed to get her unobserved inside my house. Creeping noiselessly up the stairs I took her to one of my dusty, disused attics in preference to my sitting-room, and there she locked herself in. Not, however, before I had pressed her hand in silence as assurance that she might place her trust in me.

A few moments later I found my old housekeeper in the kitchen, and having given her directions to go on an errand for me to a farm about a mile and a half distant, I started off up to the Hall upon as strange an errand as man has ever gone, namely to steal a dress belonging to his love.

I had, of course, disregarded my appointment with Pink, and not wishing to meet the searchers or the doctor himself, I reached the Hall by the bypath that led from Lowick, passing along the edge of the Monk's Wood wherein I had met Lolita.

On entering the mansion I found that the startling news of the tragedy had just reached there, for the servants were all greatly alarmed. They crowded about me to learn the latest details, but I passed quickly on to my room and for a few minutes pretended to be engrossed in correspondence, although my real reason was to await an opportunity to reach her ladyship's room after the servants' bell had sounded and the faithful maid Weston had gone down to breakfast.

At last the bell clanged, and I stole along the corridor in order to watch the neat maid's disappearance with the others. She seemed longer than usual, but presently she came, and after she had passed along to the servants' hall I quickly ascended the main staircase, and sped along the two long corridors to my love's room—a large, well-furnished apartment with long mirrors and a dressing-table heaped with silver-mounted toilet requisites.

Without a moment's hesitation I opened the huge wardrobe, and after a brief search discovered a dark tweed tailor-made coat and skirt which I recognised as one she often wore for walking, and these I hurriedly rolled up and together with a pair of buttoned boots carried them off. I noticed that the bed, with its pale blue silken hangings, was fortunately tumbled as though it had been slept in, therefore Weston evidently did not suspect that her young mistress had been absent all night.

Not without risk of detection, I managed to convey the dress and boots down to my own room, where I packed them in a neat parcel and carried them with all speed back to Sibberton.

Mrs Dawson, who was a somewhat decrepit person, had not returned, therefore I carried the parcel up to the attic, and ten minutes later her ladyship came down looking as fresh and neat in her tweed gown as though she had only that moment emerged from her room.

Leaving her cloak and muddy dinner-dress in my charge, she escaped by the back and away down the garden, expressing her intention of returning to the Hall as though she had only been out an hour for a morning walk, as was so frequently her habit. She had thanked me fervently for my assistance, and in doing so uttered a sentence that struck me as remarkably strange, knowing what I did.

"You have saved me, Willoughby. You can save my life, if you will."

"I will," was my earnest reply. "You know my secret," I added, raising her fingers to my hot passionate lips before we parted.

She made no mention of the tragedy, and what, indeed, could I remark?

My journey to London I was compelled to postpone in view of what had occurred. She had not referred to it, and to tell the truth I felt that my presence beside her just then was of greater need. Thus, after awaiting my housekeeper's return in order to preserve appearances, I ate my breakfast with the air of a man entirely undisturbed.

Just before nine the doctor came in, ruddy and well-shaven, and throwing himself into an armchair exclaimed—

"You didn't keep your promise! I called and found nobody at home. You were out."

"I'd gone down the village," I explained.

"Well, I've been up into the park with the police. They've sent that blundering fool Redway—worse than useless! We've been over the ground, but there's so many footprints that it's impossible to distinguish any—save one."

"And what's that?"

"Well, strangely enough, my dear fellow, it's a woman's."

"A woman's!" I gasped, for I saw that all my work had been in vain and in my hurry I must have unfortunately overlooked one.

"Yes, it's the print of a woman's slipper with a French heel — not the kind of shoe usually worn in Sibberton," remarked the doctor. "Funny, isn't it?"

"Very," I agreed with a sickly feeling. "What do the police think?"

"Redway means to take a plaster cast of it — says it's an important clue. Got a cigarette?"

I pushed the box before him, with sinking heart, and at the same time invited him to the table to have breakfast, for I had not yet finished.

"Breakfast!" he cried. "Why, I had mine at six, and am almost ready for lunch. I'm an early bird, you know."

It was true. He had cultivated the habit of early rising by going cub-hunting with the Stanchester hounds, and it was his boast that he never breakfasted later than six either summer or winter.

"Did they find anything else?" I inquired, fearing at the same time to betray any undue curiosity.

"Found a lot of marks of men's boots, but they might have been ours," he answered in his bluff way as he lit his cigarette. "My theory is that the mark of the woman's shoe is a very strong clue. Some woman knows all about it — that's very certain, and she's a person who wears thin French shoes, size three."

"Does Redway say that?"

"No, I say it. Redway's a fool, you know. Look how he blundered in that robbery in Northampton a year ago. I only wish we could get a man from Scotland Yard. He'd nab the murderer before the day is out."

At heart I did not endorse this wish. On the contrary the discovery of this footmark that had escaped me was certainly a very serious *contretemps*. My endeavours must, I saw, now all be directed towards arranging matters so that, if necessary, Lolita could prove a complete *alibi*.

"Do you know," went on the doctor, "there's one feature in the affair that's strangest of all, and that is that there seems to have been an attempt to efface certain marks, as though the assassin boldly returned to the spot after the removal of the body and scraped the ground in order to wipe out his footprints. Redway won't admit that, but I'm certain of it — absolutely certain. I suppose the ass won't accept the theory because it isn't his own."

I tried to speak, but what could I say? The words I uttered resolved themselves into a mere expression of blank surprise, and perhaps it was as well, for the man before me was as keen and shrewd as any member of the Criminal Investigation Department. He was essentially a man of action, who whether busy or idle could not remain in one place five minutes together. He rushed all over the country-side from early morning, or dashed up to London by the express, spent the afternoon in Bond Street or the Burlington, and was back at home, a hundred miles distant, in time for dinner. He was perfectly tireless, possessing a demeanour which no amount of offence could ruffle, and an even temper and chaffing good-humour that was a most remarkable characteristic. The very name of Pink in Northamptonshire was synonymous of patient surgical skill combined with a spontaneous gaiety and bluff good-humour.

"I've given over that bit of white fur to Red way," he went on. "And I expect we shall find that the owner of it is also owner of the small shoes. I know most of the girls of Sibberton—in fact, I've attended all of them, I expect—but I can't suggest one who would, or even could, wear such a shoe as that upon the woman who was present at the tragedy, if not the actual assassin."

"Redway will make inquiries, I suppose?" I remarked in a faint hollow voice.

"At my suggestion he has wired for assistance, and I only hope they'll get a man down from London. If they don't—by Gad! I'll pay for one myself. We must find this woman, Woodhouse," he added, rising and tossing his cigarette-end into the grate. "We'll find her—at all costs!"

Chapter Seven
Is Full of Mystery

The doctor's keen desire to solve the mystery caused me most serious apprehension. His bluff good-humour, at other times amusing, now irritated me, and I was glad when he rose restlessly and went out, saying that he had wired to Doctor Newman at Northampton, and that they intended to make the post-mortem at two o'clock.

Presently, after a rest, which I so sorely needed, I walked along to the *Stanchester Arms* and had a private consultation with Warr in the little back parlour of the old-fashioned inn. Standing back from the road with its high swinging sign, it was a quaint, picturesque place, long and rambling, with the attic windows peeping forth from beneath the thatch. Half-hidden by climbing roses, clematis and jessamine it was often the admiration of artists, and many times had it been painted or sketched, for it was certainly one of the most picturesque of any of the inns in rural Northamptonshire, and well in keeping with the old-world peace of the Sibberton village itself.

Having again impressed upon the landlord the necessity of delivering the letter to Lolita in secret, as well as remaining utterly dumb regarding the stranger's visit, I was allowed to view the body of the unknown victim. It lay stretched upon some boards in the outhouse at rear of the inn, covered by a sheet, which on being lifted revealed the cold white face.

We stood there together in silence. In the dim light of the previous night and the uncertain glimmer of the lantern, I had not obtained an adequate idea of the young man's features, and it was in order to do this that I revisited the chamber of the dead.

For a long time I gazed upon that blanched countenance and sightless eyes, a face that seemed in those few hours to have altered greatly, having become shrunken, more refined, more transparent. The closely-cropped hair, the very even dark eyebrows, and the rather high cheek-bones were the most prominent features, and all of them, combined with the cut of his clothes and the shape of his boots, went to suggest that he was not an Englishman.

In those moments every feature of that calm dead face became photographed upon the tablets of my memory, and as it did so I somehow became convinced that he was not altogether a stranger. I had, I believed, met him previously somewhere—but where I could not determine. I recollected Warr's evasion of my question. Was he also puzzled, like myself?

Outside the inn half Sibberton had assembled to discuss the terrible affair, many of the village women wearing their lilac sun-bonnets, those old-world head-dresses that are, alas! so fast disappearing from rural England. The other half of the village had entered the park to see the spot where the terrible tragedy had been enacted.

For a moment I halted talking with a couple of men who made inquiry of me, knowing that I had first raised the alarm. And then I heard a dozen different theories in as many minutes. The rural mind is always quick to suggest motive where tragedy is concerned.

At noon I walked up to the Hall again, wondering if my love would show herself. I longed to get up to London and make inquiries at that pawnbroker's in the Westminster Bridge Road, as well as to call at the address she had given me in Chelsea. As she had said, only myself stood between her and death. The situation all-round was one of great peril, and I had, at all costs, to save her.

As I entered and crossed the hall, Slater, the old butler, approached, saying—

"His lordship would like to see you, sir. He's in the library."

So I turned and walked up the corridor of the east wing to that fine long old room with its thousands of rare volumes that had been the chief delight of the white-headed old peer who had spent the evening of his days in study.

"I say, Woodhouse!" cried the young Earl, springing from his chair as I entered, "what does this murder in the park last night mean?"

"It's a profound mystery," I replied. "The murdered man has not yet been identified."

"I know, I know," he said. "I went down to the inn with Pink this morning and saw him. And, do you know, he looks suspiciously like a fellow who followed me about in town several times last season."

"That's strange!" I exclaimed, much interested. "Yes, it is. I can't make it out at all. There's a mystery somewhere—a confounded mystery." And the young Earl thrust his hands deeply into his trousers pockets as he seated himself on the arm of a chair.

Tall, dark, good-looking, and a good all-round athlete, he was about thirty, the very picture of the well-bred Englishman. A few years in the Army had set him up and given him a soldierly bearing, while his face and hands, tanned as they were, showed his fondness for out-door sports. He kept up the Stanchester hounds, of which he was master, to that high degree of efficiency which rendered them one of the most popular packs in the country; he was an excellent polo player, a splendid shot, and a thorough all-round sportsman. In his well-worn grey flannels, and with a straw hat stuck jauntily on his head, he presented the picture of healthy manhood, wealthy almost beyond the dreams of avarice, a careless, easy-going, good-humoured man-of-the-world, whose leniency to his tenants was proverbial, and whose good-nature gave him wide popularity in Society, both in London and out of it.

By the man-in-the-street he was believed to be supremely content in his great possessions, his magnificent mansions, his princely bank balance, his steam yacht and his pack of hounds, yet I, his confidential friend and secretary, knew well the weariness and chagrin that was now eating out his heart. Her ladyship, two years his junior, was one of the three celebrated beauties known in London drawing-rooms as "the giddy Gordons," and who, notwithstanding her marriage, still remained the leader of that ultra-smart set, and always had one or two admirers in her train. She was still marvellously beautiful; her portraits, representing her yachting, motoring, shooting or riding to hounds, were familiar to every one, and after her marriage it had become the fashion to regard the Countess of Stanchester as one of the leaders of the London *mode*.

All this caused her husband deep regret and worry. He was unhappy, for with her flitting to and from the Continental spas, to Rome, to Florence, to Scotland, to Paris and elsewhere, he enjoyed little of her society, although he loved her dearly and had married her purely on that account.

Often in the silence of his room he sighed heavily when he spoke of her to me, and more than once, old friends that we were, he had unbosomed himself to me, so that, knowing what I did, I honestly pitied him. There was, in fact, affection just as strong in the heart of the millionaire landowner as in that of his very humble secretary.

"I had the misfortune to be born a rich man, Willoughby," he had once declared to me. "If I had been poor and had had to work for my living, I should probably have been far happier."

At the present moment, however, he seemed to have forgotten his own sorrows in the startling occurrence that had taken place within his own demesne, and his declaration that the man now dead had followed him in London was to me intensely interesting. It added more mystery to the affair.

"Are you quite certain that you recognise him?" I inquired a few moments later, wondering whether, if this were an actual fact, I had not also seen him when walking with the Earl in London.

"Well, not quite," was my companion's reply. "A dead man's face looks rather different to that of a living person. Nevertheless, I feel almost positive that he's the same. I recollect that the first occasion I saw him was at Ranelagh, when he came and sat close by me, and was apparently watching my every movement. I took no notice, because lots of people, when they ascertain who I am, stare at me as though I were some extraordinary species. A few nights later on, walking home from the Bachelors', I passed him in Piccadilly, and again on the next day he followed me persistently through the Burlington. Don't you remember, too, when Marigold held that bazaar in the drawing-room in aid of the Deep Sea Mission? Well, he came, and bought several rather expensive things. I confess that his constant presence grew very irritating, and although I said nothing to you at the time, for fear you would laugh at my apprehension, I grew quite timid, and didn't care to walk home from the club at night alone."

"Rather a pity you didn't point him out to me," I remarked, very much puzzled. "I, too, have a faint idea that I've seen him somewhere. It may have been that when I've walked with you he has followed us."

"Most likely," was the young Earl's reply. "He evidently had some fixed purpose in watching my movements, but what it could be is an entire mystery. During the last fortnight I was in town I always carried my little revolver, fearing—well, to tell you the truth, fearing lest he should make an attack upon me," he admitted with a smile. "The fact was, I had become thoroughly unnerved."

This confession sounded strange from a resolute athletic man of his stamp whom I had hitherto regarded as utterly fearless and possessing nerves of iron.

"And now," he went on, "the fellow is found murdered within half a mile of the house! Most extraordinary, isn't it?"

"Very remarkable—to say the least," I said reflectively. "The police will probably discover who and what he is."

"Police!" he laughed. "What do you think such a fellow as Redway could discover, except perhaps it were a mug of beer hidden by a publican after closing-time? No, I agree with Pink, we must have a couple of men down from London. It seems that Pink has found the print of a woman's shoe at the spot, while in the dead man's hand was grasped a piece of white fur. The suspicion is, therefore, that some woman has had a hand in it. I think, Willoughby, you'd best run up to London and get them to send down some smart man from the Criminal Investigation Department. Go and see my friend Layard, the Home Secretary, and tell him I sent you to obtain his assistance. He'll no doubt see that some capable person is sent."

I suggested that he should write a note to Sir Stephen Layard which I would deliver personally, and at once he sat down and scribbled a few lines in that heavy uneven calligraphy of his, for he had ever been a sad penman.

The net seemed to be slowly spreading for Lolita, yet what could I do to prevent this tracking down of the woman I loved?

The mystery of the man's movements in London had apparently thoroughly aroused the young Earl's desire to probe the affair to the bottom. And not unnaturally. None of us care to be followed and watched by an unknown man whose motive is utterly obscure.

So I was compelled to take the note and promise that I would deliver it to Layard that same evening.

"I mean to do all I can to find out who the fellow was and why he was killed," the Earl declared, striding up and down the room impatiently. "I've just seen Lolita, who seems very upset about it. She, too, admits that she saw the man watching me at Ranelagh, at the bazaar, and also at other places."

"I wonder what his motive could have been," I remarked, surprised that her ladyship should have made such a statement.

"Ah! That we must find out. His intentions were evil ones, without a doubt."

"But he didn't strike you as a thief?" I asked.

"Not at all. He was always very well-dressed and had something of a foreign appearance, although I don't believe he was a foreigner."

"How do you know?"

"Because I heard him speak. His voice had rather a Cockney ring in it, although he appeared to ape the Frenchman in dress and mannerisms, in order, I suppose, to be able to pass as one."

"An adventurer—without a doubt," I remarked. "But we shall know more before long. There are several facts which may afford us good clues."

"Yes, in the hands of an expert detective they may. That's why we must have a man down from London. You go to town and do your best, Willoughby, while I remain here and watch what transpires. The inquest is fixed for to-morrow at three, I hear, so you had better be back for it. The Coroner will no doubt want your evidence." And with that we both walked out together into the park, where the constabulary were still making a methodical examination of the whole of the area to the left of the great avenue.

I had intended to obtain another interview with Lolita, but now resolved that to keep apart from her for the present was by far the wisest course, therefore I accompanied the Earl as far as the fateful spot, and then continued my way home in order to lunch before driving to Kettering to catch the afternoon express to St. Pancras.

In the idle half-hour after my chop and claret, eaten by the way with but little relish, I lounged in my old armchair smoking my pipe, when of a sudden there flashed upon me the recollection of the ring I had secured from the dead man's hand. I ran up to my room, and taking it from the pocket of my dress-waistcoat carried it downstairs, where I submitted it to thorough and searching examination.

It was a ring of no ordinary pattern, the flat golden scarabaeus being set upon a swivel, while the remaining part of the ring was oval, so as to fit the finger. I put it on, and found that the scarabaeus being movable, it adapted itself to all movements of the finger, and that it was a marvellously fine specimen of the goldsmiths' art, and no doubt, as I had already decided, a copy of an antique Etruscan ornament.

The thickness of the golden sacred beetle attracted me, and I wondered whether it could contain anything within. Around the bottom edge were fashioned in gold the folded hairy legs of the insect just showing beneath its wings, and on examining them I discovered, to my surprise, that there was concealed a tiny hinge.

Instantly I took a pen-knife and gently prised it open, when I discovered that within it was almost like a locket, and that behind a small transparent disc of talc was concealed a tiny photograph—a pictured face the sight of which held me breathless. I could not believe my eyes.

Revealed there was a portrait of Lady Lolita Lloyd, the woman I loved, which the dead man had worn in secret upon his finger!

Chapter Eight
Wherein I Make Certain Discoveries

Alas! how I had, in loving Lolita, quaffed the sweet illusions of hope only to feel the venom of despair more poignant to my soul.

During the journey up to London my thoughts were fully occupied by the discovery of what that oddly-shaped ring contained. That portrait undoubtedly linked my love with the victim of the tragedy. But how? I believed myself acquainted with most, if not with all, of her many admirers, and if this unknown man were an actual rival then I had remained in entire and complete ignorance.

As the express rushed southward I sat alone in the compartment calmly examining my own heart and analysing my own feelings. Hope gilded my fancy, and I breathed again. I found that I loved, I reverenced woman, and had sought for a real woman to whom to offer my heart. Inherent in man is the love of something to protect; his very manhood requires that his strongest love should be showered on one who needs his strong arm to shelter her from the world, with all its troubles, all its sorrows, and all its sins. I wanted a companion, pure, loving, womanly; one who would complete what was wanting in myself; one whom I could reverence—and in Lady Lolita I had found my ideal.

Yet the difference of our stations was an insurmountable barrier in the first place, and in the second, if the young Earl knew that I, his secretary, had had the audacity to propose to his favourite sister, my connexion with the Stanchesters would, I knew, be abruptly severed. Nevertheless, I had with throbbing heart confessed my secret to my love, and being aware of my deep and honest affection she allowed me to bask in the sunshine of her beauty, and she was trusting in me to extricate her from a peril which she had declared might, alas! prove fatal.

Poor Stanchester! I pondered over his position, too—and I pitied him. Awakened from the temporary aberration which made him take as wife Lady Marigold Gordon, the racing girl and smart up-to-date maiden; conscious that the *camaraderie* of the billiard-room, the stable, and the shooting-party and the card-room was after all but a poor substitute for the true companionship of a wife. The young Countess, well-versed in French novels of doubtful taste, accomplished in manly sports, a good judge of a dog, capable of talking slang in and out of season, inured to cigarettes and strong drinks, had been an excellent "chum" for a short time, but she now preferred the freedom of her pre-matrimonial days, and drifted about wherever she could find pleasure and excitement. Indeed, she seemed to have more admirers now that she was the wife of the Earl of Stanchester than when she had been merely one of "the giddy Gordon girls."

The smoky sunset haze had settled over the Thames as I crossed Westminster Bridge in search of the pawnbroker's whose voucher had been found in the dead man's pocket, and a copy of which I had obtained before leaving Sibberton. It had been a blazing August day and every Londoner who could afford to escape from the city's turmoil was absent. Yet weather or season makes no appreciable difference to those hurrying millions who cross the bridges each evening to rush to their 'buses, trams or trains.

At six o'clock that summer's evening the crowd was just as thick on Westminster Bridge as on any night in winter. The million or so of absent holidaymakers are unnoticed in that wild desperate fight for the daily necessaries of life.

Without difficulty I found the shop where a combined business of jeweller's and pawnbroker's was carried on, and having sought the proprietor, a fat man in shirt-sleeves, of pronounced Hebrew type, I requested to be allowed to see the pledge in question.

He called his assistant, and after the lapse of a few minutes the latter descended the stairs carrying a small well-worn leather jewel-case which he placed upon the counter. The instant I saw it I held my breath, for upon it, stamped in gold, was the coronet and cipher of Lady Lolita Lloyd!

The pawnbroker opened it, and within I saw a necklet of seed pearls and amethysts which I had seen many times around my love's throat, an old Delhi necklace which her father had bought for her when in India years ago. In her youth it had been her favourite ornament, but recently she had not worn it.

Was it possible that it had been stolen—or had she made gift of it to him?

I took up the familiar necklet and held it in the hollow of my hand. I recollected how Lolita, with girlish pride, had shown it to me when she had received it as a present on her eighteenth birthday, and how, on occasions at parties and balls at Government House afterwards, it had adorned her white neck and its rather barbaric splendour had so often been admired.

"It's unredeemed, you know," remarked the black-haired Jew. "You shall have it for twenty pound—dirth cheap."

Ought I to secure it? The police would, no doubt, soon institute inquiries, and finding the coronet and cipher upon the case would at once connect my love with the mysterious affair. But I had by good fortune forestalled them, therefore I saw that at all hazards I must secure it.

I pretended to examine it in the fading light at the window, lingering so as to gain time to form some plans. I had not twenty pounds in my pocket; to give a cheque would be to betray my name, and the banks had closed long ago.

At last, after some haggling, more in order to conceal my anxiety to obtain it than anything else, I said, with affected reluctance—

"I haven't the money with me. It's a pretty thing, but a trifle too dear." And I turned as though to leave.

"Well, now, ninetheen pound won't hurt yer. You shall 'ave it for ninetheen pound."

"Eighteen ten, if you like," I said. "What time do you close?"

"Nine."

"Then I'll be back before that with the money," I answered, and I saw the gleam of satisfaction in the Hebrew's eyes, for it had been pawned for five pounds. He, however, was not aware that it was I who was getting the best of the bargain.

I drove in a cab back to the Constitutional Club, where I had left my bag for the night, and the secretary, a friend of mine, at once cashed a cheque, with the result that within an hour I had the necklet and deposited-it safely in my suit-case, gratified beyond measure to know that at least I had baffled the police in the possession of this very suspicious piece of evidence.

From the Jew I had endeavoured to ascertain casually who had pledged the ornament, but neither he nor his assistant recollected. In that particularly improvident part of London with its floating population of struggling actors and music-hall artistes, each pawnbroker has thousands of chance clients, therefore recollection is well-nigh impossible.

Having successfully negotiated this matter, however, a second and more difficult problem presented itself, namely, how was I to avoid delivering the letter to Sir Stephen Layard, the Home Secretary—the Earl's request that the Criminal Investigation Department should hound down the woman I adored?

My duty was to go at once to Pont Street and deliver the Earl's note, but my loyalty to my love demanded that I should find some excuse for withholding it.

I stood on the club steps in Northumberland Avenue watching the arrivals and departures from the *Hotel Victoria* opposite, hesitating in indecision. If I did not call upon Sir Stephen, then some suspicion might be aroused, therefore I resolved to see him and during the interview nullify by some means the urgency of the Earl's request.

The Cabinet Minister, a middle-aged, clean-shaven man with keen eyes and very pronounced aquiline features, entered the library a few minutes after I had sent in my card. He was in evening clothes, having, it appeared, just dined with several guests, but was nevertheless eager to serve such a powerful supporter of his party as the Earl of Stanchester.

We had met before, therefore I needed no introduction, but instead of delivering the letter I deemed it best to explain matters in my own way.

"I must apologise for intruding at this hour, Sir Stephen," I commenced, "but the fact is that a very curious and tragic affair has happened in the Earl of Stanchester's park down at Sibberton, and he has sent me to ask your opinion as to the best course to pursue in order to get the police at Scotland Yard to take up the matter."

"What, is it a mystery or something?" inquired the well-known statesman, quickly alert.

I described how the body of the unknown man had been discovered, but added purposely that the inquest had not yet been held, and there that were several clues furnished by articles discovered in the dead man's pockets.

"Well, the Northampton police are surely able to take up such a plain, straightforward case as that!" he remarked. "If not, they are not worth very much, I should say."

"But his lordship has not much faith in the intelligence of the local constabulary," I ventured to remark with a smile.

"Local constables are not usually remarkable for shrewdness or inventiveness," he laughed. "But surely at the headquarters of the county constabulary they have several very experienced and clever officers. With such clues there can surely be little difficulty in establishing the man's identity."

"Then you think it unnecessary to place the matter in the hands of the Criminal Investigation Department?" I remarked.

"Quite—at least for the present," was his reply, which instantly lifted a great weight from my mind. "We must allow the coroner's jury to give their verdict, and, at any rate, give the local police an opportunity of making proper inquiries before we take the matter out of their hands. I much regret being unable to assist the Earl of Stanchester in the matter, but at present I am really unable to order Scotland Yard to take the matter up. If, however, the local police fail, then perhaps you will kindly tell him that I shall be very pleased to reconsider the request, and, if possible, grant it." This was exactly the reply I desired. Indeed, I had put my case lamely on purpose, and had gradually led him to this decision.

"Of course," I said, "I will explain to his lordship the exact position and your readiness to order expert assistance as soon as such becomes absolutely imperative. By the way," I added, "he gave me a note to you." And I then produced it, as though an after-thought.

He glanced over it and laid it upon his table, repeating his readiness to render the Earl all the assistance he could when the proper time came—the usual evasive reply of the Cabinet Minister.

Then he shook hands with me, and I left him, reassured that I had at least prevented the introduction of any of those clever experts in criminal investigation. The suspicions against Lolita grew darker every hour, yet even though they were well-grounded I was determined to save her.

That broad-shouldered man with whom I had seen her strolling in the early morning after the tragedy puzzled me greatly. Had I only obtained sight of him, I should, perhaps, have learnt the truth. Yet when I reviewed the whole of the mysterious circumstances my brain became awhirl. They were bewildering, for the mystery had become even more inscrutable than it at first appeared.

That my love had some connexion with the affair, I could not for a moment disguise. Her manner, her very admissions in themselves convicted her. Therefore I felt that with the facts of which I was already in possession I had greater chance than the most expert detective of pursuing my own inquiries to a successful issue.

On leaving Sir Stephen Layard's about nine o'clock, I resolved to ascertain what kind of house was number ninety-eight in Britten Street, Chelsea, the place where lived the Frenchwoman, Lejeune. I recollected the desperate words of my love on the previous night and wondered whether the death of the unknown man might not have altered the circumstances. Somehow I had a distinct suspicion that it might, hence I resolved not to reveal my presence at the place until I had again consulted Lolita.

The darkness was complete when I alighted from the cab in the King's Road, Chelsea, and turned down the rather dark but respectable street of even two-storied, deep-basemented houses that ran down towards the Embankment. It was one of those thoroughfares like Walpole Street and Wellington Square, where that rapacious genus, the London landlady, flourishes and grows sleek upon the tea, sugar and bottled beer of lodgers. In the night the houses seemed most grimy and depressing, some of them half-covered by sickly creepers, and others putting forward an attempt at colour with their stunted geraniums in window-boxes.

The double rap of the postman on his last round sounded time after time, by which I knew he was approaching me, therefore I retraced my steps into the King's Road and awaited him.

He had, I noticed, finished his round, therefore a cheery word and an invitation to have a drink at the flaring public-house opposite soon rendered us friendly, and without many preliminaries I explained my reason for stopping him.

"Oh!" laughed the man, "we're often stopped by people who make inquiries about those who live on our walks. Number ninety-eight Britten Street—a Frenchwoman? Oh, yes. Name of Lejeune. She doesn't have many letters, but they're mostly foreign ones."

"What kind of people live there?" I inquired, whereupon he eyed me rather strangely, I thought, and asked—

"You're not a friend of theirs, I suppose?"

"Not at all. I don't know them."

"Well, I'll tell you in confidence. Mind, however, you don't let it out to a single soul—but the fact is that the house is under the observation of the police, and has been for some time. Sergeant Bullen, the detective, is on duty up there at the end of the road," and he jerked his thumb in that direction. "He said good-night to me only a minute ago."

"The place is being watched, then?" I gasped in surprise.

"Yes. They've been keeping it under observation night and day for a week or more. Bullen told me one day that they expect to make an arrest which will cause a great sensation."

"For whom are they lying in wait?"

"Oh, that I'm sure I can't tell you! The 'tecs, although I know 'em well, don't talk very much, you know." And then, after some further questions to which I received entirely unsatisfactory answers, we parted.

Chapter Nine
Tells Some Strange Truths

Along the dark street, quiet after the glare and bustle of the King's Road, I retraced my steps, when, about half-way up, I met a man dressed as a mechanic, idly smoking a pipe. He glanced quickly at me as I passed beneath the light of a street-lamp, and I guessed from his searching look that he was the detective Bullen.

Without apparently taking notice of him I went along almost to the end of the street, until I discovered that the house which Lolita had indicated differed little from its neighbours save that it was rendered a trifle more dingy perhaps by the London smoke. And yet the large printed numerals on the fanlight over the door gave it a bold appearance that the others did not seem to possess. The area was a deep one, but the shutters of the kitchen window were tightly closed. With the exception of the light in the hall the place seemed in darkness, presenting to me a strange, mysterious appearance, knowing all that I did. Why, I wondered, was that police officer lounging up and down keeping such a vigilant surveillance upon the place? Surely it was with some distinct motive that a plain-clothes man watched the house day and night, and to me that motive seemed that they expected that some person, now absent, might return.

There is often much mystery in those rows of smoke-blackened uniform houses that form the side-streets of London's great thoroughfares, and the presence of the police here caused me to ponder deeply.

My first impulse had been to try and get sight of the mysterious Frenchwoman and her associates, but to escape the observation of that vigilant watcher was, I knew, impossible. So I passed along down to the Embankment, where the river flowed darkly on and the lights cast long reflections.

I was puzzled. I could not well approach the detective without making some explanation of who I was, and by doing so I recognised that I might inadvertently connect my employer's sister with whatever offence the inmates of the mysterious house had committed.

Yet when I recollected that wild terrified declaration of Lolita's on the previous night, how she had told me that if the Frenchwoman withheld her secret "it must result in my death," I felt spurred to approach her at all hazards. There are moments in our lives when, disregarding our natural caution, we act with precipitation and injudiciously. I fear I was given to hot-headed actions, otherwise I should never have dared to run the risk of arousing suspicion in Bullen's mind as I did during the hours that followed.

From the fact that the house was in darkness there seemed to me a chance that the woman Lejeune was absent and that she might return home during the evening. The detective was apparently keeping watch at the King's Road end of the street, therefore I resolved to keep a vigilant eye on the Embankment end. She might perchance approach from that direction, and if she did I hoped that I should be able to stop her and obtain a few minutes' conversation. It was true that I did not know her, yet I felt sufficient confidence in my knowledge of persons to be able to pick out a Frenchwoman in a half-deserted London thoroughfare. The gait and manner of holding the skirts betray the daughter of Gaul anywhere.

Patiently I lounged at the corner, compelled to keep an eye upon the detective's movements lest he should notice my continued presence. Apparently, however, he had no suspicion of a second watcher, for he stood at the opposite end of the street gossiping with all and sundry, and passing the hours as best he could. Presently a ragged newsvendor came up, and after exchanging words the man shuffled along the street in my direction, while the detective went off to get his supper. Then I knew that the ragged man was one of those spies and informers often employed by the London police and who are known in the argot of the gutter as "policemen's noses."

I avoided him quickly, well knowing that such men are as keen-eyed and quick-witted as the detectives themselves, being often called upon to perform observation work where the police would be handicapped and at once recognised. Many a crime in London is detected, and many a criminal brought to justice by the aid of the very useful "policeman's nose," whose own record, be it said, is often the reverse of clean.

It was then nearly eleven o'clock. The newsvendor had seated himself upon a doorstep half-way up the road and almost opposite the house with the number upon the fanlight, munching his supper, which he had produced from his pocket. I had watched him from around the corner and was turning back towards the Embankment, when of a sudden I heard footsteps.

On the opposite side, by the parapet which divided the roadway from the river, two persons were walking slowly, a man and a woman. In an instant I strained my eyes in their direction, and as they passed beneath one of the lamps I saw that the woman was young, dark-haired, thin-faced and rather well-dressed, while her companion was older, bearded, with a reddish bloated face which betokened an undue consumption of alcoholic liquors. As they passed on towards Britten Street I stepped across the road and walked behind them when, next instant, I recognised by the man's dress and his broad back view that he was none other than he whom I had observed walking with Lolita in the wood that morning—the stranger whose face I had not then plainly seen!

My curiosity was aroused immediately, for on hearing the woman make an observation in French I knew that she must be the person of whom I was in search.

Was she, I wondered, aware that the police were watching her house? Should I not, by placing her on her guard, ingratiate myself with her? My object was to get her to speak the truth and thus save Lolita, therefore I should have greater chance of success were I her benefactor.

She and her companion, whoever he was, were stepping straight into the trap laid for them, therefore on the spur of the moment, regardless of the fact that I might be the means of enabling certain criminals to escape from justice, I stepped boldly up to her just before they turned the corner into Britten Street and, raising my hat, said—

"Excuse me, mademoiselle, but your name, I believe, is Lejeune?"

The pair started quickly, and I saw that they were utterly confused. They were evidently endeavouring to reach the house by the less-frequented route.

"Well, and what if it is?" inquired the broad-shouldered man in a harsh bullying tone, speaking with a pronounced Cockney accent and putting forward his flabby bull-dog face in a threatening attitude.

"There's no occasion for hot blood, my dear sir," I replied quietly. "Just turn and walk back a few yards. I'm here to speak with mademoiselle—not with you."

"And what do you wish with me?" the young woman inquired in very fair English.

"Come back a few yards and I'll explain," I responded quickly. "First, let me tell you that my name is Willoughby Woodhouse, and that I am private secretary to the Earl of Stanchester."

"Woodhouse!" gasped her companion involuntarily, and I saw that his face went pale. "You are Mr Woodhouse!"

"Yes," I continued, "and I have been sent here to you by Lady Lolita Lloyd to warn you that your house is being watched by the police."

"The police!" ejaculated the man. "Are they there now?"

"They are. A detective has been keeping observation all the evening."

"Then we must fly," he whispered quickly. "By Jove! we've had a narrow escape! And, sir, I can only apologise for what I've just said. Of course I didn't know who you were. The fact is I thought you were yourself a detective."

"No apology is needed," I smiled. "I've only one further word to deliver from her ladyship," I added, turning to the young Frenchwoman, "and it is that, having given you this timely warning, she hopes that you will not fail to let her know your whereabouts. She also says that you are to regard myself as the intermediary between you."

"Tell her that I shall not fail to recognise this kindness," was the woman's answer in her broken English. "But for her we might both have fallen into the hands of the police. I've been absent a fortnight, but thought that all was clear, otherwise I should not have dared to return here."

"Come, let's get away," urged her companion anxiously.

It was on the tip of my tongue to remark upon his presence in the Monk's Wood with her ladyship, but perhaps fortunately I held my peace. He seemed more in fear of detection than she did, for his face had gone ghastly pale and his bloodshot eyes were turned back upon the street-corner.

"Have you any message for her ladyship?" I inquired eagerly of the woman.

"Only my thanks to her."

"But," I said, bending to her and speaking in a low very earnest voice, "she is in grave peril. Only the truth, spoken by yourself, can save her. Recollect by giving you this warning she is saving you from the police."

"I know. I know!" she replied. "I am fully aware of the disaster which threatens her. Tell her that I have not yet myself learned the whole truth. When I do, I will write to her."

"But you will surely tell what you know?" I urged quickly.

"At risk of incriminating myself? Not likely," was her reply.

"Then when the blow falls—as fall it must—it will kill her," I said, disregarding the man's presence, for I felt that he must certainly be aware of everything.

"Perhaps," was her vague answer, in a hard strained voice. "If I could help her I would. At present, however, it is utterly impossible."

"Not after this great service she has rendered to you? She has rescued you, remember."

"Because it is not to her own interests that she should be connected with the affair," she remarked with what seemed a sneer.

Then, for the first time, I realised what a terrible mistake I had committed. The warning I had given this woman she actually believed to be an additional sign of weakness on the part of my well-beloved!

"But her very life depends upon your words," I cried. "You surely will not now withhold the truth?"

"I can say nothing—at least at present," she responded evasively.

"But you must—you hear?" I cried. "You must!"

"I shall not until it suits me," was the woman's defiant answer, as her dark eyes flashed quickly upon me, and I recognised with what kind of person I had to deal. "Tell her that in this matter the stake is her life, or mine—and I prefer to keep my own." And she laughed that harsh discordant laugh of a Frenchwoman triumphant.

"Then you refuse to tell the truth?" I demanded fiercely.

"I do."

In that instant a bold plan had suggested itself. She expected to escape, but now she defied me I had no intention that she should; therefore I sprang forward, seized her, and at the same time shrieked with all my might—

"Murder! Murder! Help—*help!*"

Her companion flung himself upon me, beating me about the head, but I had gripped them both, and in a few moments there sounded hurrying footsteps and several persons, including the detective Bullen, came tearing round the street-corner.

Next second the pair recognised how very neatly they had been trapped.

Chapter Ten
The Earl of Stanchester Speaks his Mind

"Let me go!" cried the woman, speaking in French in her excitement. "Let us cry quits and I will tell the truth. If I am arrested, Lady Lolita must also fall into the hands of the police. You do not know everything or you would not do this! Let us go—and save her."

There was something in her quick argument that struck me as truthful. If the pair were arrested they might certainly lay some counter-charge, true or false, against my love, therefore with as sudden an impulse as I had raised the alarm I released my hold, saying—

"Very well. That's a bargain. I shall hold you both to it, remember. Get away as quickly as you can."

And before the detective, the newsvendor and the two other men attracted by my shouts could reach the spot, the pair had sped along the Chelsea Embankment as fast as their legs could carry them and turned into a narrow thoroughfare running parallel with Britten Street.

The detective had, of course, not recognised them and when he inquired what was the matter I merely explained that two drunken men had struck me on the head when passing, and that I had been alarmed.

"Well," he grunted, "you needn't have kicked up such a fuss. We thought you were being killed, at least!"

"The fact is," I responded lamely, "I was frightened. I'm from the country, you see, and don't appreciate the horseplay of your London hooligans."

"Then you'd better not take evening walks along this place," was the man Bullen's response, while the ragged newsvendor picked up my battered silk hat, and handing it to me with a grim laugh, said—

"You'll want a new 'un, sir. Them 'ooligans likes toppers. Some o' Jimmy Boyle's gang agin, I 'spect."

To which the detective answered—

"I expect so. They'll get into trouble one of these nights."

And so the curious incident ended. I walked with them to the further end of Britten Street, taking leave of the unsuspecting detective in the King's Road. He returned to his vigil, but I laughed within myself knowing how ingeniously the wily pair had slipped through his fingers.

On my drive back to the club I wondered whether I had acted wisely. At any rate I had made the acquaintance of the woman Lejeune, and had succeeded in showing her that I was prepared to aid her in exchange for the secret upon the knowledge of which Lolita's future depended. Whether she would keep faith with me was quite another matter.

I deeply regretted that I had not been able to ascertain the name of the man who had been Lolita's companion and had talked so earnestly with her in the wood. Without doubt he knew of the tragedy in the park—if, indeed, he were not the actual murderer. This latter suspicion became somehow impressed upon me. His face had gone ashen grey when I had revealed to them that a detective was awaiting them round the corner.

Was it possible that he had come to London in order to hide, knowing that the Metropolis is the best place to secrete oneself in all the world.

Next day at noon I sat in the schoolroom at Sibberton, listening to the opening of the Coroner's inquiry into the tragedy. The facts having already got into the papers, the small room was crowded to suffocation by villagers and outsiders. The jury had viewed the body over at the *Stanchester Arms* opposite, and after a few introductory remarks from the Coroner, a solicitor from Northampton, I was called as the first witness.

I told how I had obtained the assistance of the publican Warr, and described how we had found the body of the murdered man. Then, when I had concluded, the foreman of the jury, a man who combined the avocation of baker and local preacher, asked—

"What first aroused your attention?"

"I heard a noise," I replied. I did not intend to tell them the truth— that it was a woman's cry. "A noise from behind the trees in the avenue," I added. "It was very dark at that point."

"You saw no one?"

"Nobody. I came to the village at once for assistance."

"Any other questions to ask?" inquired the Coroner of the jury.

"I would like, sir, to inquire whether Mr Woodhouse had any suspicion of the body having been searched before he discovered it?" asked Redway, the police officer.

My answer was a negative one. I feared he was about to question me regarding the footprints, and held my breath in fear and expectation.

"What time elapsed between the hour when you heard the noise and the discovery of the tragic occurrence?" the Coroner asked.

"About half an hour."

A dozen other questions upon points of detail were put to me, but they were of no importance. Neither was the evidence given by Warr or any other of the witnesses, except perhaps that of Dr Pink, who, in his sharp way and using many medical terms which conveyed no meaning to the majority of those in the room, explained that the result of the post-mortem was that the man had been fatally stabbed.

"The instrument used was not an ordinary knife," the doctor continued. "From the appearance of the wound it must have been inflicted by a long thin triangular instrument almost like a skewer. With a sharp point this would penetrate the man's clothing much more easily than a knife or dagger, which requires considerable force to drive to the heart. My colleague, Doctor Newman, agrees with me that such an instrument as was used could be used fatally with very little force. It was, at the point, almost as sharp as a needle, and each of the three sides were keen-edged as razors—a terrible weapon. I don't think it was much more than a quarter of an inch across at its widest part."

The public heard this and sat mystified.

"Then it would appear very much as though the crime were a premeditated one," remarked the Coroner, looking up when he had finished laboriously writing down the depositions with his scratchy quill.

"Undoubtedly," replied the doctor. "The man is a complete stranger, and no doubt kept an appointment at that spot and was done to death. The steel inflicted a mortal wound, and he must have expired in a few moments."

"Any questions to ask the doctor?" inquired the Coroner turning to the twelve villagers who sat in a row in their Sunday clothes.

There was no response, therefore Redway was called, and the public, to whom he was well-known, were instantly on the alert.

"Philip Redway, inspector, Northamptonshire Constabulary," he commenced, giving his evidence with the business-like air of police officials. "I was called by Constable Knight of Sibberton at five AM on the 18th of August and drove back with him to a spot in Sibberton Park where the deceased had been discovered. I examined the ground carefully and found certain marks of footprints, casts of which I have taken. I afterwards saw the body of the deceased, but do not identify him. His description has been circulated throughout the Kingdom, but up to the present no one has recognised him. I have also had the body photographed."

"These footprints?" asked the Coroner, laying down his pen and looking at the inspector. "Are you of opinion that they will form any substantial clue to the assassin?"

"The marks were those of a woman's feet," Redway explained, whereat there was a stir of sensation among the public, who sat so quiet and open-mouthed that the proverbial pin might hitherto have been heard had it been dropped.

"Recent?"

"No doubt," was his reply. "There were also the marks of the boots worn by deceased—and of others. The latter were probably those of Mr Woodhouse, Mr Warr and Constable Knight. They were so overtrodden that it was very difficult to recognise any distinctly. One fact, however, that I might mention, sir, and which adds a peculiar mystery to this case, is that I discovered that certain footprints had been deliberately erased."

"Erased!" exclaimed the Coroner, surprised. "How do you mean?"

"Scratched over by some person who was able to visit the spot before I could arrive there."

"Some accomplice?"

"It seems so. The spot was unfortunately left unguarded during Knight's absence to warn me, and in that time it would appear that some one went there and deliberately set about to defeat the ends of justice."

"This seems very curious and suspicious, gentlemen," remarked the Coroner, re-adjusting his gold pince-nez as he turned to the twelve expectant jurymen. "If the theory of the police is true, then some second person, having knowledge of the crime, risked arrest and actually went to the spot and effaced those tell-tale marks. That the assassin had an accomplice is thus proved without a doubt. Therefore I think that under such peculiar circumstances you should leave the matter in the hands of the police to investigate. They will, I hope, be able both to establish the dead man's identity, and to fix the crime upon the guilty person. In cases such as this it is always best for the jury to return a verdict of 'Wilful Murder against some person or persons unknown,' as it allows the police an entirely free hand afterwards, and prevents them from being compelled in evidence to disclose the nature or direction of the inquiries."

"Redway's a fool. He'll discover nothing," whispered the Earl to me, as he stood beside me in the further corner of the schoolroom. "If Sir Stephen had stirred up Scotland Yard we might have hoped for success. But now it's in Redway's hands we may rest assured it will be bungled from the very first."

"I fear so," was my reply, although at heart I was honestly glad that the inquiries were left to the local constabulary.

"Well, sir," exclaimed the foreman of the jury to the Coroner, "we are, I think, entirely in your hands."

"You've heard the evidence, and that is as far as we can proceed to-day," he said. "Of course if you deem it wiser to adjourn for a week you may do so. You are here to decide not who committed the murder but to inquire by what means the deceased came by his death. About the latter I think you can have no doubt, and if you return a verdict in accordance with the evidence—a verdict of wilful murder—then the police will push their inquiries, I hope, to some successful issue. Are you all agreed?"

The twelve villagers in their Sunday tweeds whispered together and the local baker at last replied in the affirmative. Then the verdict was signed, and Knight in a loud voice thanked the jury for their attendance and declared the court closed.

Thus ended the official inquiry into the death of the man unknown—the man who had carried secreted within his vest the paper with those strange cabalistic numbers written upon it, and who, strangest of all, had worn in the ring upon his finger a portrait of my love!

Chapter Eleven
Certain Questions and their Answers

The inquest concluded, I walked back to the Hall with the Earl. The latter was annoyed that the Home Secretary had not acted upon his suggestion. He was young, and therefore impetuous sometimes, as a man of his great wealth is perhaps apt to be. Since his marriage he had, I noticed, become more quick-tempered, restless and rather less good-humoured than in his buoyant bachelor days. The gay irresponsibility of Marigold, his wife, worried him, I knew, and I therefore looked upon his irritability as only natural.

"The whole thing's a confounded mystery, Woodhouse," he remarked after a long silence as we went up the avenue, glad of the shade, for it was a blazing day. "I haven't yet told that thick-headed fool Redway about the fellow watching me in London. Do you think I ought?"

"No," I answered. "Let him find out for himself. He's got lots of self-assurance, therefore he may, I think, be allowed to show his great talent as a tracker of criminals."

"By Jove! you're right," he laughed. "If it were not for the fact that I should be aiding him, I'd pay a smart private detective myself to look into the matter. What's all that rot he says about finding a woman's footprint there? I expect it's only where one of the maids from the Hall has passed along. I've lots of times seen courting couples from the village going along on the grass parallel with these trees, so as to avoid being noticed by any of us." I did not remark that neither the girls of Sibberton nor the maids at the Hall were in the habit of wearing Louis XV heels. On the contrary, I entirely agreed with my employer's remarks.

He wanted to see Frank Blew, his huntsman, therefore we struck across the wide level park to the curious old building, the gate of which, flanked by two circular towers, presented the appearance of an ancient castle, and entered the celebrated kennels of the Stanchester Foxhounds.

Blew and his assistants were in the paved courts, wearing long white smocks over their clothes and engaged in feeding the hounds as we entered. The instant we passed the low wicket-gate a dozen of them were pawing us, while the Earl, knowing each of the pack by name, cried—

"Down Jason! Down Jerry! Down Bound-away." And each addressed by name obediently returned to his companions.

"I've decided the date, Blew," the Earl said. "We begin cubbing three weeks on Monday, so you'll have everything ready."

"Yes, m'lord."

"We'll commence in the covers around the park, as usual, you know. I shall fix the first meet at Spring Wood, at five. Her ladyship will be back, and both she and Lady Lolita intend cubbing this season."

"Glad to hear that, m'lord. Last season all the Hunt regretted that the Countess came out so very little."

"Well, let's hope we kill as many cubs as we did last back-end. I wish all of you the best of good luck."

"Thank you, m'lord; we shall all of us do our best, I assure you." And the sharp-nosed, thin-faced, thin-legged huntsman, one of the "cracks" of England, touched his cap to his master to whom he had always been devoted ever since the days when he was only a stable "helper" and young Lord Sibberton used to ride to the meets on his pony.

There is still among hunting-men in England, both master and servant, a genuine *camaraderie* that exists in no other sport. In the hunting-field the Master is supreme to control and direct; and after that millionaire and farmer, countess and vicar's daughter, squire and horse-breaker are all on equality, all keen upon the running down of the crafty marauder of the hen-roost.

Therefore it was not really surprising that Blew was the Earl's adviser in all connected with the pack and with the hunt, and that in his absence at San Remo in the latter part of the winter season, or in London, he left the hounds for Frank Blew to hunt, and surely a better huntsman there was not in all the shires. After leaving Sibberton he had graduated in the Belvoir, and the Quorn kennels, and had returned to the old Earl's service as kennel-huntsman and subsequently as huntsman.

Some conversation followed regarding the condition of the puppies, the bad epidemic of distemper, and the consequent fatality among them; the naming of some fresh puppies which were to be put out to "walk" with farmers on the estate, and then, with Blew accompanying us to the gate and raising his cap, we struck away across the park, back again to the Hall.

I lunched alone, and about four o'clock had finished the correspondence. My brain was on fire. I wanted to see Lolita, for truth to tell I wished to ascertain from her how much she knew regarding the dead man who had worn her portrait in secret.

When I had met her in that draggled condition in the wood I had purposely made no mention of the crime and its discovery, preferring to allow her to make some mention of it herself. But she had made no remark. Perhaps she, too, had been waiting for me to broach the unwelcome subject. One thing was, however, plain: with the exception of that unfortunate footprint of which Redway had taken a cast, she had succeeded in very cleverly hiding the fact that she had been absent from her room that night, or that she had had any connexion whatsoever with the tragedy.

I thought of the necklet which I now had locked safely in my room down in the village, and wondered how it possibly could have come into the young man's possession a year ago. It surely had not been stolen, otherwise she would have remarked upon her loss. Had she given it to him? That was the question which constantly held me thinking and wondering.

I awaited my opportunity to encounter her when tea was served in the hall and, there being no visitors, she seated herself at the great silver tray and handed me my cup. The Earl had ridden over to Laxton, therefore we were alone, except for the irritating presence of Slater, the grave-faced old butler.

She was dressed to go out walking, her brown tailor-made gown fitting her like a glove and her smart straw *canotier* to match gave her that *chic*, almost Parisienne appearance which was so characteristic of her well-bred style. She always dressed well, without any undue show of laces and trimmings, but with that exquisite taste which betokens the well-turned-out woman who is an aristocrat.

I stood before the great old fireplace with its enormous bright steel dogs of an age bygone, and chatted to her, noting that in her face there was no trace of anxiety, so well did she conceal her feelings before the servants. Our conversation was rather strained, it was true, mostly about a tennis tournament over at Drayton and regarding the decision of her brother to cut down and grub-up Oxen Wood, a favourite cover which he had suddenly taken it into his head to sweep away. Then, when tea had finished, she announced her intention of walking across the park to Stanion village and invited me to accompany her.

This I eagerly did, and a few moments later we were out in the bright afternoon sunshine. Our way led first up the north avenue across the deer park for half-a-mile, then along a narrow path through one of the densest woods in the district, called Geddington Chase, and afterwards skirted the river for some distance to Stanion mill, and thence by the high road to the village.

"You have been to London," she exclaimed in a low voice as soon as we were safely out of hearing from the Hall. "Well, did you recollect what I told you?"

"I did, and I acted according to your directions," was my quiet answer.

"And what did the woman say?" she inquired, turning to me eagerly, her face suddenly anxious and changed.

"She told me nothing. She refused to speak."

"Ah!" my idol gasped, and I saw the light of hope at once die from her countenance. "As I expected! Just as I feared!"

"She says she cannot yet tell the truth," I hastened to explain. "But I have made a compact with her."

"How?"

Then I explained how I had discovered the house in Britten Street watched by the police; and how I had been able to give the Frenchwoman warning.

"But," I said, "will you pardon me, Lolita, if I remark upon one most peculiar circumstance?"

She started visibly and held her breath, for the tragedy had never been mentioned between us, and it seemed as though she feared I would broach it.

"You will recollect," I went on, "that when I met you early yesterday morning you were accompanied by a man who—"

"Ah, you saw him, then!" she gasped, interrupting me.

"I did. And moreover I met that same man in Mademoiselle's company last night."

"With her!" she cried. "Never! Why, he doesn't know her."

"I met them walking together on the Chelsea Embankment," I persisted in a quiet tone, wondering the reason of her utter amazement.

"How? Where? Tell me all about it?" she urged quickly. "There's mystery here."

In obedience to her wish I explained the circumstances just as I have already recorded them; how I had first implored her to divulge her secret, and then in order to threaten her, had called the police, afterwards making a solemn compact with her and allowing them both to escape.

She heard me in silence to the end, nervously pulling her veil beneath her chin and twisting it to keep it tight. Then sighing, she remarked, turning her wonderful eyes upon me—

"She is not the woman to keep any promise, Willoughby. It is just as I feared! She is afraid to tell the truth lest she herself should suffer. Her words only confirm that."

I recalled what she had said, and was bound to agree.

"But surely," I cried, "the outlook is not so black as you anticipate? If this woman, in order to safeguard herself, refuses to speak, are there not other means by which the truth could be revealed?"

"No—none!" was her despairing answer as she shook her head.

"Perhaps I acted unwisely in allowing them to slip through the fingers of the police?" I suggested.

"No. It was wise, very wise. Had they been arrested they would both have sought to seriously incriminate me—and—and the blow would have fallen. I—I should have killed myself to avoid arrest," she added in the low hoarse voice of a woman absolutely desperate.

"Oh, don't speak like that, Lolita," I urged earnestly. "Recollect you have at least in me a true and loyal friend. I will defend you by every means in my power. You refuse to tell me this strange secret of yours; nevertheless I am ready to serve you without seeking to penetrate the mystery which you are so determined to withhold."

"I would tell you everything if I dared," she assured me with a sweet grateful look upon her countenance, and I saw that upon her veil a teardrop glistened. I saw too how agitated she was, and how she longed to take me entirely into her confidence—yet dared not do so. Why, I wondered, had she made no remark upon the tragedy or upon the Coroner's verdict that morning. Was that, too, a subject which she dare not mention?

I glanced at the boots she was wearing, and saw that they were small dark-brown ones but with those same Louis XV heels that had left such tell-tale traces.

"Is your secret such a terrible one that you fear to entrust it to me?" I asked gravely after a brief pause.

"You couldn't understand—you couldn't believe the real facts even if I told you," was her reply. "Besides, this refusal of the woman Lejeune prevents me knowing the real truth myself. She intends that I shall suffer— that I shall pay the penalty of the crime of another. She vowed revenge and, alas!" she sighed, "she has it now."

"But she's quite a common person," I remarked, for knowing the Continent as I did, and being some thing of a cosmopolitan, I put her down as of the lower class.

"It is her foreign ill-breeding that renders her such a bitter enemy. She has no pity and no remorse—indeed what Frenchwoman has?"

"Then I was a fool to let her escape! Had I known, I would have given the pair into the detective's hands and faced the worst."

"And by so doing you would have caused my death!" was her low remark in a hard strained voice. We had climbed the hill and arrived at the edge of Geddington Chase, where we halted at the old weather-worn stile which gave entrance to the wood.

"Yet by allowing them to escape it seems that I have unwittingly been their accessory!" I remarked. "You do not anticipate that this woman Lejeune will reveal the truth and thus place you in a position of safety. Therefore, why should we shield her?"

"I feel sure she will not—now that she is friendly with Joseph Logan."

"You mean the man who was with you at early morning?"

She nodded in the affirmative, and with a sigh declared: "The interests of the pair are entirely identical. Even if she wished to reveal what she knew, he would prevent her. I never anticipated that they would become acquainted and thus unite their evil intentions against myself!"

"Against you?" I cried. "Why?"

"It is an intrigue—a vile and ingenious plot against myself and certain persons who are innocent and unoffending. Ah! If you only knew the woman Lejeune as I have reason to know her, you would not ask such a question. You, too, would be well aware that the man or woman unfortunate enough to fall into her cunningly-devised pitfalls may at once abandon all hope of the future—for death alone can release them from the bond." I failed to understand the true meaning of those words which sounded to my ears so wild and tragic. The mystery of it was all-consuming. I tried to discern some light through the dark cloud that had so suddenly fallen and enveloped my well-beloved, but all was utterly inscrutable.

We crossed the stile and walked on into the dim lonely gloom of the Chase. I took her hand and felt that she was trembling. Of what, I wondered, was she in fear? Was it because of the sudden return of that rough seafarer, Richard Keene? Was it of some denunciation that could be made by Mademoiselle Lejeune; or was it because of what had occurred down in that damp hollow behind the beeches in the south avenue—that spot that bore the imprint of her shoes?

"Lolita," I said at last in a soft, low voice, "are you aware of the terrible affair—I mean the discovery in the park?"

"Yes," was her mechanical answer, without, however, daring to look me in the face. "I have heard all about it."

"Well," I said, "the unfortunate young man is unidentified except—" and I hesitated.

"Except what?" she gasped quickly. "What have they discovered?"

"They have discovered nothing," I assured her. "But I myself have discovered that the man now dead pawned, a year ago, your amethyst and pearl necklet—the one your father, the Earl, gave you for a birthday present in India, and, further, that he wore upon his finger a ring containing your portrait!"

"The police!—do they know these facts?" she gasped, halting and glaring at me.

"They are known only to myself," I answered in a grave, low tone. "What have you to say?" For a moment she stood with her countenance blanched to the lips, and a strange haunted look in her eyes. Summoning all her courage, her gloved fingers clenching themselves into the palms, she bowed her head and answered hoarsely—

"I have nothing to say—nothing—nothing!"

I stood in silence regarding her, utterly mystified. Was it guilt that was written so vividly upon her face, or was it the fierce desperation of an innocent woman hounded to her death?

Ah! had I known the startling truth at that moment, how differently would I have acted!

Chapter Twelve
Love and Lolita

To press her further was out of the question. I had sufficiently explained that I held the knowledge to myself, and that I did not intend to divulge to the police what I had discovered.

That she had been fully aware of the unknown's death was quite plain and equally so that she feared lest the inquiries might lead the police in her direction.

The silent manner in which she had changed her mud-bedraggled dress was in itself sufficient to show that she was well aware that I suspected her of being implicated in the young man's death, and her mute thankfulness was also very marked.

In silence we walked on through the forest gloom where the damp smell of the moss and dead leaves was welcome after the dry August heat outside, until presently, after debating within myself whether it were wise to place her upon her guard, I suddenly put my hand upon my love's arm, saying—

"Lolita, you know that your interests in every particular are mine, therefore it is, I think, but right that you should know that the police have already made a discovery in connexion with the—the unfortunate affair in the park. They have found at the spot the marks of small shoes with French heels. Casts have been taken of those imprints, and it is suspected that they are of your shoes!"

"My footprints!" she gasped, turning and glaring at me with wide-open frightened eyes. "Ah! I—I never thought of that! It never occurred to me!" And then I saw how she trembled visibly from head to foot. She had striven to remain calm, but had now utterly broken down.

"The situation is perilous," I said quite quietly, "inasmuch as the man Redway has taken casts, and knowing that only you in this district are in the habit of wearing such shoes, I fear he suspects. He will, no doubt, seek some secret means, probably through the servants, to compare his cast with the boots you are in the habit of wearing."

"Ah! I see," she remarked thoughtfully. "Then I must either hide or destroy them all, unknown to Weston."

"That is best. I will help you," I said. "We will do it as soon as we return. If you will collect them all I'll pack them in my suit-case and send them up to the cloak-room at St. Pancras. They'll be safe enough there for a few months."

"An excellent idea," she said. "I must get rid of them at all costs. I'll order some others from Francis—shoes with flat heels, although I hate them."

I could not, however, help noticing that she had actually admitted being present at the spot where the dead man was discovered, yet she had made no mention of him. My object was to learn his name and who he really was, but with a woman's cleverness she vouchsafed no information. I think she saw that I suspected her of the crime, although my intense love for her prevented me withdrawing from her in loathing as would otherwise have been the case.

That strange cipher that I had found secreted in the dead man's waistcoat occurred to me, and I longed to be in possession of its key. I knew a man who often amused himself in deciphering such things, and counted himself something of an expert in such matters, but I had not yet had time to submit it to him and obtain his opinion.

As we continued our way she expressed a hope that the man Redway would not make investigations in her wardrobe during her absence.

"He may bribe Weston, you know," she suggested in an apprehensive tone. "And if he found that his cast corresponded with my foot, the result would surely be fatal. I could not live to face it, Willoughby. How could I?"

"Don't let us anticipate such a thing. Redway will not be able to enter the Hall without some very good excuse, that's very certain. Up to the present only two persons are aware that you were out in the Park all night—the man whom I afterwards found with the Frenchwoman, and myself."

"Ah! yes, thanks to you I succeeded in returning home as though I had only been out for an early walk. The manner in which you accomplished it was most ingenious. It has freed me from suspicion. Yet in the footmarks has arisen another and much more serious matter."

"The boots you must leave to me. I will get rid of them, never fear," I assured her; and she pressed the gloved hand I held, as though to confirm her trust in me.

Yet was I acting as accessory to a foul and dastardly crime. A man, unarmed and unsuspecting, had been cruelly and secretly done to death, and I, because I loved her, was seeking by all means in my power to throw the police off the scent and dispel even those grave suspicions that were so strongly increasing in my own mind daily, nay hourly.

Walking at her side I tried to argue with myself. But I was too loyal to her. That face drawn and haggard, the paleness of which even her veil failed to hide, was the countenance of a woman whose heart was torn with conflicting emotions—one whose enemies had triumphed, leaving her friendless, crushed—and guilty before the face of the world.

We went on, past the smithy, into Stanion village, an old-world place with its grey church-spire the most prominent figure in the landscape. The sun was setting, and our long shadows lay in front of us upon the dusty highway.

Young Sampson, the squire of Ashton, over near Oundle, whirled past us in his ten-horse Panhard, enveloping us in a cloud of dust, passing before he became aware of who we were. Then we turned into the rectory, where in the cool little drawing-room Lolita had a brief conversation with the worthy rector's wife concerning a forthcoming sale of work. Oh! those everlasting jumble sales and sales of work.

As she sat there, her veil raised, coolly discussing such things as stalls, stall-holders, fancy needlework and church expenses, she smiled sweetly and certainly did not in the least present the woeful picture that she had done as we passed through the Chase. They even discussed the tragic discovery in the park. With the well-bred woman's natural tact she could control her outward appearance marvellously. The wife of the estimable rector would certainly never have dreamed the subject of our conversation a quarter of an hour before. They strolled across the tennis lawn together, and her neat figure and graceful swinging carriage was surely not that of a woman suspected of a heartless and brutal assassination.

Yet when I argued coldly and methodically with myself; when I recollected her admission, and her eager anxiety to get rid of those boots with the small high heels, I could not disguise from myself the hard fact that if she were not the actual assassin she was, at any rate, an accessory.

There had been some strong motive why that young man should die. That was plain, and without the slightest shadow of doubt.

I strolled beside the pair in the garden until my love took leave of her hostess, and then we walked home in the calm golden glow of the sundown.

Before the dressing-bell rang I surreptitiously carried my old suit-case, empty, up to her room, and half-an-hour later fetched it down. It was packed full of all her French boots, and having locked it securely I tied upon it an address-label inscribed to myself to be left at St. Pancras cloak-room "till called for." Then I rang for a servant, and dispatched it to Kettering station.

The blazing August days went slowly by. The body of the nameless victim had been laid in its grave in Sibberton churchyard, and the inquiries conducted by the obsequious Redway resulted in nothing. As was to be expected, he and his assistants haunted the village continually, endeavouring to gather all they could, but fortunately no suspicion was cast upon the sweet woman whom I loved. An active search was made for the boots with the Louis XV heels, in which Pink, the doctor, joined, but it never once occurred to them that they had belonged to Lolita. Or, if it did, the theory had no doubt been dismissed as a wild and unfounded one.

Eager to escape from the place which was undoubtedly so full of tragic memory, Lolita, in the early days of September, went up to Strathpeffer to stay with her aunt, Lady Clayton, as was her habit each year.

On the morning just before she left, however, she came to my room ready dressed for her departure, and again, for the first time since our walk to Stanion, referred to the tragedy.

"Recollect, Willoughby, I am now entirely in your hands," she said, standing at the window with her eyes fixed aimlessly across the broad level park. "I cannot bear to remain here now, for I feel every moment that I am being watched, suspected—that one day that awful person Redway will enter my room with—perhaps a warrant for my arrest."

"There is no evidence," I pointed out, first ascertaining that there were no eavesdroppers in the corridor outside. "We have been able to efface everything. The police are utterly puzzled."

"Thanks to you," she said, turning her great blue eyes sweetly upon me. Surely she did not at the moment present the appearance of a murderess, and yet the circumstances all pointed to one fact—that there was a motive in the death of that young man who had remained unidentified. "You told me the other day," she went on, "that the necklet had been pawned. My connexion with the poor young fellow may be established through that. You see I do not conceal my fears from you, Willoughby—my only friend," she added.

"You need fear nothing in that direction," I responded. "I purchased the necklet, and I have it at this moment safely at home."

"You have!" she cried, a great weight lifted from her mind. "Ah! you seem to have left nothing undone to secure my safety."

"For the reason I explained to you on the night of the unfortunate affair," I responded, taking her small soft hand in mine and raising it slowly to my lips. She did not attempt to withdraw it. She only sighed, and a slight shiver ran through her as my lips came in contact with her fingers. What did that shudder mean?

Was it that I was actually kissing the hand that had committed murder?

"Lolita!" I said a moment later when I had crushed from my heart the gradually increasing suspicion. "You have received from the innkeeper, Warr, a letter left for you by a rough uncouth stranger."

"Ah," she sighed, "I have. Richard Keene has returned! You don't know what that means to me."

"The letter contained news that has filled you with serious apprehension, then?"

"It contained certain information that is utterly astonishing!"

I explained how I had seen the stranger and overheard his conversation with Warr, whereupon she said—

"I expected that he would return, but it seems that he does not intend to do so. He fears, perhaps, to call upon me—just as I fear that he may reveal the truth."

For some time I was silent, pretending to occupy myself with some papers, but truth to tell I was considering whether the question I wished to put to her was really a judicious one. At last I decided to speak and make a bold demand. Therefore I said—

"And now, Lolita, that I have rendered you all the assistance I can, I want to ask you one single plain question—I want you to answer me truthfully, because what you tell me may in the future be of greatest assistance to me. Recollect that in this affair I am combating the efforts of the police, therefore I wish to know the name of the man who is dead."

"His name!" she exclaimed, looking straight at me. "His name—why do you wish to ascertain that?"

"First, because of curiosity, and, secondly, because in dealing with your enemies it will give me advantage if I am aware of facts of which they are in ignorance."

But she shook her head, while her brows knit slightly, by which I knew that she was firm.

"Your knowledge of the affair is surely sufficient, Willoughby," was her answer. "You see in me a miserable woman, haunted by the shadow of a crime, a woman whom the world holds in high esteem but who merits only disgrace and death. You pity me—you say that you love me! Well, if that is so—if you pity me, and your love is really sincere, you will at least have compassion upon me and allow me to retain one secret, even from you—the secret of that man's name!"

"Then you refuse to satisfy me," I exclaimed in bitter disappointment.

"Is it a proof of love and confidence to wring from a woman a name which is her secret alone?" she asked reprovingly.

"But I am trying to act as your protector," I argued.

"Then have patience," she urged. "His name does not concern you. He is dead, and his secret—which was also my secret—has gone with him to the grave." Then, almost in the same breath, she bade me farewell, and a few moments later I saw the station-brougham receding down the long avenue.

Chapter Thirteen
The Young Countess Makes a Statement

The harvest had been garnered and on the glorious "first" the young Countess returned from the Continent, just in time to receive her annual house-party.

The instant she arrived Sibberton always put on an air of gaiety which it never wore during her absence. Full of verve and go, she lived only for excitement and pleasure, and always declared the Hall as dull as a convent if it were not full of those clever, well-known people who constituted her own particular set. Therefore she seldom brightened the place with her presence unless she brought in her train a dozen or so merry men and women of the distinctly up-to-date type, some of whom were fashionable enough to have scandal attached to their names.

Has it ever occurred to you that feminine beauty in the higher circle of society is unfortunately, but very surely, deteriorating? It is remarkable how the type has of late years changed. When our grandmothers were celebrated and toasted in old port as beauties, quite a different ideal reigned. The toast was then something *petite*, womanly, of a pink complexion, of a delicious plumpness and animated by a lively and natural emotionalism. But with the introduction of athletic, open-air exercise, motors and mannish achievements, we have developed an entirely different type.

The modern athletic girl is generally ugly. She begins early, and continues till after her marriage to cycle, shoot, ride and play golf and tennis, all of which ruin her figure and consequently her health. She shoots up tall, flat-chested, colourless and lacking in reasonable proportions, with one hip larger than the other if she rides regularly to hounds. She becomes wried and atrophied by rough wear and unseemly habits, and the womanly delicacy shrinks and withers from the form of health and beauty.

Glance over any social function in town or country, any meet of hounds, or any shooting-party where ladies are included, and you will not fail to recognise how women, by overtaxing their physique, are fading and gradually becoming asexual.

The Countess of Stanchester's house-parties were always merry ones, and generally included an Ambassador or two, a Cabinet Minister, a few good shots, and a number of ladies of various ages. The gigantic place was liberty hall, and both the young Earl and his wife carried out to the letter the traditions of the noble house for boundless hospitality. There was no better shooting in all the Midlands than that furnished by the Earl of Stanchester's huge estate, extending as it did for nearly thirty miles in one direction; and the bags were always very huge ones.

Twenty-eight guests arrived on the same day that the young Countess returned home, and dinner that night was served as it always was on the first night of the shooting-season, upon the historic service of gold plate presented by Queen Elizabeth to the first Earl of Stanchester. I was invited to dine, and after music in the blue drawing-room retired with the men to the cosy panelled smoking-room with the grotesque carvings over the mantelshelf.

Many were the anecdotes and low the laughter, until at about midnight I rose and went back to my study, intending to get through some correspondence before retiring.

I suppose I must have been writing half-an-hour when the door opened and the Countess entered, greeting me merrily, saying—

"Well, Mr Woodhouse! I've had no time to talk to you to-night. And how have you been all this time?"

"As usual," I responded, smiling, for notwithstanding her faults she was so beautiful, merry and witty that her companionship was always pleasant. "Is there anything I can do?"

"Yes. I want you, please, to send out cards for dinner next Tuesday to this list." And she handed me half a sheet of note-paper on which she had hastily scribbled some names. "These county people, as they call themselves, are a fearful bore, and their women-folk are a terribly dowdy lot, but I suppose I must have them. It's only once a year—thank Heaven."

I laughed, for I knew that outside her own set she had withering sarcasm for the lower grade of society. With poor people she was always pleasant and popular, but with that little circle which called itself "the county," and which consisted of hard-up "squires," country parsons, men who had made money in the city and had bought properties, and the tea-and-tennis womankind that came in their wake, she had no common bond. They were a slow, narrow-minded lot who held up their hands at what she would term a harmless game at baccarat, and would be horror-stricken at tennis-playing or even bridge on Sundays.

Yet from time immemorial these people had been invited to dine at the Hall once during the shooting-season, and it was her husband's wish that all the old customs of his noble house should be strictly observed. For hospitality, the house of Stanchester had always been noteworthy. The Earl's grandfather, whom many aged villagers in Sibberton could still remember, used to keep open house every Friday night, and any of his friends could come up to the Hall and dine with him at six o'clock, providing they left or sent their cards on the previous day, in order that the cook should know how many guests would be present. It was the one evening in the week when his lordship entertained all his hunting friends, and on that day he did them royally for the port was declared the best in the country.

In these modern go-ahead days, however, with the giddy young Countess as chatelaine, this sort of thing was of the past. She tolerated people only as long as they amused her. When they ceased to do that, she calmly and ruthlessly struck them off her list. In town, she petted young foreign musicians and got them to sing or play at her concerts and brought them into notoriety by paying them cheques of three figures for their nightly services. But their reign usually lasted only half the season, when they were cast aside, disappointed and dejected, and other popular favourites rose to take their places.

She noticed my cigarettes in the big silver box the Earl had given me, and walking across, selected one, and slowly lit it with that free-and-easy air that was essentially that of the latter-day woman. An exception to the general rule that beauty in women of the higher class is growing rarer, she was extremely good-looking—fair-haired, grey-eyed, with handsome regular features and a clear pink complexion devoid of any artificial "make-up."

Her dress was magnificent, the latest Paquin creation for which I had sent a cheque only the week before for one hundred and ten guineas. It was a study in cream, and trimmed with sparkling sequins which caused the gauze to shimmer and sparkle with every movement. The curves of her figure were graceful in every line, and at her throat she wore the magnificent collar of rubies which Queen Anne had given to the beautiful Countess of Stanchester, wife of Her Majesty's Ambassador to France.

With careless abandon she threw herself into an armchair opposite where I sat, stretched out her tiny shoes upon the rug, gazing steadily at me, and blew a cloud of blue smoke from her lips. Yes, as I gazed upon her I really did not wonder how completely Lord Sibberton had been fascinated. Magnificent was the only word that described her.

"I've only just heard about this awful affair in the park," she commenced. "George says he knows nothing very much about it. He says you found a man murdered. Tell me all about it—I'm interested." And she placed the cigarette to her lips and gazed lazily at me through the haze of smoke. Knowing the strong bond of friendship existing between her husband and myself, she always treated me with a flippant equality that would be viewed with some surprise in any other circle of society. But to-day it seems that the more daring a wealthy woman is in words and actions, the greater is her popularity.

"Yes," I answered, turning towards her upon my revolving writing-chair. "It is a mystery—an entire mystery." And then I briefly related the curious facts, omitting, of course, all mention of the connexion between the murdered man and her sister-in-law, whom, be it said, she secretly ridiculed as a pious stay-at-home.

Lolita did not care for the ultra-gay set who formed the shooting parties, therefore was absent from them when she could escape. She hated bridge and baccarat, and had nothing in common with those women about whom scandalous tales were told in boudoirs and smoking-rooms.

"I suppose Doctor Pink has been exercising his talents in trying to discover the assassin?" she remarked.

"Yes. But the young man has remained unidentified," I answered. "And for my own part, I believe the affair will remain an absolute mystery."

"Why? What causes you to anticipate that?"

"Because there are certain features which are utterly incomprehensible. The young man came along the avenue that night to keep a secret appointment—that's very certain. And the person who met him coolly murdered him."

"Yes. But it really isn't very nice to have a tragedy at one's very door, and yet be unaware of the identity of the assassin! Who was the murderer? Who is suspected?"

"A woman," I responded, whereupon, to my great surprise, I noticed in her eyes a strange expression, but whether of fear or of surprise I could not determine.

"A woman!" she repeated. "How is it that the police suspect a woman?"

I told her how Redway had discovered certain footmarks, and how at least two of the prints were those of a woman's shoe.

"That's very strange! Most interesting!" she remarked. "Sounds almost like what you see in a drama on the stage—a dark wood, man meets a woman who stabs him, then rushes away full of remorse—green lights, and all that sort of thing. You know what I mean."

"But this is no theatrical effect," I said. "It is a hard solid tragic fact that an unknown man has been murdered in the park here not half-a-mile away, and the affair is still a complete mystery except, as I have said, a woman was certainly present."

"Exactly. She might have been present—and yet innocent," she said, with a slightly triumphant ring in her argument, I thought. Was it possible that she, too, knew something of Lolita's secret and, suspecting her, sought to divert suspicion from her?

Her beautiful face was sphinx-like. She continued to discuss the startling affair, and I somehow felt convinced that she knew rather more of its details than she would admit. Yet probably she had read some report of it in the papers. Nevertheless, certain remarks of hers were distinctly curious, especially her eagerness to know exactly what suspicions the police entertained, and in what direction their inquiries were at present directed.

As to the latter, I could tell her nothing, for I had not met Redway for several days. Indeed I had not heard of his presence in the neighbourhood, and I had begun to believe that he and his men were giving up the matter as a mystery that would never be solved save by confession or by mere chance. They were evidently pursuing that policy of masterly inactivity of which local police officers are past-masters. Gossips all of them, they are full of pretended activity on false scents, and prone to discover clues wherever beer chances to be deposited.

"I hear that Warr, the innkeeper, was with you when you found the man," the Countess presently remarked. "If the dead man were not an absolute stranger surely he, of all men, would have recognised him!"

"But he was an entire stranger—and apparently a gentleman," I said. "From his clothes, his appearance was that of a foreigner—but of course that's only mere surmise. He may have been abroad and purchased foreign clothes there."

"A foreigner! And who in Sibberton could possibly have any business with a foreigner?" she laughed. "Why, half the villagers haven't been as far away from their houses as Northampton, and I don't believe, with the exception perhaps of our studsman James, that any one has crossed the Channel."

"Yes," I admitted, "the whole affair is a profound puzzle. All that is known is that a certain young man who, from his exterior appearance and clothes, was well-bred, met in the park a certain woman, and that afterwards, he was found stabbed in the back with some long, thin and very sharp instrument. That's all!"

"And the police are utterly confounded?"

"Utterly. They photographed the unfortunate man."

"Did they? Where can I see a copy?" asked the Countess quickly, bending forward to me in her eagerness. "I would so very much like to see one. Could you get one?"

"I have one here," I replied. "The police sent it to me a week ago, in response to my request." And unlocking a drawer, I took out the inartistic picture of the dead man.

So keenly interested was she that she sprang from her chair, and came quickly to the edge of my writing-table in order to examine the picture.

"God!" she gasped, the colour of her cheeks fading pale as death as her eyes glared at it. "The woman has killed him, then—just as I thought! Poor fellow—poor fellow! The police don't even know his name! It is a mystery—then let it remain so. They regard it, you say, as a strange affair. Yet if the real truth were known, the remarkable romance of which this is the tragic *dénouement* would be found to be most startling—one so curious and mysterious indeed as to be almost beyond human credence. Yes, Mr Woodhouse," she added in a low voice as she straightened herself and looked at me, "I know the truth—I know why this man was sent to his grave—and I know by whom!"

Chapter Fourteen
Concerns a Gay Woman

The open declaration of the Countess held me in weak indecision. No doubt she was well aware of the motive of the crime, and therefore guessed who had struck the fatal blow. Yet she boldly expressed her intention of concealing her knowledge, which seemed strange on the face of it. A murder had been committed, therefore if she really had no reason to defeat the ends of justice she might surely reveal the dead man's identity and explain all she knew concerning him. I argued this with her, but she shook her head and remained firm in her decision of silence.

Did she entertain, as I did, a grave suspicion of Lady Lolita?

This vague suggestion occurred to me as I sat staring straight up into the grey eyes of that brilliant woman before me. She knew the truth. She had told me so, yet next instant she seemed to regret the words had escaped her and sought lamely to modify her assertion.

She appeared to regard her statement as an error of judgment, and with all the tact of a clever woman ingeniously endeavoured to mislead me.

"One person could, I believe, tell us something," I remarked presently, in order to show her that I was in possession of other facts that I had not revealed.

"Who's that, pray?"

"A certain man named Richard Keene." It was quite a haphazard shot, only made in order to ascertain whether the name really conveyed anything to her.

"Richard Keene!" she echoed, her brows knit in quick apprehension. "Did you know him?"

"I do know him," was my calm response. "I have seen him down in Sibberton, if I am not very much mistaken."

"Seen him!" she cried hoarsely. "Why, if you've seen him you've met an apparition. He died long ago."

"No," I declared. "I have seen Richard Keene in the flesh. He is not dead."

"Impossible! You're deceiving me," she exclaimed. "The man cannot possibly be alive."

"How do you know?"

She hesitated, for she saw that to reply to my question was to expose her own knowledge. Her face was ashen grey. My announcement, I saw, held her rigid in terror and surprise.

"Because his death is common knowledge to those who—well, those who knew him," she replied lamely.

"I tell you that Richard Keene has eaten cold meat and drunk beer in the tap-room at the *Stanchester Arms*. He came to Sibberton to make inquiries regarding the Earl and the occupants of this house."

"He did!" she gasped aghast. "Are you quite certain of that?"

"I heard him with my own ears. He questioned Warr, who is not, however, very communicative to strangers, especially if they are not very well-dressed."

"How long ago?"

"On the evening of the tragedy."

"Ah!" she sighed, and the light died out of her countenance again. "But are you really certain that it was Richard Keene?—does Lolita know this?"

"Yes. He wrote to her."

"Wrote to her! Then there is no mistake that the fellow is still alive?" she cried, dismayed.

"None. He told Warr that he had only just arrived home from abroad. And he looked very travel-stained and weary. He seemed to be on tramp."

"Without money?"

"On the contrary, he appeared to have plenty. It struck me that his penurious exterior was assumed for some purpose of his own."

"Then if he really has returned, he means mischief—serious mischief," exclaimed the Countess, still very pale. "The fact that he is not dead, as we had all supposed, alters entirely my theory regarding the crime and its motive."

"You believe then that he is the guilty one?"

"No. That could not be," was her quick reply.

"There are strong reasons—very strong reasons—why there can be no suspicion against him."

"Is he such a very estimable person, then?" I inquired, hoping to obtain some further facts from her.

"Estimable!" she ejaculated. "Why, he is the one person in all the world who—but no!" she added, suddenly breaking off. "You are George's friend!"

"And therefore I must not be told the truth," I remarked disappointedly.

"You must not know the secret of his sister Lolita," she answered quite calmly. "I cannot betray her confidence."

I felt assured that the real reason of her refusal to tell me was because she feared lest I might betray her to her husband, and not on account of Lolita at all. She and I had somehow never been very close friends. I distrusted all women of her stamp, and treated them with that same light airy irresponsibility with which they treated me. The Countess of Stanchester could not be taken seriously. She was one of those women who, though married, live for the admiration and flattery of the opposite sex, and who indeed, according to her enemies, would court the admiration of her footman, provided no other male of higher status were available. Often she had set herself to win from me some complimentary speech, but had, probably to her chagrin, always found me blind to all her feminine blandishments. That she was amazingly handsome could not for a moment be denied, but the open manner in which she coquetted under her husband's nose filled me with anger and contempt.

How different she was from Lolita. The latter possessed all that calm, well-bred dignity, that inflexible moral principle which had ever been characteristic of the noble Catholic line of Stanchester. Her early years had been passed with the good nuns of the Sacred Heart at Provins, in France, and even now she gave the impression of one who had passed under the ennobling discipline of suffering and self-denial; a melancholy charm tempered the natural vigour of her mind; her spirit seemed to stand upon an eminence and look down upon the world as though it were not of it; and yet when brought into contact with that world which she inwardly despised, she shrank back with all the timidity natural to her convent education.

Marigold, on the other hand, possessed all the worst traits of the Gordons of Glenloch, that ill-fated house whose men were gamesters and whose women had for two centuries been noted only for their personal beauty. Successions of Gordons had ruined the estates, now mostly in the hands of Jew mortgagees, and the present generation, still reckless and improvident, were consequently very poor. Lady Gordon had successfully schemed to marry her three dashing daughters to wealthy men as a means of saving the last remnant of the estate from passing out of her husband's hands and of the trio of girls who, for two seasons in London, were the most admired and most courted, Marigold, now Countess of Stanchester, was perhaps the most confirmed flirt. She had set all the *convenances* at naught then, just as she did now. The golden bond of matrimony never for a moment, galled her. She found the world most amusing, she declared, pouting if her husband reproved her, and surely she might be allowed to amuse herself!

She differed very little from thousands of other wives—women of our latter-day degenerate stock which has neither code of honour to husband nor to tradesmen. Debts trouble them not, they fear neither man nor God, but skip arm-in-arm with the devil down to ruin and disgrace. If, however, the husband chances to be wealthy and their extravagance makes no difference to his income, they will, strangely enough, instead of descending to destruction, rise to a pinnacle of notoriety, become popular leaders of Society, and have their daily doings chronicled by the papers as assiduously as those of the princes of the earth. But, after all, conscience is the padlock that we try to put on our inclinations.

I tried to ascertain the reason why the announcement of the man Keene's return should concern her so deeply, but she was far too clever to betray herself. From her manner, as soon as she grew calmer again after the first startling shock which the truth had given her, I saw that she was trying to exercise her blandishments upon me. She had some motive in this, I felt convinced. Was it that she was trying to win me over to her side as her friend?

"I really think the less we discuss the unfortunate affair, Mr Woodhouse, the better," she exclaimed at last, standing upon the hearthrug and facing me with her hands clasped behind her back. The lamplight caught the magnificent ornaments on her throat and bodice, causing them to dance with a thousand flashing fires.

"You yourself approached the subject," was my cool response. "I quite agree that we may well leave the matter in the hands of the police."

"But there is one thing I would implore you, as Lolita's friend—for she is very fond of you, I know—and as my own friend also—and that is to keep this man Keene's return a profound secret from every one—more especially from George. Do you understand?"

"No, I don't," I answered. "At least I don't understand your reason for endeavouring to conceal the fact."

"Of course not," she exclaimed in quick earnestness. "Because you don't know the truth—you don't know what exposure means to me—or to Lolita."

"To you? Then you wish me to assist you in preserving the secret?"

"You have guessed aright, Mr Woodhouse. I confess that I am in fear lest George shall learn that this man Keene has been to Sibberton. He must be kept in ignorance of it at all hazards. Besides yourself, who knows of his return?"

"The innkeeper, Warr."

"Ah!" she gasped quickly. "Then you must see him and make him promise to say nothing—either to the police or to any person Whatsoever."

"I will act as you wish," I responded. "But Lolita has already told me of her own peril."

"Yes, she no doubt foresaw it, just as I do. If you will assist me in this matter, which is purely confidential between us, you will earn my everlasting gratitude," she declared.

Then after a brief pause she turned from me, as though to hide her face, and said—

"I know quite well, Mr Woodhouse, that you hold me in little esteem. I daresay that if I dared I should be your open enemy, but knowing the friendship my husband has for you, I am prevented from acting as I would perhaps otherwise act. I confess to you, however, that no one is better aware of my own failings than I am myself. People believe that because I like to amuse myself, I am a woman without a heart. But I tell you that George is the only man I care for, even though I may laugh and allow others to pay court to me. George will not believe me when I say this, but some day I will show you, as I will show him, the strength of my love for him. I will, in a word, redeem my character as a woman worthy to bear his honourable name."

I was utterly dumbfounded at this sudden outburst of confidence. There was a strange catch of emotion in her voice by which I knew that the words came direct from her heart, that remorse had at last seized her, and she intended to make atonement for all the grief and pain she had caused the devoted man who was her husband.

"If I can assist you in any way in this, Lady Stanchester, I will willingly do so," I replied, deeply in earnest.

She turned her handsome countenance to me, and I saw that her grey eyes were dimmed by tears.

"I ought not, I suppose, to make you my confidant," she went on, "yet if you will really take pity upon me, a helpless woman, you can at least prevent the one thing I dread from becoming known—you can help me to show George that I love him fondly after all—that I will try to make him as happy as is my duty. You have no belief in me, that I know full well. You believe that if it suited my purpose I would betray any confidence of yours to-morrow, and laugh in your face for being such a fool as to trust me. That is my exact character, I admit; but if you will preserve the secret of Richard Keene's return and promise to act as my friend as well as Lolita's, I swear to you that I will keep faith with you and endeavour when the day comes — as it certainly must ere long — to show George my heart is his, and his alone."

I could scarcely follow her true meaning, except that she was in deadly fear that the Earl should learn of the stranger's presence at the *Stanchester Arms*.

I promised to remain secret and, if possible, to secure Warr's silence, yet in her words there was some hidden meaning that even then I could not fathom. She seemed to anticipate an event in the near future by which her love for her husband would be sorely tried. How strange it was that she, gay and giddy woman that she was, had been seized by a genuine remorse on learning of the return of that dusty, down-at-heel stranger!

I looked at her and became convinced that the words she had spoken were by no means idle ones. Her slim white hand, laid upon the edge of my table, trembled, her pale lips were set, and in her grey eyes was a strange hard light as she said —

"Then I trust you, as you will trust me. In future, Mr Woodhouse, we will be friends, and I assure you that you will find your friendship has not been misplaced."

"Remember," I pointed out, "that I do not unite with you against the Earl."

"No, of course not," she cried in a low intense voice. "But by your silence you can give me a chance to atone for all the past — you — you can save me!"

Chapter Fifteen
The Track of the Truth

When the Countess had gone, leaving behind her a sweet breath of "Ideale," that newest invention of the Parisian perfumer, I sat with my elbows idly upon the table, pondering over her strange words and becoming more than ever puzzled.

Beauty may be only skin-deep, yet it makes a very deep impression. The brilliant woman who was my dear friend's wife had never captivated me. Nevertheless I had seen in her a genuine desire for reform and had therefore given her my promise. Still the mystery of it all seemed to increase, instead of diminish.

The Earl of Stanchester had, of course, seen the dead man on the morning after the discovery, but had not recognised him. At least it was quite clear that he had no suspicion whatever of who the young man really might be.

From a drawer I took that piece of paper with those puzzling numerals upon it which I had managed to obtain in secret. The cipher was, however, utterly unreadable. Staring at the paper I sat wondering what was written there. If only I could learn the meaning of those figures, then I knew that the truth would quickly become revealed.

Only that morning I had received a response from an expert in cipher—one of the officials at the Record Office in London—to whom I had submitted a copy of that tantalising document.

"This," he wrote, "is what is known as the checker-board cipher, a numerical cipher invented by a Russian revolutionist some forty years ago, and of all secret means of correspondence is the most complicated and ingenious. It is absolutely undecipherable unless the keyword or words agreed upon by the two correspondents be known, and it is therefore much used by Anarchists and Revolutionists. The meaning of the present cipher can never be solved until you gain knowledge of the keyword used, for in writing it the numbers representing each letter of that word are added to the numbers representing each letter of the message. Therefore, in deciphering, the proper subtraction must be made before any attempt can be successful in learning the message contained. I enclose you a copy of the checker-board used in writing the cipher, but without knowledge of the keyword this can be of no use whatever. It will, however, serve to show you what an extremely ingenious cipher it is, devised as it has been by a Russian of quick and subtle intellect, and used as means of secret communication in the constant plots against the Russian aristocracy. In the Russian prisons this square with its five numbers and twenty-five letters is used in a variety of ways, for most political prisoners have committed it to memory. If two persons are in separate cells, for instance, and one wishes to communicate with the other, who in all probability is acquainted with the use of the square, he will ask, 'Who are you?' by rapping on the wall, thus, 5 raps, a pause, 2 raps, a pause (W); 2 raps, a pause, 3 raps, a pause (H); 3 raps, a pause, 4 raps, a pause (O); and so on until the whole question is rapped out. This is the way in which the cipher you have submitted to me is written, but in this case, as I have said, with the numbers of the keyword added. Discover that, and the secret here will be yours."

Enclosed was a half sheet of note-paper on which was drawn the following device:—

```
- 1 2 3 4 5
1 A B C D E
2 F G H I K
3 L M N O P
4 Q R S T U
5 V W X Y Z
```

Ah! If only I could read what was written there! I placed the key beside the message, but saw that all the numbers were higher than those of the checker board, showing that the unknown keyword had been added, thus rendering the cipher secure from any save the person aware of the pre-arranged word. If, however, the expert failed to decipher what was written there, how could I hope to decipher it? I therefore replaced the papers in the drawer regretfully, locked it, and went upstairs to the long, old-fashioned room set apart for me when I dined and slept at the Hall.

My thoughts were full of Lolita and of the curious effect the news of Richard Keene's return had produced upon the Countess. For a long time I sat gazing out across the park, flooded as it was by the bright white light of the harvest moon.

My window was open, and the only sound that reached me there was the distant barking of the hounds in the kennels and the bell of the old Norman church of Sibberton striking two o'clock.

Over there, beyond the long dark line of the avenue, was the spot where the tragedy had been enacted, the spot where, in the clay, was left the imprints of Lolita's shoes. Time after time I tried to get rid of those grave suspicions that ever rose within me, but could not succeed. The evidence against my love, both confirmed by her own words and by the circumstances of the affair, was so strong that they seemed to convey an overwhelming conviction.

Yet somehow the Countess herself seemed to have united with Lolita in order to preserve the secret. Their interests, it seemed, were strangely identical. And it was this latter fact that rendered the enigma even more puzzling than ever.

Next day the guests shot over at Banhaw, the Countess accompanying them, but "cubbing" having just opened, the Earl was out with the hounds at five o'clock at the Lady Wood.

A letter I received by the morning post from Lolita at Strathpeffer told of a gay season at the Spa, for quite a merry lot of well-known people always assemble there in early autumn and many pleasant entertainments are given. One passage in the letter, however, caused me considerable apprehension. "If Marigold should question you regarding the re-appearance of a certain person at the inn in Sibberton, tell her *nothing*. She must not know."

What could she mean? Unfortunately her warning had come too late! I had told the Countess exactly what was contrary to my love's interests. Could any situation be more perilous or annoying?

When I recollected her ladyship's words of the previous night I saw with chagrin how clever and cunning she was, and with what marvellous tact she had succeeded in eliciting the truth from me.

Pink came in during the afternoon, and flinging himself into the armchair opposite me, took a pinch of snuff with his usual nonchalant air.

"Thought you'd be out cubbing this morning," he commenced. "Too early for you—eh? We killed a brace in Green Side Wood. Frank Gordon was there, of course. He's as keen a sportsman as he ever was, and rides as straight as half the young ones. Wonderful man! They say he used, back in the fifties, to ride seventy miles to the meet, hunt all day, and ride home again. That's what I call a sportsman!"

"Yes," I said. "There are few left nowadays like old Frank Gordon. He was one of the hunting crowd at the Haycock at Wansford in the old days when men rode hard, drank hard, and played hard. He did the first, but always declares that his present good health is due to abstinence from the other two."

The old gentleman we were speaking of was the *doyen* among hunting-men in the Midlands. He had hunted with the Belvoir half a century ago, and was as fine a specimen of an Englishman as existed in these degenerate days when men actually go to meets in motor cars.

The doctor himself hunted, as indeed did every one, the parson of Sibberton included, and the opening of "cubbing" was always a time of speculation as to what the season was to be, good or bad. The Earl had been delighted at his success at winning the cup for the best dog-hound at the Hound Show at Doncaster back in July, and certainly the pack was never in better form even under the old Earl than it was at present. Of course he spent money lavishly upon it, and money, as is so often the case, meant efficiency. The thousand pounds or so subscribed annually by the Hunt was but a drop in the ocean of expenditure, for a Master of Hounds, if he wishes to give his followers good sport, must be a rich man and not mind spending money to secure that end.

"I had a funny adventure last night," the doctor remarked presently, after we had discussed the prospects of hunting and all appertaining to it. "Devilish funny! I can't make it out. Of course you won't say a word of what I tell you, for we doctors aren't supposed to speak about our patients."

"I sha'n't say anything," I assured him.

"Well, I was called out about eleven last night, just as I was going up to bed, by an old labourer who drove into Sibberton in a light cart, and who told me that a woman was lying seriously ill at a farmhouse which he described as beyond Cherry Lap. It was out of my district, but he told me that he had been into Thrapston, but one doctor was out at a case and the other was away, therefore he had driven over to me. From what he said the case seemed serious, therefore I mounted my horse and rode along at his side in the moonlight. The night was lovely. We went by Geddington Chase, through Brigstock, and out on the Oundle Road, a good eleven miles in all, when he turned up a narrow drift for nearly half-a-mile where stood a small lonely farmhouse on the edge of a spinney. The place was in darkness, but as soon as I had dismounted the door opened, and there appeared a big powerful-looking man, holding a candle in his hand, and behind him was the figure of an old woman, who made a remark to him in a low voice. Then I heard a man somewhere speaking in some foreign language."

"A foreign language?" I remarked, quickly interested.

"Yes. That's what first aroused my suspicion," he said. "I was taken upstairs, and in a rather poorly-furnished room found a person in bed. The light had been purposely placed so that I could not see the features distinctly, and so dark was the corner where the patient lay that at first I could distinguish nothing.

"My daughter here has—well, she's met with a slight accident," the sinister-looking fellow explained, standing behind me, and then as he shifted the paraffin lamp a little there was revealed a young woman, dark-haired and rather good-looking, lying pale and insensible. Upon the pillow was a quantity of blood, which had, I saw, flowed from an ugly gaping wound on the left side of the neck—distinctly a knife-wound.

"'Accident!' I exclaimed, looking at the man. 'Why, she couldn't have inflicted such a wound as that herself. Who did it?' 'Never mind, doctor, who did it,' the fellow growled surlily. 'You sew it up or something. This ain't the time for chin—the girl may die.' He was a rough customer, and I did not at all like the look of him. I was, indeed, sorry that I had entered there, for both he and the woman also in the room were a very mysterious pair. Therefore I got the latter to bring some warm water, and after a little time succeeded in sewing the wound and properly bandaging it. Just as I had finished, the young woman gradually recovered consciousness. 'Where am I?' she inquired in a faint, rather refined voice. 'Hold your jaw!' roughly replied the fellow. 'If you don't it'll be the worse for you!' 'But, where's George?' she demanded. 'Oh, don't bother about him,' was the gruff injunction. 'Ah!' she shrieked suddenly, raising herself in her bed and glaring at him wildly. 'I know the truth! I remember now! You caught him by the throat and you strangled him?—you coward! You believe that Dick Keene doesn't know about the Sibberton affair, but he does. They've seen him, and told him everything—how—' The man turned to her with his fist raised menacingly saying, 'Lie quiet! you silly fool! If you don't, you'll be sorry for it! No more gab now!' Then turning to me he said with a short harsh laugh, 'The girl's a bit off her head, doctor. Come, let's go downstairs!' And he hurried me out lest she should make any more allegations.

"My first inclination was to remain and question her, yet it seemed clear that I was among a very queer lot, and that discretion was the best course. Therefore I followed the man down, although my patient shrieked aloud for me to return."

"By Jove!" I exclaimed, aroused to activity by mention of the man Keene. "That was a strange adventure—very strange!"

"Yes," he continued. "The fellow evinced the greatest anxiety that I should leave, pressed into my hand half-a-sovereign as a fee, and again assured me that the girl's mind was wandering. Again and again she called after me 'Doctor! doctor!' but in a room beyond I again heard men's voices, speaking low in a foreign language, therefore I hesitated, and presently mounted my mare and rode away. Now," he added, taking another long pinch of snuff, "what do you make out of it, Woodhouse?"

"Seems very much as though there's been another tragedy," I remarked. "I wonder who the injured girl is?" I added, utterly amazed at his narrative.

"I wonder," he added, "and who is this man Keene who knows all about the Sibberton affair? Could she have been referring to the tragedy in the park, do you think?"

"Yes, undoubtedly," I said quickly. "We must return there, get to see her in secret, and hear her story."

"The worst of it is that as I was there at night, just at a time when the moon was hidden behind the clouds, I doubt whether I'll be able to recognise the place again."

"Let's try," I suggested eagerly, springing up. "Don't let us lose an instant. I have a suspicion that we're on the track of the truth."

Chapter Sixteen
The Story of Mr Thomas Hayes

By half-past four we had covered the eleven miles that lay between the old-world village of Sibberton and that point beyond Brigstock on the Oundle road which skirts that dense wood called Cherry Lap.

Both of us were well-mounted, the doctor on his bay hunter, while I rode my own cob, and our pace had all along been a pretty hard one. Being both followers of hounds we knew all the bridle-roads across Geddington Chase, and over the rich pastures between them and the road at Cat's Head. Beyond Brigstock, however, we never hunted, for at that point our country joined that of the Fitzwilliam Hunt. Therefore, beyond Cherry Lap the neighbourhood was unfamiliar to both of us.

We hacked along on the grass by the side of the broad highway for a couple of miles or so, but the doctor failed to recognise the field by which he had turned off on the previous night. By-roads are deceptive in the moonlight.

"The gate was open when I passed through," he remarked. "And if it's closed now it'll be difficult to find it again. The country is so level here, and all the fields are so much alike. I recollect at the time looking around for some landmark and finding nothing until I got to the top end of the field, over the brow of the hill."

"We'll go on slowly," I said. "You'll recognise it presently."

We passed half a dozen fields with rough cart-roads running through each of them. Indeed, after harvest each field generally bears marks of carts in its gateway. In the darkness my companion had not been able to see what had been grown, except that the crop had been cut and carried.

For another couple of miles we rode forward, the doctor examining every field but failing to recognise the gateway into which he had turned, until at length we came to the junction of the road from Weldon, when he pulled up, saying—

"I didn't come as far as this. We'd better turn back."

This we did, slowly retracing our way in the sunset, the doctor now and then expressing disgust at his own failure to recognise the path.

Presently we encountered an old labourer plodding home from work with bag and scythe across his shoulder, and pulling up, the doctor asked, pointing over the hill—

"Which is the way to the farm across there?"

"What farm?" asked the man blankly, in his broad Northamptonshire dialect.

"I don't know the name, but there's a road goes in across one of these fields."

"Oh! you mean Hayes's, sir! Why, there's a way across that there next field. 'Bout 'arf a mile oop."

"Who lives there?" I asked.

"Why, ole Tom Hayes an' his missus."

"Anybody else?"

"Not as I knows of. Bill used to live with the ole man, but 'e's gone away this twelvemonth. Ole Tom don't make much of a thing out o' the farm nowadays, for 'e's nearly blind."

We thanked him, and rode eagerly onward, Pink opening the gate with his hunting-crop. Up the hill we cantered, skirting a broad stretch of pasture land and presently coming into sight of a small old redbrick house with tall square chimneys and quaint gable ends, while at a little distance were several barns and cow-houses.

Pink recognised the place in an instant, and we resolved that while I dismounted, tied my horse to a tree and walked on to the house, he should approach boldly and inquire after his patient of the previous night.

I had found a convenient tree and was walking in the direction of the farm when I saw a decrepit blear-eyed old man leaning on a stick, emerge from the door and hold a conversation with Pink, who had not dismounted.

A moment later my friend beckoned to me, and as I hurried forward he cried dismayed—"They've gone. We're too late."

"Gone!" I cried in disappointment, turning to the old farmer for explanation.

"Yes, sir," the old fellow answered. "I've just been telling this 'ere gentleman. They were a funny lot, an' I was glad to get rid of 'em out o' my house."

"Tell us all about them," exclaimed Pink dismounting, tying his horse to a ring in the wall, and entering the house with us. It was a poor, neglected, old-fashioned place, not over-clean, for it appeared that both Hayes and his wife were very infirm and kept no woman-servant.

"Well, gentlemen, it happened just like this," explained the decrepit old fellow, when we were in his stone-floored living room, with its great open hearth and big chimney corner. "One evening, back in last month, a gentleman called here. He'd walked a long way, and was very tired, so the missus, she gives 'im a mug o' milk. He would insist on me 'avin a shillin' for it, and then 'e sat here smoking 'is cigar—an' a good un it wor. After we'd been talking some time and he got to know we were livin' alone 'e asked whether we wouldn't care to let four of our rooms to some friends of 'is up in London, who wanted to come and stay in a farm-'ouse for a month. What people wanted to come and stay in this 'ere place in preference to their own 'omes I couldn't quite understand. Still, as 'e offered us five poun' a week, I an' the missus agreed. 'E stayed with us that night, 'ad a bit o' supper, and went to bed. Next morning 'e went away, and in the afternoon 'e came back with one of his friends, a young man who was called Ben, while the older man they called Dick."

"Dick what?" I inquired breathlessly.

"I don't know. I never 'eered his other name." Was it possible that the stranger who had walked so far was none other than Richard Keene? I inquired what day of August he had arrived.

"It wor the night of the sixteenth," was old Hayes's reply.

The very night of the tragedy in Sibberton Park! I asked him to describe the man known as Dick, but his description was somewhat hazy on account of his defective sight. Having, however, no doubt that the man who had arranged for apartments for the others was really the mysterious wayfarer, I allowed him to proceed with his highly-interesting narrative:

"The two stayed 'ere about a week, but 'ardly went out. I'd got some old fishin' tackle, so they spent their time mostly down at the river yonder. They were very pleasant gentlemen, both on 'em, and at the end o' the week they gave me a five-poun' note. Then they went away sayin' that their friends were comin' soon to occupy the rooms. At the end o' the next week there arrived, without any notice, a young lady—the one you saw last night, Doctor—the big man with a beard, named Logan, two other younger men, and an old woman-servant. The two men were foreigners, as well as the woman-servant, but Logan seemed to be head of the household, and the young lady was 'is daughter. At least 'e said so, but I don't think they were related at all. Well, from the very first 'our they were in the 'ouse they puzzled me: Logan took me aside, and explained that he and his friends wanted perfect quiet, and they didn't want a lot o' gossipin' about what they did, and where they went. He told me to open my mouth to nobody, and if he found I kept my own counsel he'd make me a present o' an extra five poun'. They seemed to 'ave plenty o' money," remarked old Hayes in parenthesis:

"So it seems," I observed. "Well, and what then?"

"Well, they occupied the four upstairs rooms, the two younger men occupying one room. They were thin-faced, dark-eyed fellows, whom I never liked at all, they seemed so sly and cunnin', always whispering to themselves in their own language. If anybody chanced to come up 'ere I saw how alarmed they all were. That's what first aroused my suspicions."

"Why didn't you speak to the constable at Brigstock?"

"And lose my five poun'? Not likely! They did me no harm, even if they were forriners. Well," he went on, "they all five of 'em remained 'ere, and like the men Dick and Ben, hardly ever went out in the day-time. The servant, an ugly old woman, did their cookin' an' looked after 'em while the three men amused themselves very often by playin' cards for 'ours and readin' their forrin' papers. I've kept some of 'em—'ere they are," and he took from a chair several well-thumbed newspapers, which I saw were the Italian *Avanti*, and other Continental journals of advanced socialistic policy.

"They had no letters?"

"Only one. The man Logan received it about four days ago."

"But the young lady. Was she English?" I asked.

"I suppose so. But she would talk with the forriners just like one o' themselves. I rather liked 'er. She was very kind to my missus, and seemed quite a lady, much more refined than that big bullyin' fellow who said he was her father."

"They gambled, you said, merely to kill time—or for money?" inquired Pink.

"I never saw 'em play for money. They used to play a forrin' game and I could never make anythin' out of it. After some little time the young lady went back to London for a day or two. While she was absent the man Dick called. He was differently dressed and took Logan out for a walk in the wood, in order to talk, I suppose. Logan came back alone, and I saw from his face that 'e was in a vile temper, so I suppose the two 'ad quarrelled. Howsomever, next day the young lady, who was known as Miss Alice, rejoined her friends, and that night they sat talkin' together till very late. I listened at the door, and 'eard 'em one by one a-arguin', it seemed, in their forrin language. It was just as though they were 'olding a council about something, but the tone of their voices showed that something alarmin' had happened. What it was, of course, I didn't know. But when I went up, I told my old woman that there was something unusual in the wind. Nothin' happened, however, till last night."

"And what happened last night?" I asked quickly.

"Well, as you'll remember, it was a beautiful evening, and after supper they all four went out for a walk, leaving the servant at home with us. When they'd been gone nearly two hours, I saw Logan return in the moonlight across the grass-field from the wood, smoking 'is pipe leisurely. When he saw me sittin' in the shadow outside the door, 'e said 'e'd missed the others and been wandering about the wood in the dark for more'n 'arf a hour. This struck me as rather peculiar, but I went inside with 'im, and presently went up to bed. I 'adn't been there long afore I 'eard a great scufflin' and whisperin', and on lookin' out o' my door saw the two forriners a carryin' Miss Alice upstairs to her room! I inquired what was the matter, but they said she'd only fainted and 'ud be better presently. So I went back to bed. Logan, howsomever, seems to 'ave gone out to old Jim Pywell's cottage down the hill and sent him for a doctor, telling 'im not to get one close at hand, but from a distance. Pywell called you, sir," he added turning to Pink, "and the first time I knew that anythin' was wrong was after you'd gone and the poor thing began to cry out and say that an attempt had been made to kill 'er. Both me and my ole woman are a bit 'ard o' hearin', an' they brought you very quietly up the stairs that I'd no idea you were in the 'ouse."

"And what occurred afterwards?" Pink inquired eagerly.

"They were evidently frightened lest what the poor girl had said in 'er ravings might arouse your curiosity a bit too much, for they were early astir this mornin', and by eleven they paid me and all of 'em left, walkin' by separate ways over to Oundle station, Jim Pywell a-takin' in their trunks on a wagon."

"But the young lady?" the doctor exclaimed. "Was she well enough to walk?"

"Yes. She was bandaged, of course, but she 'ad one o' them big feather ruffles that 'id her throat an' the lower part of 'er face. When she said 'good-bye' to me she looked like a corpse—poor thing."

"Then she said nothing about Logan's attack upon her?" I asked. "She appeared anxious to get away with the others?"

"Very," replied the old farmer. "She seemed to fear that she had said somethin' which would reveal what they were all tryin' to keep secret."

"Now tell me, Mr Hayes," I said, facing him very seriously. "Tell me one thing. Have you ever heard any of your mysterious visitors mention the name of Lejeune?"

The old fellow leaned heavily on his stick, scratched his white head and thought hard a moment.

"Ler—june,—Ler—june," he repeated. "Why, I believe that's the name by which the gentleman called Dick addressed the young lady when he came to see Mister Logan the other day! I recollect quite distinctly now. I've been a-tryin' an' a-tryin' to remember it—an' couldn't. Yes. It wor Ler—june—I'm certain. Do you happen to know her, sir?"

Chapter Seventeen
Which Concerns a Guest at the Hall

The old fellow's recognition of the name made it clear that the mysterious Mademoiselle, on her escape from Chelsea, had taken refuge in that house, together with certain other persons who were either accomplices, or who had formed some conspiracy in which she was implicated.

To the doctor, of course, this declaration of the man Hayes conveyed but little, but to me it threw an entirely fresh light upon the extraordinary affair. To Pink I gave a false explanation of the reason of my question. Some cunning plot seemed to be in progress, until the attack upon the young Frenchwoman and its subsequent exposure had, it appeared, put them all to flight.

Richard Keene had apparently gone straight from the *Stanchester Arms* and taken up his abode in that lonely house, ingratiating himself with the old people, in order, it seemed, to obtain a safe retreat for Mademoiselle, the man Logan and his two companions.

For what reason? Was this man Logan the same person who had walked with Lolita when I had discovered her after the tragedy?

I endeavoured to obtain a minute description of him from both the doctor and the farmer, but somehow his appearance, as described by my friend, was not as I had met him in those exciting moments on the Chelsea Embankment. Yet, perhaps, on that night, when he was secretly returning to Britten Street, his countenance might have been disguised. If he suspected that the police were watching, he would, no doubt, try and alter his personal appearance.

We both questioned old Mrs Hayes, a white-faced old woman in a silk cap with faded ribbon, but we could get nothing very intelligible from her, for she seemed upset and nervous regarding the hurried departure of the mysterious foreigners.

"I'm very sorry, sir, we 'ad anything to do with 'em," she declared, shaking her head. "Only the first gentleman 'as come was so nice, an' made us laugh so much with 'is funny stories that we thought any friends of 'is'n must be just so nice. He'd been at sea, and told us a lot about places abroad."

"Oh! he'd been at sea, had he?" I remarked, as that statement confirmed the suspicion that the man called Dick was actually Richard Keene—the person whose return had struck terror in the heart of both Lolita and the Countess.

"He said so," was her answer. "'E also said that he knew something of these parts, and made a lot of inquiries about the death of old Lord Stanchester, the present Earl's marriage and all that. In fact it somehow struck me that he had known the family long ago, and was anxious to hear about the recent happenings over at the Hall."

"He made no remark about the man found dead in the park?" asked the doctor.

"No. Not to my recollection. But Mr Logan did. He seemed very concerned about it, and I believe he went over to Sibberton one evening to see the spot. Only he didn't tell us. We knew from the ostler at the *Fox and Hounds* in Brigstock, where he hired a trap."

This negatived the theory that Logan was the man I had met in Chelsea, for if he were, he would surely not have wished to visit a place he had already seen. Indeed, he would, no doubt, have kept away from it as far as possible.

Compelled as I was to veil from my companion the reason of my inquiries, he regarded them, of course, as unnecessary, and did not fail to tell me so in his plain blunt fashion.

"There's one thing quite certain," he remarked as we cantered home together in the crimson sundown, "there's a lot of mystery connected with those people. I wonder if there really has been a tragedy, and if the man Logan actually made an attempt upon the young fellow, as the girl had declared. It's a great pity," he added, "that we don't know their surnames."

"Yes," I agreed. "If we did, we might perhaps establish their connexion with the affair in Sibberton Park."

"Is it wise to tell Redway what we've heard?" he suggested.

In an instant I saw that to do such a thing would be to break my promise to Mademoiselle, therefore I expressed myself entirely against such a course, saying—

"My own idea is that if we conduct our inquiries carefully and in secret, we'll be able to learn much more than the police. Personally, I've no faith in Redway at all."

"I haven't much, I confess," he laughed. "Very well. We'll keep our own counsel, and find out all we can further."

To me the enigma had assumed utterly bewildering proportions. The mystery of it all, combined with the distinct suspicion resting upon the woman I loved so fondly, was driving me to madness. Sleeping or waking, my one thought—the one object of my life—was the solution of this problem that now constituted my very existence.

I would have followed Mademoiselle at once, and questioned her further, had I known her whereabouts. But, unfortunately, she had again escaped me, and I still remained powerless and in ignorance of the truth, which proved afterwards to be so utterly astounding.

We passed through Brigstock, and cantering on set out along the long white highway. Both of us were silent, deep in thought. From the west poured an infinite volume of yellow-gold light. A wonderful transfiguring softness covered the earth. Far above the transfiguring gold in the west was a calm clear-shining blue, and into the blue softly blended colour into colour so artistically that any painter's brush would be defied.

Suddenly, the rays of the sun stretched up from behind the dark hill-tops and the whole became an illimitable blaze of gold and crimson. The sun seemed standing on the edge of the world, and its mystery was mirrored upon my heart.

The life of the day was nearing its end, and in the hush of silence we went onward, onward—towards home. And as we rode on I reflected that life was like an April day of alternate showers and sunshine, laughter and tears, flashes of woe and spasms of pain. One sun alone can brighten our gloom, and that sun is love. Without it, we have only the darkness of desolation.

Lolita! Lolita! The pale troubled refined face arose ever before me, haunting me sleeping or waking; that terrified look that had settled upon her matchless countenance at the moment when she had told me in her desperation that Keene's return meant death to her, I could by no means efface from my mind. It had been photographed indelibly upon my memory.

I received a letter from her next morning, a brief friendly note containing, as usual, no words of affection, only an expression of intimate friendship and trust. Was she guilty? If so, of what?

Could such a woman be really guilty of a crime?

In my quiet room at the Hall I sat with a pile of the Earl's correspondence before me. The letter-bag always contained a strange assortment of communications; some pathetic, many amusing, and at rare intervals notes on coloured paper in a feminine hand which, not being for my eyes, I re-enclosed in a plain envelope without reading.

Sibberton had had before his marriage what is known in club parlance as "a good time." His name had been coupled with more than one lady; he had driven a coach, given wonderful luncheons at the Bachelors', kept a house-boat up at Bray, was a well-known man about town, and an equally well-known figure at the tables at Monte Carlo. He had shot big game on the Zambesi, caught tarpon in Florida, potted tiger in the Himalayas, and had otherwise run the whole gamut of the pleasures of life as are opened to the wealthy young Englishman. On the day of his marriage with Marigold, he became a changed man, and now having assumed the responsibilities of an enormous estate, he declared himself to be gradually developing into an old fogey.

I had at last managed to stifle down my conflicting thoughts, and was busy replying to the pile of letters before me, when the Earl, in riding breeches, strode in from "cubbing." He had been out at five, and now, at eleven, had finished the day's sport and returned to his guests.

"Want to see me, Willoughby?" he asked, for it was usual for him to look in each morning to see whether I wished for any directions upon matters which I could not decide myself.

"Nothing of urgent importance," was my reply. "Benwell, the agent at Brockhurst, suggests buying about a thousand acres that adjoin the estate and are in the market."

"He means Haughmond Manor, I suppose?"

I replied in the affirmative.

"Tell him to buy if he can at a reasonable price. I fancy the Manor House isn't let just now. Tell him to get a good tenant for it."

I knew the place, a fine old sixteenth-century house, with beautiful terraces and gardens, one of the prettiest places in all Shropshire.

"What about visitors? Who's coming?" he asked. "Has Marigold given you another list?"

"Yes," I responded, taking out a slip of paper the Countess had handed me on the previous day, giving the names of some thirty persons, with the dates of their arrival and departure.

Having scanned them down quickly he gave a grunt of distinct dissatisfaction, for certain of the names were of persons of whom I knew he did not approve.

"I see she's asked Goffe, after all—hang the fellow. You must put him off, Willoughby. I won't have such a blackguard under my roof—and I told her I wouldn't! I'm no saint myself, but I'm not going to ask my guests to meet such a person. It's simply a marvel to me," he added, striding up and down the room, his spurs clinking as he walked, "how the papers talk about him. To-day you read he is staying with Lord This, and to-morrow he is at the Duchess of That's house-party, and the next day he meets the King at Doncaster. People must really think he's the most popular man alive."

"Sends the paragraphs to the editor himself, I suppose," I remarked.

"Suppose so. There's Marigold's friend Lady Laxton, who boasts that she pays two hundred a year to some poor devil of a journalist up in town to puff her every other day in the papers, and scatter her portraits about in the ladies' journals. That's why you see 'Lady Laxton at Home,' 'Lady Laxton on her motor,' 'Lady Laxton and her Chow,' 'Lady Laxton walking,' 'Lady Laxton riding,' and all the rest of it," he laughed. "The Laxton boom costs a couple of hundred a year, but it's cheap to a draper's wife, for it's put her into a good set where she wouldn't otherwise have been."

I joined in his laughter, for like all his class he hated cheap notoriety, and was far too conservative to discern that no success, social or commercial, is achieved in these modern days without judicious advertising.

"Oh, by the way!" he exclaimed suddenly. "I see she hasn't put Smeeton on the list—write it down, David Smeeton. You've never met him, I think. He's a good fellow. I asked him down for a fortnight's shooting. He's a magnificent shot—was with me up the Zambesi."

"When does he come?"

"To-morrow—five-forty at Kettering. See after him, won't you? Introduce him, and all that. I shall shoot over at Harringworth, and can't be back till late."

"Very well," I said, for it usually fell to me to put guests in the ways of that enormous house.

That day, and the following, passed uneventfully, and I heard nothing of any tragic discovery being made beyond Brigstock, therefore the suspicion that a second crime had been committed seemed negatived. I had driven over to Gretton in the afternoon to give instructions to one of the keepers, and returning about seven o'clock, was walking along the corridor to my room when, at the further end, in the fading light, I saw two figures, one a guest, and the other Slater, the butler.

"This is Mr Smeeton, sir," the old servant explained. "He's just arrived, and been shown his room. His lordship said you would entertain him until he and her ladyship returned."

The newly-arrived guest came forward from the shadow to greet me, and as he did so the light fell straight across his face.

I stood open-mouthed, unable to utter a word in response.

The guest was none other than Richard Keene himself!

Chapter Eighteen
Which Teaches the Value of Silence

The man's audacity in coming there openly and boldly as Lord Stanchester's guest so utterly astounded me that my very words froze upon my lips. Was this some further development of the intrigue in which one man had already lost his life?

Yet the visitor, bluff and hearty of speech, stood smiling at me with a calmness that was absolutely amazing. In the first instant, I wondered whether the dim light of the corridor had deceived me, or whether his face only resembled in a marked degree the dusty wayfarer who had refreshed himself with such gusto at the *Stanchester Arms*. Suddenly I recollected that although I had watched him on that hot afternoon, he had been unable to see me where I remained in the publican's back parlour. There was a screen on purpose to hide any person seated in the little low inner room from the vulgar gaze of those in the tap-room, and at the moment he had faced me I had been peeping round the corner watching him. As I crossed the room he had seen my back, of course, but his self-assurance at the moment of our meeting made it quite plain that he did not recognise me.

The dim light having concealed my surprise, I quickly regained my self-possession, and with effusive greeting asked him into my room.

"Lord Stanchester, her ladyship, and most of the party are still out," I explained. "There's been a big shoot to-day. He asked me to entertain you until he returned," I said, when he had seated himself in an armchair.

His tall figure seemed somewhat accentuated; his dark face, however, no longer wore that expression of weariness, but on the other hand he seemed hale and hearty, and had it not been for his rather rough speech, he might, in his well-cut suit of grey tweed, have passed for a gentleman.

"Oh! her ladyship is at home, then?" exclaimed the man who called himself Smeeton. "I've not yet had the pleasure of meeting her. In fact I haven't been in England since the Earl's marriage."

"You're a big-game hunter, I hear," I remarked.

"I shoot a little," was his modest rejoinder. "I shot with Lord Stanchester in Africa, one season, and we had fair sport. I notice that he has some of his trophies in the hall. By Jove!" he added. "He's a splendid sportsman — doesn't know what fear is. When we were together he got in some very tight corners. More than once it was only by mere chance that there was an heir left to the title. It wasn't through recklessness either, but sheer pluck."

He at any rate seemed to possess an unbounded admiration for my friend.

"You spend most of your time abroad?" I remarked, hoping to be able to gather some further facts.

"Well, yes. I have a house abroad," he answered. "I find England a nice place to visit occasionally. There's no place in the world like London, and no street like Piccadilly. But I'm a born wanderer, and am constantly on the wing in one or other of the five continents, yet at infrequent intervals I return to London, stand for a moment beside the lions in Trafalgar Square, and thank my lucky planet that I'm born an Englishman." He laughed in his own bluff hearty way.

And this was the man of whom both Lolita and Lady Stanchester lived in such mortal terror!

He took a cigarette, lit it, and leaned back in the chair with an easy air of comfort, watching the smoke ascend.

"Pretty country about here, it seems," he remarked presently. "The drive from Kettering station is a typical bit of rural English scenery. The green of the fields is refreshing after the scorched lands near the Equator. What's the partridge season like? It seems an age since I shot a bird in England."

"Oh! They're fairly strong," I replied. "The spell of wet was against them in the early season, but I believe the bags are quite up to the average."

"And who's here just now?"

I enumerated a list of his fellow-guests, in which I saw he was greatly interested.

"There's Lord and Lady Cotterstock, Sir Henry Kipton, General Bryan, Captain Harper, the Honourable Violet Middleton, Count Bernheim, the German Ambassador, Lady Barford, Mr Samuel Woodford—"

"Sammy Woodford!" he exclaimed, interrupting me. "How long has he been here?"

"Ever since the opening of the season. Are you acquainted?"

"Well—not exactly," he responded evasively. "I've heard a good deal about him from mutual friends. I'll be glad to meet him. He's the man who was in the Chitral affair. They swear by him in India."

"So I believe," I remarked, puzzled at the strange expression which crossed his features when I mentioned the name of the Earl's very intimate friend. Mr Samuel Woodford, or "Sammy" to his intimates, was a district superintendent of Bengal Police, who was home on two years' leave, a short well-preserved fair-headed man, a splendid athlete, a splendid shot, a splendid tennis and polo player. At Sibberton, where he had been a guest on several occasions, he was a great favourite, for he was always the merriest of the house-party and the keenest where sports or games were concerned.

Stanchester liked him because he was so perfectly honest and straight. The very look in his clear steel-grey eyes spoke truth, uprightness and a healthy life, and after their first meeting, one season at Cowes, his lordship had taken a great fancy to him.

"Anybody else I'm likely to know?" asked the visitor, with a carelessness which I knew was assumed.

"Well, there's the Marchese Visconti, of the Italian Embassy, young Hugh Hibbert from Oxford, and 'Poppa,' as they call the newly-made Lord Cawnpore. And the honourable Lucy Whitwell, the daughter of Lady Drayton."

"Is she here also?" he exclaimed, looking at me in quick surprise, which he did not attempt to disguise. "She's with her mother, of course?"

I responded in the affirmative, and recognised by his manner that the presence of the lady in question somewhat nonplussed him. Possibly she might be acquainted with him as Richard Keene, seafarer, and he anticipated an awkwardness about his introduction as the celebrated big-game hunter.

I anticipated a scene when the Countess met him, and was inwardly glad that at least Lolita was absent.

Ought I to warn the Countess, I wondered? She had, I remembered, appealed to me to assist her, and surely in this I might. Nevertheless, if her husband were in ignorance of the man's real identity, it was not likely that he would expose it willingly, or seek to injure her ladyship, or make any demonstration before her guests. On the one hand, I felt it my duty to give her warning of the stranger's arrival, while on the other I feared that by doing so I might be defeating the ends which the man Keene might have in view, namely, the discovery of the real author of the crime in Sibberton Park.

Thus I remained, undecided, continuing to chat with him, watching his attitude carefully, and seeking to learn from his conversation something regarding his intentions.

"I should imagine Lord Stanchester to be a very lucky fellow," he remarked presently. "If the photographs one sees in the papers are any criterion, her ladyship must be a very beautiful woman."

"Yes," I answered, smiling. He was very cleverly trying to impress upon me the fact that they had never met. His shrewd cunning showed itself in the sidelong glance he gave me.

At that moment the door suddenly opened, and Lord Stanchester, in his rough shooting kit, came in.

"Halloa, Smeeton! Welcome, my dear fellow!" he cried, wringing his guest's hands. "Excuse my being away, won't you? I've got a lot of people here, you know, and had to go out with them. By Jove! When you said good-bye to me and left the boat at Zanzibar, I never expected to see you again?"

"Well, here I am—turned up in England again, you see!" he replied merrily. "When we parted I had no intention of coming back. But somehow, on occasions, a longing for home comes over me, and I'm drawn back to London irresistibly. I see," he added, "some of the trophies are up in the hall."

"Yes," laughed his lordship. "I had them all mounted. And often when I look at them, they bring back pleasant recollections of those many weeks we were together. Well," he added, "I'm very pleased, Smeeton, to see you here at Sibberton—very. My wife knows you're here; she'll be delighted to meet you. I'm sure. I've often spoken of you, and told her how you saved me from that lioness. By Jove! I was within an ace of being done—and should have been if you hadn't been such a dead shot."

"Oh, that's enough," laughed the guest, modestly. "I can't shoot partridges—that you'll see."

The Earl walked to the mantelshelf, took a cigarette, and lit it, saying—

"I see Woodhouse has been making you at home. This is Willoughby Woodhouse, my friend as well as my secretary," he exclaimed. "I spoke of him, I believe."

"You did, on several occasions," and turning, Smeeton added, "I'm delighted to make your acquaintance, Mr Woodhouse. His lordship said all sorts of kind things about you."

But I scarcely heeded the newcomer's remarks. I was wondering what would occur when he met her ladyship face to face.

"I want you to have a good time, my dear fellow," exclaimed the Earl to his guest. "Just make yourself at home. You'll find the house a big barrack of a place, too big in fact—but with the aid of the servants you'll very soon discover the proper trails. If you don't, just go into the nearest room, ring the bell and wait. That's what most people do. My wife was fully six months before she could find her way about properly—it's a fact! She wanted to shut up the place and live in the new wing. But," he added, "the old guv'nor always kept it up properly, and I feel it my duty to do just as he did."

That a cordial friendship existed between the pair was plain, and yet I had only once heard his lordship mention him, and that was in the smoking-room when daring feats of big-game hunting and the achievements of Selous and others were being discussed. Then he had declared that he knew a man that held his own with them all—a man named Smeeton, who had spent the greater part of his life exploring and hunting, some of whose trophies, sold to well-known dealers, were the finest in the world.

His lordship was never a boastful man, and had not referred at all to his acquaintance with this renowned hunter, nor to his own African exploits, which were in no way a mean achievement.

He had just ordered Slater to bring in whiskies-and-sodas, as it was his habit to have a "peg" before dressing, when there sounded out in the corridor a light quick footstep, and the scamper of a dog, and the next instant the door opened, and the Countess of Stanchester halted on the threshold, facing the man she held in such deadly fear—Richard Keene!

Chapter Nineteen
Face to Face

"My friend Smeeton—Lady Stanchester," exclaimed the Earl, introducing them.

Their gaze met, and I saw that in a moment her heart became gripped by a nameless terror, her countenance blanched, and she halted rigid, as utterly dumbfounded as I had been; while the mysterious guest bowed, expressing his pleasure at making her acquaintance, and thus allowing her a chance to recover her self-possession.

I saw that he had darted a meaning look at her—a glance which she apparently understood, for next second she held her breath, stifling down her apprehension, and then managed to stammer out the usual expression of gratification at meeting any of her husband's friends.

"We have only a moment ago, Lady Stanchester, been recalling memories of our days on the Zambesi. We were both, I think, a little more reckless then than we are now," he said laughing.

"You're right, Smeeton," declared the Earl. "Playing the fool as I did, I narrowly escaped with my life half-a-dozen times over. But I've profited by your advice and experience."

"George is quite a steady-going old fogey nowadays, you must know, Mr Smeeton," exclaimed her ladyship. "He's a member of all sorts of committees for this and for that, and sits on the bench of magistrates with the row of fat butchers and bakers."

"And is pretty hard on poachers, I suppose?" he laughed. "In the eyes of county magistrates the snaring of a hare is, I've heard, regarded as one of the worst crimes in the calendar."

"Of course. Because it is generally the only crime that personally concerns the bench," remarked his lordship, while his wife had crossed to the fireplace and stood slightly behind her husband, in order, I noticed, to conceal the agitation now consuming her. Why had the man come there in the guise of her husband's friend? That they had shot together in Africa was certain, for she had heard of this man's prowess as a big-game hunter, but it was a revelation to her, as to me, that Smeeton and Richard Keene were one and the same person.

Old Slater returned with the "pegs" and the men drank them while her ladyship busied herself pretending to try and find a book in the large bookcase behind me. She chatted to them all the time, but managed to keep her face concealed.

At last the dressing-bell sounded, and the Earl accompanied his guest to his room, exclaiming with a laugh—

"I'd better show you the way, old chap, or you'll be wandering about like one of the lost tribes." Then, the instant the door had closed and their footsteps retreated, the Countess turned quickly to me, her face white and drawn, her eyes terrified, whispering—

"What does this mean, Mr Woodhouse? What can it mean?"

"Well, it seems as though the fellow had some object in coming to stay here as a guest," I said. "What that object is you yourself know best."

"Of course he has a motive," she cried in despair. "But what am I to do? Why didn't you warn me that you had recognised him?"

I explained briefly how to warn her had been impossible.

"Do you think George noticed my confusion when I opened the door and saw him here?" she asked anxiously.

"I think not," was my reply. "You so quickly recovered yourself."

"Ah! But you don't know how sharp his eyes are. He's really absurdly jealous sometimes."

I smiled within myself to think that a woman so fond of admiration and flattery should complain of her husband's jealousy.

"At any rate, in this affair, you'll have to act with the greatest caution and discretion, Lady Stanchester," I said. "The man is here for some sinister purpose—of that I feel quite sure. He arrived in Sibberton a little while ago, tramping along the highway, tired and hungry, a shabby wayfarer, upon whom Warr looked with suspicion. To-day he is your husband's welcomed guest, to whom he expects you to act with kindness and attention."

"Kindness!" she ejaculated. "Kindness to that man!"

"Is he such an enemy of yours?" I asked in a low tone. "Why don't you take me further into your confidence, Lady Stanchester? Surely you can rely upon my discretion?"

"I have taken you into my confidence as far as I dare," was her answer, uttered in a tone of desperation. "I want you now to assist me in combating this man's intentions, whatever they are."

"I promise to render you what assistance I can, but on one condition, recollect," I said. "The condition is that what I do is in order that you shall be afforded opportunity to convince George of your true affection."

"I know, I know," she cried quickly. "I will adhere to my part of the compact. Believe me, I will," and she stood before me a pale apprehensive figure in her Norfolk jacket and short tweed skirt—a woman whose attitude showed me that Keene's presence there held her terrified.

The truth of it all I could not guess. A vague suspicion arose of some curious romance in the days prior to her marriage; of some skeleton in her cupboard, which she feared must now be brought out to the light of day before her husband's eyes. I saw written in her countenance, as she stood before me, an all-consuming fear which seemed to hold her there immovable.

"I'm wondering whether I ought not to make some excuse to go away on a visit somewhere," she suggested after a pause. "I can't really stay under the same roof with him, meet him each day at table, and be compelled to chat with him. It's utterly impossible."

"But how can you leave all these people?" I asked. "Besides, if you did, he might perhaps revenge himself—that is, if you are wholly in his hands. Are you?"

"Utterly," she answered hoarsely, as though that confession were wrung from her.

"You fear him, while he has no need to fear you. Is that so?"

She answered in the affirmative in the same hoarse unnatural tone.

"Then you must not run further risk by attempting to escape him," I said decisively. "You must remain, act diplomatically, and endeavour to maintain a bold front. Recollect that he is here in order to take advantage of the first sign of apprehension on your part. Show no fear of him," I urged. "Disclaim all knowledge of him if necessary. Assert to his face that you have never met before, should he speak to you alone and endeavour to recall the past. We live for the present or the future, Lady Stanchester, not for the past—whatever it may have been. Courage!" I said. "If you really love George and are now hounded by this man, I will help you in every way."

"Ah!" she said gratefully. "I know you will, Mr Woodhouse. Believe me, I am at this moment sorely in need of a friend. I know, alas! what evil tongues have said of me, and what a reputation I have for giddiness and flirtation. Yet every action of a woman of my age and position is magnified and exaggerated in order that it may furnish food for gossips and hints for scandal. But I tell you I am not so black as I am painted. I still have a heart— and that heart is my husband's. He is your friend, and if you assist me to defeat this man you will be rendering him the greatest service one man can render to another—and you will save me."

"I have promised," I answered. "You must go now and meet the man on perfect equality, with perfect friendship. Your mind is blank regarding the past, and you have never met him before in all your life. No matter what he threatens to reveal, or what he tells you his revenge will be, you must not admit that you have been previously acquainted."

"It will be difficult—terribly difficult," she said. "He can unfortunately recall certain facts which—well, which I fear I cannot deny."

"But you must," I urged. "Deny everything. Then he will expose his hand, and we shall know how to deal with him in order to checkmate his plans."

"Very well," answered the desperate woman. "I'll do my best. But if I fail you must not blame me."

"You are clever, Lady Stanchester, and with your woman's diplomacy and quick inventiveness I am sure you can face the difficulty and overcome it. Go," I urged. "You must appear at dinner gay and merry, as though you had not a serious thought in the world. Your careless attitude will then puzzle him from the very outset. Act as I tell you, and if you want advice at any moment, come to me."

She thanked me, and turning slowly went out to dress for the terrible ordeal which she knew too well was before her. And when she had gone I sat in my chair for a long time, plunged in thought.

The mystery was assuming even greater and more remarkable proportions. The chief problem at the moment was the motive of the mysterious guest.

Who was this man Keene of whom both Lolita and Lady Stanchester were in such deadly fear? What power did he possess over them?

Times without number had I asked myself that self-same question, but no solution of the enigma presented itself. The mystery was now even more dark and inscrutable than it had been at the outset. The puzzle was maddening. So I rose with a sigh, and went up to my room to dress with a distinct feeling precursory of some untoward event about to occur in the Stanchester household, and a fervent hope that the young Countess would hold her own successfully in the desperate fight with this man whom she declared to be her very worst enemy.

The situation was surely a most grave and remarkable one, and her position was certainly unenviable. Knowing her abject terror of the man I felt apprehensive of the result, for I felt confident that one single sign of weakness would give the desperate game entirely into his own unscrupulous hands.

In the big white drawing-room where the visitors assembled before dinner, the Countess appeared in a marvellous gown of pale turquoise and cream, and wearing the diamond collar and bodice-ornament which was her husband's wedding gift, and which cost a sum which to many a man would have represented a fortune. Her coiffure was beautifully arranged without a hair awry, and her white neck and arms seemed like alabaster. Truly she was a magnificent woman, and well merited the description a certain royal prince had once uttered of her—"Taking face and figure, the prettiest woman who ever came to Court during the present reign."

She was laughing gaily with old Lord Cotterstock as she entered, chaffing him about his sleepiness after luncheon and missing several birds, and as her gaze met mine I saw that the manner she had reassumed, that nonchalant air that she usually wore, was little short of marvellous. One would hardly have recognised in her the white-faced, terrified and despondent woman of half-an-hour before.

In the corner of the room stood Smeeton, a tall, commanding figure in faultless dress clothes, and a small but fine diamond in his shirt, chatting to two women, Lady Barford and the Honourable Violet Middleton, to whom he had just been introduced. Her ladyship was of that middle-aged type of stiff-backed lion-hunter who sought London through to get the latest poet, painter or *littérateur* to go to her weekly "At Homes," and had already, it seemed, buttonholed the renowned hunter of big game.

Old Slater appeared at the door, bowing with that formality acquired by long service in that noble family, and announced in a voice loud enough to be heard by all—

"Dinner is served, m'lady."

Then the Countess walked boldly up to Smeeton and asked to be taken in by him, while I linked myself up with a rather angular girl in a pale rose gown that had seen long service, the daughter of a Squire from a neighbouring village who was this evening eating his annual dinner at the Hall.

Through dinner her ladyship preserved an outward calm that was remarkable. She chatted and laughed amiably with her guest seated at her right hand, and as I watched narrowly I detected that he was already amazed at her self-possession. That night she was even more brilliant than ever. Her conversation sparkled with wit, and her remarks and criticisms caused her guests in her vicinity to roar with laughter at frequent intervals.

From where I sat little escaped my watchful eyes. Once or twice she turned her gaze upon me, as though to ask whether she were acting her part sufficiently well, then fired off some epigrammatic remark to one or other of the gay crowd of well-dressed people around her.

Dinner ended, the ladies retired, the cloth was removed, the port was circulated in decanters in silver stands along the bare table of polished oak, in accordance with the custom that had obtained at Sibberton ever since the Jacobean days. The Stanchester cellars had always been celebrated, and assuredly there was not a finer port in the whole country than that which they contained. Among the men, as they drank their wine, the newly-arrived visitor became the centre of attraction. Sportsmen all of them, Lord Stanchester had told them of Smeeton's keenness after big game, and many questions were being put to him regarding the practicability of shooting expeditions in East Africa.

At last an adjournment was made into the huge vaulted hall, the stained glass and architecture of which reminded me of a church, where there was music every evening. In the high roof hung those faded and tattered banners carried by the Stanchesters in various battles historic in English history, and around the walls stands of armour in long and imposing rows.

Her ladyship was an excellent musician, and although in these days of mechanical piano-playing music will, it is feared, soon be a neglected art, she always played on the grand piano for the entertainment of her guests. Some songs were sung—mainly from the comic operas, *San Toy*, *The Geisha*, *The Country Girl*—and some even with a chorus heartily joined in by those lords and ladies of illustrious name. It was Liberty Hall, and in the evening the fun always grew fast and furious.

Presently the bridge tables were set, parties were made up, cards were dealt and played, money rattled and very soon there were high stakes in various quarters and a good deal of money began to change hands.

With two or three exceptions the whole party played bridge. Myself, I could not afford to lose, and therefore never played. While among those who declined the invitation was Smeeton, who remained an interested onlooker at his hostess's table.

Only by the slight trembling of her bejewelled hands could I detect in her any sign of fear, but when she rose as midnight chimed out from the turret clock over the stables, as a signal for the ladies to retire to their rooms, he had, I noticed, disappeared. Perhaps he wished to obtain a secret interview with her, therefore I was quickly on the alert, and succeeded in gaining a point at the junction of two corridors that ran at right angles, and down which I knew she must pass. In order to escape notice I slipped into one of the rooms and stood in the dark with the door slightly ajar.

She came at last alone, her silken skirts sweeping with loud frou-frou, her diamonds glistening in the light as she advanced. Her guests had passed out into the new wing, but she habitually reached her room by this corridor, which was a short cut and ran through a portion of the vast mansion not generally used.

She had almost gained the doorway wherein I stood, when I heard hurrying steps behind her, and next moment Smeeton caught her roughly by the wrist, exclaiming in a quick determined whisper as he bent to her—

"Marigold! Marigold! Have I so changed that you don't know me? I told you that I should return and here I am! You thought you could escape by marrying this man—but you can't! The awkward little matter outstanding between us still remains to be arranged, and I think you know Dick Keene well enough to be aware that in an affair of this sort he's not a man to be trifled with. So you know well enough what I'm here for, and what a word from me to these fine friends of yours will mean to you. Do you hear me?" he added, with a hard ring in his voice. "What have you to say?"

Chapter Twenty
Richard Keene Makes a Revelation

The Countess, unconscious of my presence, halted quickly, and turning upon him with a start exclaimed—

"I—I really don't understand what you mean, Mr Smeeton!"

"Understand what I mean!" he echoed with a short dry laugh. "I suppose you'll deny acquaintance with me next!"

"I certainly do not recollect having met you before," she answered with admirable hauteur.

"What?" he exclaimed, in undisguised surprise at her bold attempt to disclaim any previous acquaintance. "Do you actually affirm that we have never previously known each other?"

"Never until this evening," was her response. "That is why I don't understand what you mean in addressing me in this manner."

He burst out laughing, treating her bold denial with derision. Yet she remained firm, and in indignation exclaimed—

"Let me pass. I think, Mr Smeeton, you have forgotten yourself this evening."

"No," he said. "I never forget a debt that is owing me. I am here for repayment."

"I really don't understand you. It's late, and one of the servants may pass this way and overhear you. Let us resume this highly interesting discussion in the morning," she suggested. "This must no doubt be a case of mistaken identity. I can only suppose I resemble somebody you know."

"There was but one Marigold Gordon," he replied, in a hard firm voice. "There was but one Marigold who wrecked one man's happiness, and who afterwards married another because of his wealth and position—yourself."

"Oh! this is insupportable!" she cried indignantly. "I shall tell my husband that I'm insulted by his guest—a man from nowhere. Let me pass—I say!"

"Yes, a man from nowhere," he sneered. "Richard Keene is always from nowhere, because he has no fixed home. He comes to-day from nowhere and goes to nowhere. But before he goes he means that his account with you shall be settled. Understand that!"

"Well, you've said so already," she laughed. "Is it the action of a gentleman to utter all kinds of vague threats like this?"

"Vague threats! You'll find that they are more than vague. What I say I mean. You think," he added, "to escape by denying all previous acquaintance with me. But you'll discover your mistake when too late."

"I have no reason to escape," she declared with a nonchalant air that amazed me, knowing how at heart she feared him. "I shall merely tell my husband of this indignity, and leave him to act as he thinks best."

"Ah!" he remarked, "you are a clever woman, Marigold—you always were. Is it really necessary to remind you of those ugly events of three years ago in which you and Lolita were so intimately concerned, or that there still exists a certain woman named Lejeune?"

"I desire no reminder of any matters which concern me," she replied coldly. "This does not."

"But it concerns Lolita—and what concerns her concerns you. She fled to the north the instant she heard that I had returned, for she feared to meet me."

"Her affairs are not mine," declared the Countess unmoved. "You are speaking of something of which I am in utter ignorance. Why don't you explain your meaning?"

"Shall I speak openly?" he said. "Very well, if you prefer it, I will. If you recollect nothing else, perhaps you will remember that a young man named Hugh Wingfield was found dead in the park here quite recently— murdered."

"I heard of it. I was at Aix-les-Bains," she replied.

"You saw his photograph—your husband showed it to you after your return, and you recognised who the dead man was who had remained unidentified."

"How could I recognise a person whom I had never seen before?"

"Then you also deny acquaintance with Hugh Wingfield, the poor young fellow who fell into the trap so cunningly set for him?"

"Certainly. Why?"

"Well, because you are a more wonderful woman, Marigold, than even I believed," he answered in his deep rather rough voice. "You're a perfect marvel."

"Not at all," she answered quite calmly. "First, I do not see what gives you permission to call me by my Christian name; and secondly, I don't see the motive you have in endeavouring to fix upon me knowledge of certain matters of which I am in entire ignorance. Perhaps you'll explain why, being my husband's guest and only a few hours in this house, you arrest me like this, and commence all these extraordinary insinuations? You claim acquaintanceship with me, while I declare that I didn't know you from Adam until my husband introduced us just before dinner."

"Then what I have to reply is the reverse of complimentary. If you had been a man I should have told you to your face that you were a liar."

"You may disbelieve me as you will," she responded still unruffled. "But I merely tell you that I have no further desire to stand here and be insulted," and although she tried to pass him he again clutched her wrist fiercely and prevented her.

"You shall answer me!" he whispered angrily. "You are Marigold Gordon, now Countess of Stanchester; you are the woman I am here to meet, to speak with calmly, and to come to an amicable settlement—if possible. You know, as well as I do, that Lolita's future in is your hands, just as it is in mine. A word from either of us can ruin her. It would mean for her arrest, disgrace, condemnation. Now, do you intend to speak and to save her; or will you still deny previous acquaintance with me and consequently all knowledge of the affair? Lolita is in peril. If you will you can save her, although she is your enemy—although I know how you hate her."

I stood aghast at this fresh development of the mystery. I had actually urged this woman to disclaim all that the man Keene might allege, yet in utter ignorance that, by so doing, she was bringing ruin upon my love! My ears were open to catch every word. The Countess was Lolita's enemy! Could that be the actual truth? Did this woman whose beauty was so remarkable so mask her real feelings towards her husband's sister that, while outwardly showing great affection for her, she had secretly plotted her ruin and disgrace?

"I know nothing," was her persistent reply.

"Then you prefer that Lolita shall suffer," he said in a calm hard voice. "Remember that her enemies are unscrupulous, relentless. The word once spoken can never be recalled. Do you intend that her life shall actually be sacrificed?"

"How?"

"She intends to take it by her own hand the instant the truth is known. I have been up to Scotland."

"And you have, I suppose, threatened her, as you have me?" sneered her ladyship.

"I have no necessity to threaten her," was his answer. "She knows quite well enough the peril in which she is placed by those who have sought her downfall."

"Well, and what does her future concern me, pray?" asked the woman coldly.

"Only that you can save her," he argued. "Think if, in a moment of despair, she took her life, what a burden of remorse would be yours."

"There is no such word as remorse in my vocabulary," she laughed. "If there were I should have entered a convent long ago."

"Yes," he said. "You speak the truth, Marigold. You are one of those few women who are, perhaps fortunately, untroubled by conscience. The past is to you a closed book, would that it were also to me! Would that I could forget completely that affair at which you and I exercised such dastardly cunning and scandalous duplicity. But I cannot, and it is for that reason I am here to beg—to beseech of you to at least save poor Lolita, who is being driven to extremity by despair!"

Lolita! I thought of her, desperate and unprotected, the victim of a vile and yet mysterious conspiracy—the victim of this woman who was, after all, her secret enemy. Heaven formed me as I was, a creature of affection, and I bowed to its decree in living but for love of her. Upon the tablet of my heart was graven Lolita, and death alone could efface it. I was no sensualist; thank heaven I had not brutalised my mind, nor contaminated the pure ray of my divinity. I loved with truth, with ardour, and with tenderest affection, from which had arisen all those ecstasies that constituted the heaven of loving. True, I was jealous—madly jealous. I was a tyrant in the passion that consumed me, but none can truly love who would receive it when divided.

Poverty claimed wealth—ambition craved for honour—kings would have boundless sway—despots would be gods—and I merely asked for love. Where was my crime in claiming a return for that already given? Or if it could never be mine, why should I dash at once to earth the air-drawn vision of felicity?

Fate was inscrutable; and sanctioned by its will, I determined to yield without a sign to my reward, be it love or be it misery.

Each pleasure has its pain, nor yet was ever mortal joy complete. In those days before the advent of Richard Keene in Sibberton I had been lulled by bliss so exquisite that reason should have told me it was but a dream. I had forgotten everything in the great vortex of love which had, till then, overwhelmed me. And as I stood there listening to every word that passed, I felt that I alone had power to save the woman I adored.

There was a plot, some vile dastardly plot, the mystery of which was inscrutable. And she was to be the victim. Was it right that I should remain silent and make no effort to rescue her from the doom which this man Keene declared must be hers?

"How can I save her, when I am in ignorance?" asked the woman, still persistent in the disclaimer I had so foolishly urged upon her.

"Then you still deny all knowledge of the affair?" he said in his deep earnest voice. "You still dare to stand there and tell me that you are not the woman who assisted Marie Lejeune—the woman for whom the police still hold a warrant, but who do not seem to recognise a common criminal in the person of the Countess of Stanchester. Think for a moment what a word from me to the police might mean to you," he added in a threatening tone.

"And think also, Mr Smeeton—or whatever you choose to call yourself— that I also possess knowledge of a fact which, if known to Scotland Yard, would prevent you in future from pushing your unwelcome presence into a house where you were not wanted. Do you understand?"

"No, I don't."

"Well, as you've spoken so plainly," she said in an angry tone, "I will also tell you what I mean to do. You are here bent upon mischief; you intend to carry out the threat you made long ago. Good! From the very start I openly defy you," and she snapped her slim white fingers in his face. "Tell my husband any lie you like! Do your worst to injure my reputation, but recollect that from to-night, instead of being friends, we are enemies, and I shall tell the police something which will be to them of enormous interest. You wish to quarrel with me, therefore let it be so. My husband shall know of your insults at once, and that will allow you an opening to denounce me as one of the worst women in England. The result will be interesting— as you will see. One of us will suffer—but depend upon it it will not be myself," she laughed defiantly.

"I have no wish to quarrel," he assured her quickly. "I said I had come here to make terms with you and to save Lolita."

"What do you wish? That I should incriminate myself?" she asked. "Lolita does not concern me in the least, neither do you, for the matter of that. I've given you the ultimatum," she added. "If you wish to pick a quarrel, then my own safety will be assured."

"You misunderstand me," he said in a tone more conciliatory than before.

"Yes, I certainly misunderstand your desire to bring upon yourself what must be a very serious disaster by coming here and trying to wring from me certain things which I am determined, for my own good name and reputation, to keep secret. My own opinion of you is that you are a fool, and that if you are wise you'll make an excuse, and to-morrow morning leave Sibberton."

"I shall do nothing of the kind," he responded in quick indignation. "I intend to act as I have told you."

"Very well, then, that is sufficient. I wish you a very good-night," she said passing on before the doorway where I stood hidden. "My husband shall know at once how you, a stranger to me, have dared to insult me with your outrageous insinuations and threats."

"No, I did not mean—" he commenced, as though to modify his actions.

"Enough, Mr Smeeton. I have decided upon my course of action, and you had better leave this house while there is yet time. Otherwise perhaps you will have unwelcome inquiries made after you."

The man upon whom she had so cleverly turned the tables gave vent to a muttered imprecation, while the swish of her silken flounces receded down the long dark corridor, and I stood there breathless and motionless, not daring to betray my presence.

The result of such an open quarrel as it had become I dreaded to contemplate, for I knew, alas! too well that whatever it be my love must suffer, and that she was bent upon taking her life rather than face exposure of the mysterious scandal.

Chapter Twenty One
The Saints' Garden

After breakfast on the following morning I contrived to make an appointment with the Countess to meet her at a short distance from the house in what was known as the Saints' Garden.

Her ladyship's habit was to walk in the garden for half an hour after breakfast, and I deemed that the Saints' Garden, being at a secluded spot down near the lake, and little frequented either by the gardeners or visitors, was a good place of meeting. The gardens at Sibberton were noted for their beauty. There was an old lavender garden; one for bulbs; another for roses, and—most charming of all, Lolita's pride—the Saints' Garden, the flowers of which were supposed to blossom on the days set apart for certain saints. In it were veronicas, lilies, Christmas roses, and a wild tangle of old-world flowers.

I waited in patience in this little "garden of the good," encompassed by its dark thick box hedges. The morning was bright, the dew glistened everywhere in the sunlight, and the flowers filled the air with their fragrance. It was a peaceful spot where Lolita loved to linger, and where we had often walked and talked in secret.

She came at last—the reckless, handsome woman who held my love's life in her hands.

Her fair face was smiling as she came along in her neat short skirt and fresh morning blouse, and greeted me saying—

"Really, Mr Woodhouse, I hardly think it was wise of you to meet me here. One of the gardeners or some one may see us and gossip," and she turned her eyes upon me with that look which had made many a man's head reel.

"We are safer from observation here, Lady Stanchester, than in my room," I answered in a rather hard tone, I fear. She glanced at me quickly, apparently in wonder that I was in no mood for trifling. She was, of course, unaware that I had overheard all that had passed between her and the man Richard Keene. Nevertheless she said—

"As I anticipated, he claimed acquaintanceship with me last night—stopped me in the Panelled Corridor and addressed me by my Christian name."

"Well."

"I flatly denied ever having met him before. It took him back completely. He wasn't prepared for it," she laughed.

"And you were able, I hope, to sustain the fiction until the end?" I asked, looking straight at her.

"Well," she answered, rather uneasily, "I managed to so confound him that I don't think he'll carry out what was his intention. As a matter of fact, I fancy he'll curtail his visit. George has taken him to shoot over at Islip." She made no explanation of his urgent appeal to her to save Lolita, of his threats or of her own declaration that if they were to be enemies then she would bring upon him an overwhelming disaster. She was keeping the truth to herself, suspecting my love for Lolita.

"He threatened you, of course?" I said, leaning upon the grey old weather-worn sundial and looking at her as though I were waiting for her explanation.

"Threats?" she laughed. "Oh! yes. He was full of them. But you were quite right; my denial utterly upset all his bluster. He can't make out my intentions, and therefore will hesitate to do me harm, for he doesn't know the extent of my knowledge. Really, Mr Woodhouse, you very cleverly foresaw the whole affair. I admit that I was very hard pressed for a few moments. But now—" and she paused.

"And now?" I asked.

"Well, I've met him with his own weapons. He won't dare to speak, because at heart he's afraid of me."

"Then you think he'll leave very soon?"

"Ah! I don't know. He's playing a very clever game, as he always does. Think how he has come here as George's friend, and at the same time as my bitterest enemy! His audacity is surely unequalled!"

"But is he really your enemy?" I queried, fixing her with my gaze. "Are you not his?"

She looked at me somewhat puzzled. I had put a meaning note into my voice, yet I did not intend that she should be aware that I knew the truth of her secret hatred of my love, or that I had ascertained that the name of the young man who had fallen the victim of an assassin's hand was Hugh Wingfield.

"Perhaps I am his enemy," she laughed lightly. "I have surely need to be."

"Why?"

"With a man of his stamp one must act with firmness and disregard all scruples. He will ruin me if he can. But I don't intend that he shall. Before he does that I'll give information against him myself—information that will be a revelation to certain persons in this house."

I thought of the peril of my love.

"Information I take it, that would mean ruin to a certain person—a woman!" and I held her steadily with my eyes.

Her mouth opened slightly, and I saw that she suspected that I had gained some knowledge which she believed was his alone.

"A woman," she repeated. "Whom do you mean?"

"Lolita," I replied in a low hard voice.

"Lolita?" she gasped. "Who told you that—I mean, what makes you suggest such a thing?"

"My conclusions are formed upon certain facts already known to me, Lady Stanchester," I answered coldly. "You deceived me when you sought my aid by declaring your desire to show your affection for your husband. You had a deeper and more desperate game to play—and poor Lolita is to be the victim."

"You love her, I suppose?" she snapped. "You needn't deny it. I've seen it long ago—you, her brother's secretary!" she sneered. "Why, the thing's absurd?"

"There is a wide gulf in our social positions, I admit, Lady Stanchester," was my quick angry response. "But surely it is not so strange nor so absurd that I should love a woman who is friendless, and who has so strangely incurred your hatred!"

"Incurred my hatred? What foolishness are you talking now?" she asked with that cold hauteur which she could assume to inferiors when she willed.

"I repeat what I have said. You intend that the ruin that threatens you shall fall upon Lolita. In plain words, you will sacrifice her, in order to save yourself!"

"And who's been telling you this interesting untruth, pray?" she asked. "I thought you knew Lolita sufficiently well to be aware that I have, ever since my marriage to George, been her friend."

"To her face yes, but in secret no."

"You are insulting me, Mr Woodhouse," she exclaimed, her eyes flashing. "I have always been Lolita's friend."

"Then prove your friendship by telling the truth concerning her," I said, "the truth known equally to Marie Lejeune with yourself—the truth that can save her from this unfounded charge against her."

I made a blind shot, and stood watching its effect upon the brilliant woman.

A slight hardness showed at the corners of her mouth, and a strange light shone in her eyes as she realised that I knew the truth, how she had cleverly sought to deceive me by her false declaration of that love for her husband which she had assuredly never entertained.

"I didn't know there was any charge against her. What is it?" she inquired calmly.

"Prevarication is useless. Lady Stanchester," I said determinedly. "Richard Keene has come here to get you to tell the truth concerning Lady Lolita. You have refused, and he has threatened you with exposure. You, on your part, have retaliated by threatening him, hence the position at this moment is that he fears to speak lest he should incur your revenge, while you refuse to speak the truth and remove suspicion from Lolita. You intend, therefore, that she shall fall the innocent victim. But recollect that I am her friend, and I will save her, even if compelled to go to George and tell him everything."

She bit her lip. I could see that it had never crossed her mind, that, being her husband's friend, I might lay bare the truth to him and expose the fact that Richard Keene and Mr Smeeton were one and the same.

"Ah! So you intend to give me away?" she remarked, with a quick shrug of the shoulders.

"I have no wish to do anything that will tend to cause a breach between you and your husband," I answered. "I merely say that I intend to stand as Lolita's friend, and to-night I shall go north, see her, and explain all I know. She will be interested, no doubt, to hear that a friend of your pre-matrimonial days is here as your husband's guest."

"Then you're going to tell her?" she asked with a quick start, and I saw by the way her eyebrows had contracted that she was devising some plan to counteract my intentions.

"I shall act just as I think proper, Lady Stanchester," I responded. "In this affair I have the good name of only one person to consider—the person whom you declare it is absurd for me to regard with affection."

"And so you mean to place me in a very invidious position by telling tales to everybody?" she exclaimed with a supercilious smile. "Well," she added, "go up to Scotland and see her, if you like. Tell her whatever you think proper; it will be all the same to me."

"Why?"

"Because I shall still retain the knowledge which I hold, and she cannot—she will not dare to—do anything to injure me. If she does, Mr Woodhouse—if she does—then I'll speak the truth—a truth that will astound you, and cause you to regret that you ever interfered in my affairs, or ever sought to befriend a woman guilty of a crime."

"Guilty of a crime!" I echoed. "What crime do you allege against Lady Lolita?"

She merely laughed triumphantly in my face.

"I demand a reply to my question," I cried angrily.

"Ask her yourself. It is not for me to denounce her before she has sought my downfall."

"But you make a distinct allegation!"

"And one that I can substantiate when the time is ripe," was the woman's firm fearless answer.

"But you can clear her character if it suits you!" I exclaimed quickly. "You have admitted that."

"You think fit to take the part of my enemies against me, therefore you will find me merciless," was her vague ominous reply. "Go to Scotland and see Lolita. Tell her that I have sent you—and," she added, "tell her from me to keep her mouth closed, or else the story of Hugh Wingfield shall be known, You will recollect the name, won't you?—Hugh Wingfield."

I stood silent, unable to respond, for that was the name of the young man who was so foully done to death in that hollow behind the beech avenue.

"Moreover," she went on, noticing the effect of her words upon me, "moreover, you are at liberty to tell George what you like concerning me. He loves me—and when a man's in love he believes no evil of the woman. So go!" she laughed. "And afterwards tell me what he says. I shall be so very interested to know."

Chapter Twenty Two
The Sign to the Unknown

Love knows not want—he has no such intimate as poverty; if he smiles, he has but one dread foe; if he frowns, he has but one true friend; and those both concentrate in the oblivion of death.

I loved—yes, I loved Lolita. While she lived, the soul-invigorating fire of her eyes kept alive my passion-torn frame. And yet who was I that I dared thus ally myself with heavenly beauty and terrestrial greatness? She was the daughter of an Earl and I a mere secretary, dependent upon her brother's favours. No title, no transcendent qualities were mine. And yet, was I not ennobled? Did I not wear within my heart the never-fading insignia of love, the qualifications of which were fervency and immutable truth?

The proud Countess had sneered at me. She sneered because the passion of true love had never known a place in her fickle heart. As next day I sat alone in the express travelling up to Scotland, memory of the hour came back to me when I had first gazed upon those charms I since had learned to reverence with all the fervour of matchless truth. I recollected how long, long ago, whenever I saw Lolita, my pulse beat with an unwonted motion, and the throbbing of my heart spoke to my soul in a language it had never known before—my brain became on fire, and ere I knew the term, I knew what constituted love. Yes, love—love that had not yet taught me. what presumption was, but I rather stood the awe-struck victim of his all-puissant will.

And now I was tearing with all speed to seek her, to hear the truth from her own sweet lips. Never once had she told me that my love was reciprocated, yet in her clear bright eyes I had long ago seen that mixture of tender pity, noble generosity, candour and pure refined womanly feeling open as the face of day, that told me that she was not averse to my attentions even though I was neither wealthy nor of noble birth.

Day had succeeded day since her departure for the north, and every coming dawn had proved what gave bitter anguish to my soul. A strange suspicion that seemed to envelop her like a cloud—a suspicion which somehow I could not determine—had caused the struggle of conflicting thoughts. And now I was rushing towards her, hoping fervently that her words to me might reveal the truth, and infuse into my chaotic soul one bright spark of heavenly comfort whence might blaze the inextinguishable flame of requited love.

Alone, gazing aimlessly at the fleeting panorama of hill and dale as the express rushed on from Crewe to Carlisle, my busy fancy seemed to reconcile impossibilities, and as the mariner who feebly grasps the plank surrounded by a sea of deadly horrors, so I, amid the gloom of black despair, illumined the fallacious touch of hope and wandered into the maze of gilded fallacy.

Ah! Hope, thou flitting phantom, thou gaudy illusion, thou fond misleader of the wrecked senses, that framest a paradise of airy nothingness, how strange that thou canst in pleasing dreams bring to the tortured mind a brief respite.

And yet when I recollected the dark suspicions that rested upon my love, I held my breath. When I calmly reviewed all the circumstances, life seemed all a blank to me; my reason bade me cease to hope. Yet better be warmed by madness than chilled by coward fear; better burn with jealousy than die the silent fool of black despair.

In such a mood I sat thinking and pondering until we glided into the great echoing station of Carlisle. Then I descended, bought a paper, and tried to read as the portion of the train in which I sat continued its way eastward towards Edinburgh. To concentrate my mind upon a printed page was, however, impossible. I recollected those strange, ominous words of the Countess when we had parted in the Saints' Garden, and somehow felt convinced that her position was impregnable.

Keene had distinctly declared that if Marigold failed to tell the truth, then my love must fall a victim. Why—and how? All was so mysterious, so utterly inscrutable, so bewildering that the enigma admitted of no solution.

I could not disguise the fact from myself that Lolita had gone north purposely to avoid the unwelcome stranger who had so mysteriously returned, and I now intended at all hazards to obtain from her some fact concerning the conspiracy into which he seemed to have entered.

The strange incident in that lonely farmhouse and the attack upon Marie Lejeune were again facts which combined to show what a wide-spread plot was in progress—a plot the motive of which was still enshrouded in mystery, but of which the victim was undoubtedly to be none other than my well-beloved.

Lolita, who was staying with her aunt, the Dowager Lady Casterton, at the *Royal Hotel*, in Princes Street, sprang quickly to her feet when, shortly before dinner, the waiter ushered me into their private sitting-room. Fortunately her aunt was still in her room, and we were therefore alone.

"Willoughby!" she gasped springing forward to me breathlessly. "You! Whatever brings you here—what has happened at Sibberton?"

"Nothing," I replied in order to set her at ease. "Or rather nothing in particular. Every one is very well, and the house-party has assumed its usual gaiety."

"Marigold is still at home?" she inquired, as though her first thought was of her brother's wife. I answered in the affirmative, and then slowly and with reverence raised her slim white hand to my lips. She allowed me to kiss her fingers in homage, smiling sweetly upon me the while.

She was in a magnificent dinner-dress of black net shimmering with sequins—a gown the very simplicity of which rendered it graceful, charming, and the essence of good taste. At her throat was a single row of large pearls, but she wore no other ornament. She always dressed artistically and in the latest mode, and surely her gown was exactly suited to the hotel *table d'hôte*.

I had only just had time to go to my room, change, and seek her, for I had not notified her of my coming in order that she should have no chance of avoiding me. Yet her manner of greeting was as though my presence gave her the utmost pleasure. Her cheeks flushed as I pressed her fingers to my lips, and I knew that her heart, like mine, beat quickly with the passion of affection.

In a few brief words I told her that I had taken quarters in the hotel, that I should explain to her aunt that my presence in Edinburgh was connected with the Earl's affairs, and that I desired to have a private chat with her after dinner.

"Something has happened, Willoughby," she said apprehensively. "I see it in your face! What is it? Tell me?"

"Nothing very serious," was my evasive reply, for I heard Lady Casterton's high-pitched voice outside, and wished to conceal from the snappy old dowager that the real object of my visit was to see Lolita.

Next instant the old lady entered, dressed in black and wearing a smart cap of fine old lace. Much surprised at my presence, she greeted me and commenced inquiring after the Earl and the Countess, remarking that she intended to join the house-party in November as she had to make a visit to Lord Penarth in Wales before coming to us.

"We've had a most delightful time at Strathpeffer—Lolita and I," she remarked. "And as I wanted to pay a few visits about Edinburgh, we're just here for a few days. Of course you knew from George that we were here?"

"Yes," I replied. "I have some business to do for him in Edinburgh, so I thought I would put up here."

And then, in obedience to the gong, we all three descended into the large dining-room of the hotel. A good many people were present, but no woman so beautiful or brilliant as Lady Lolita Lloyd.

I noticed how the guests turned to look at her, and then to whisper among themselves, for her beauty was remarkable and her photographs often appeared in the ladies' papers, just as did those of Mangold. A pretty woman with a title is always remarked in a hotel.

We sat at our small table chatting affably through the meal, yet I saw how intense was her desire to know the true reason of my presence. That I had some distinct object in coming north she could not doubt, and was therefore anxious for the long meal to end and for opportunity to speak with me alone.

Old Lady Casterton was a typical dowager of the days of class distinction—a stout, well-preserved, white-haired person who regarded the world through her *lorgnon* with an air of wonder, as though she were examining some interesting species. She stared at all common people, who felt themselves uncomfortable 'neath her gaze, and generally spoke in a tone loud enough to be heard by all in the vicinity. She was youngest sister of the old Earl of Stanchester, and had married the Earl of Casterton, who afterwards became one of England's most famous generals, and had been left a widow of very large and wealthy estate.

With me she was always perfectly affable, knowing the strong personal friendship existing between the Stanchesters and my own family. Hence she treated me on an equality with herself and during the meal laughed and chatted merrily about the people she and her niece had recently met.

At last, however, dinner was over, and we all three retired to the private sitting-room, where Lolita at my desire played Tito Mattei's "White Moon" serenade and the "Cavatine" from *Faust*.

"Won't you sing us something?" I urged presently when she was about to turn from the piano. At first she tried to excuse herself, but seeing that I was anxious to hear her voice she turned again, and in her clear contralto sang an old French serenade:—

> "Une reine est maitresse de mon coeur;
>   Elle reigne part tout.
>   Car ses beaux yeux.
> Sont les deux sceptres de l'amour;
>   Et quand vers moi ils tournent leurs brillantes flammes.
>   Le feu d'amour s'empare de tout mon âme.

"Heureux si j'étois souverain.
    De tout le ciel
    Peut être elle,
Ne voudras pas que j'aime en vain;
Mais comme je suis en silence je soupire;
J'ose bien aimer, mais je n'ose pas le dire."

Her gaze fell upon me as she sang, and surely she addressed those final words to me—

"But as I am, in silence I must feel
Love's sacred flame, and yet that flame conceal."

I sat gazing upon her beauty entranced. In that sweet clear voice was a touch of pathos such as I have never before heard, and I knew that she was suffering, like myself. In those moments I had wandered in the mazes of ecstatic bliss. All the world save her was lost to me. By the look in her beautiful eyes I was again launched on the wide sea of bliss; love was the pilot of my soul and the bright beam of her love-look illuminated my track, as the soft zephyrs of love filled my warm fancy, leading me to the shores of matchless beauty.

The song had ended, and with it my vision vanished. She closed the piano, rose and crossed the room to look out of the window upon the long line of lights in Princes Street with the castle frowning opposite in the starless gloom.

Her action was a natural one, yet it was succeeded by one which caused me some surprise. She had been standing for a moment at the open window, as though enjoying the cool air, then suddenly she removed a great bowl of bright dahlias that gave a welcome touch of colour to the room from a sideboard, and placed them upon the small table in the window.

Afterwards she returned to us without, however, drawing down the blind.

Had she placed those flowers there merely to give them air because the room was warm? Or had she put them in the window as signal to some one in the street below?

Her hand trembled, she grew uneasy, and then I knew that I had guessed the truth.

Those flowers were placed there to warn some one of my presence!

Chapter Twenty Three
Contains a Disclosure

When the old lady had at last retired and I stood alone with my love, I moved across to draw the blind.

"Oh! do let us have some air," she urged with a sigh. "It was so hot downstairs to-night. I feel stifled."

This could not be, for the night air in Scotland is chilly in September. Therefore I felt convinced that she wished the bowl of flowers to remain in view of some one outside, a suspicion confirmed by her quick glance at the clock upon the mantelshelf.

For whom could that signal be intended? That it was to warn some one against calling upon her was apparent, and in an instant a great uncontrollable jealousy sprang up within me. The goddess of my admiration stood there before me calmly, her eyes fixed upon my woe-worn countenance in silence. Her lips moved at last.

"Well?" she asked. "And why have you come here, to me?"

"Because I am seeking to serve you, Lolita," was my answer. "At Sibberton matters have assumed a very grave aspect. Richard Keene is staying there as George's guest."

"What?" she gasped, her face white in an instant. "Impossible! Keene as George's friend!—never?"

"He is guest at Sibberton under the name of Smeeton. George apparently met him when hunting in Africa," I said.

She stood regarding me, utterly bewildered, as I explained to her further the cunning manner in which the stranger Keene had introduced himself into the house.

"Then for me the future is utterly hopeless," she exclaimed blankly, her beautiful face pale as death. "It is just as I have feared. My enemies have triumphed—and I am their victim."

"How?"

"Richard Keene will not spare me—that I know," she cried in desperation. "Ah! Willoughby! I cannot bear it longer. I have either to endure and be accursed here, or seek my fate and still exist the creature of the wrath hereafter. Cowardice some will call my death! But can it be coward-like to spurn the certainty I have and fly to regions unexplored? Where hope exists, life would become a stake too dear to hazard, but all with me is dreariness; and if I live existence pictures to my mind one cheerless blank; a life of condemnation and despair." And she stood staring straight before her.

"But, Lolita!" I cried, taking her hand tenderly and gazing into her beautiful face, "you surely don't know what you are saying. You are my love—my all in all."

"Ah! yes," she responded bitterly, glancing quickly at me. "Until—until they tell you the truth—only until then!"

How could I determine her meaning? How could I explore the labyrinth that surrounded her?

My brain still conjured up excuse upon excuse and warred against my better reason.

"But I don't understand?" I said. "Why not speak more plainly—tell me everything?"

"Ah!" she sighed, her eyes fixed before her. "As I look back upon life's stormy sea my resolution stands appalled, and I more wonder that I am than that I should be thus. Were ever woman's trials such as mine?—or if they were, then show me that creature. Soon the busy tongue of scandal will be unfettered, and the ears of greedy calumny opened wide to swallow every breath of defamation and still add falsehood upon falsehood to blacken and condemn a helpless woman! Ah! I know," she added. "I know what the future holds for me."

"Then if so, why not allow me to assist you in arming against these enemies of yours and against Marigold especially?" I urged after those desperate words of hers had fallen upon me.

"Marigold! Why against her? She is my friend."

"No, Lolita," I responded in a low earnest tone. "She is your bitterest enemy. She knows the truth of this strange allegation against you, and she can clear you if she wishes—only she refuses."

"Refuses! Whom has she refused?"

"Richard Keene."

"How do you know?"

"I was present when he begged of her to tell the truth. But she only laughed, declaring her disinclination to implicate herself by so doing. That woman will let you sacrifice your life rather than tell the truth."

"Are you certain of this? Are you positive there is no mistake, Willoughby?"

"None. I heard her with my own ears. She is awaiting eagerly your downfall."

Lolita's hands clenched themselves, her pale lips moved but no sound came from them. The small clock chimed ten, and as it did so she crossed the room and drew down the blind. There was, I supposed, no further necessity for the signal of the bowl of dahlias.

Ah! how crooked are the paths of life; how few the sweets; how bitter the gall! the wretched, like the daisy of the field, neglected live, nor feel the withering blast of wavering fortune. The great alone are noted, and though they weather long the pitiless storm, are struck at length and down hurled to destruction. Greatness is a dream! This world's a dream—we wander and we know not whither.

"Are you sure that Marigold's friendship is only assumed?" she inquired at length.

"Quite. You told me that Keene was your enemy, yet from what I have seen I believe him to be rather your friend."

"Friend! No," she said, shaking her head. "That's impossible. He cannot be my friend. You do not know all the past."

"How long ago did you know him?" I inquired. "In the days before George's marriage. We were acquainted then," was her faint answer.

"And the woman Lejeune? Tell me, is there any reason why he should be antagonistic towards her?" I asked, recollecting that strange incident at the farmhouse.

"Not that I'm aware of. He would be her friend, most probably. Ah! if that woman would only tell me the truth. But she will not. I know that she fears to speak lest by the truth she may herself be condemned."

A silence fell between us. A heavy gloom had fallen over my heart; the world to me was darkness, and the contemplation of futurity a dream. And yet it was resolved; Kings reigned on earth, but I owned no other sway but love's, no other hope but Lolita.

"And the truth," I said very slowly and in deep earnestness. "The truth you refer to concerns Hugh Wingfield?"

The effect upon her of that name was electrical. She started, her blue eyes fixed themselves upon me with a hard, terrified look, and her lips half parted in fear were white and trembling.

"You know his name?" she gasped.

"Yes, I know the name of the dead man, the poor fellow who was so foully done to death."

"No, no, Willoughby!" she shrieked aloud, covering her face with her hands. "Spare me, spare me that!" she sobbed.

And I saw that I had acted wrongly in recalling that fatal night. Yet if she were not guilty, why did the mere mention of the dead man's name produce such an effect upon her?

I hastened to apologise, but her reply was—

"Ah! Willoughby! I am so doubly cursed that I can laugh to scorn all other ills of life. My cup of misery is full; one drop more and it must overflow, and life will ebb with it."

"But can I do nothing to help you—absolutely nothing?" I demanded, looking earnestly into her eyes.

She shook her beautiful head despondently, and her breast heaved and fell in a long deep-drawn sigh.

"You saw the Frenchwoman, and you failed," was her despairing reply. "It was the last chance afforded to me, and it is lost—lost. I know, now Richard Keene has returned, that I must suffer."

"But if Marigold can save you from this terrible fate that threatens you, why does she refuse?"

"She has, I suppose, some motive known to her in secret," was my love's reply. "You know her character just as well as I do. Before her marriage there was—well, an incident. And I presume it is this which she fears that George may know."

"But if you are aware of it, will you still conceal it though this woman is your enemy? Recollect," I said, "that she has no love for her husband. Hers was a mere marriage of convenience."

"Ah, yes, I know," she said. "But would you have me condemn a woman even though she be my enemy? No, Willoughby, that is not like you. I know that revenge is never within your heart, you are always too generous."

I regretted that I had made such a suggestion, and bowed beneath her reproachful words. Yet it somehow seemed that if she possessed the knowledge of this "incident," whatever it was, she might hold it over her enemy as a threat, and use it as a lever to obtain the information she desired from the Countess's lips.

"Poor George!" I exclaimed. "What, I wonder, can be the end of his life with such a woman? And yet he is so utterly infatuated by her. I threatened to speak to him regarding certain of her actions but she has openly defied me, saying that he is too deeply in love with her to hear any word of condemnation. And she's absolutely right, I believe," I added, sighing.

"She is right. He is more deeply in love with her than before their marriage, while on her part her open flirtations and love of admiration are little short of scandalous!" she declared.

"And yet you would protect such a woman—even though she seek your downfall?"

"The divine lesson taught us, Willoughby, is to forgive our enemies, and to allow them an opportunity for reform," she answered calmly. "Were I to hound her down by an exposure of the past, I should myself merit neither pity nor compassion."

"But she remains silent in order that you shall go to your ruin," I remarked.

"Her silence may be the result of ignorance," she suggested. "She may not really know the truth, but for some secret reason has made Keene believe she is aware of everything."

There was something in that argument which caused me to ponder, for I recollected that her whole object had been to deceive the man who was her husband's guest.

"But had you no suspicion that she knew the truth?" I asked.

"None whatever."

"It seems, however, that Marigold is also in possession of some secret concerning this man Keene, for she threatened that if he revealed his real name to her husband, or sought to expose her, that she would inform the police of his whereabouts. Does that threat of hers convey anything to you?"

"Did she really say that?" ejaculated my love in blank surprise. "If she did, then it throws a new light upon the affair. She must have met the woman Lejeune, and the latter has told her certain very important facts in order to place Keene in her power. And yet," she added, pausing, "I doubt very much if Marigold dare denounce Keene for her own sake."

"Then she is implicated in this ugly affair as well as him?" I exclaimed quickly.

She saw that she had unintentionally revealed to me one very important fact, but having made such an assertion there was no withdrawing it, therefore she was forced to respond in the affirmative.

"Ah!" she cried desperately, gripping my hand in both hers. "You do not know, Willoughby, what conflicts wring my soul. I would barter worlds to tell you the truth, yet dare not. Because if I did so I would lose all your esteem and all your fond affection. I—I cannot live in this uncertainty," she cried bursting into a torrent of tears. "I wander now a melancholy woman, and seem unthankful where most I should be grateful. Religion stays my hand from the self infliction of that blow which I have vainly sought within the jaws of death. Where can I go? Where can I hide my miserable self? A trackless desert would be paradise to all I suffer here. But it cannot be. I shall—I must—relieve my woes in everlasting sleep."

"No, no," I cried, kissing the trembling hands of my white-faced desperate love. "You must not talk like that, Lolita. You are marked down as the victim of these intriguers, but you shall not be. There is still life and love for us. Be patient, be brave—tell me the truth of the allegation against you and trust in me."

"Tell you the truth," she cried in a hoarse strained voice. "No, no, not to you—never. You would loathe and hate me then—you the man who now loves me."

"Say also the man you love," I urged tenderly, her hands still in mine.

Her lips compressed as her tearful eyes turned themselves upon me. She sighed convulsively, and then with a slight catch in her tremulous voice confessed with a sad sweet smile—

"Yes, Willoughby—the man I love."

I clasped her in my arms. I felt the heaving of her breast, my throbbing heart kept pace with that within her bosom. My lips met hers—oh!—what a melting kiss. Love held my heart, entangling every thought.

And yet what changes in our fates must here be registered; what an accumulated scene of bliss and wretchedness must stain the pages that are to follow.

Ah! if I could at that moment have read what was written upon my love's heart—if I could but have torn aside that veil of mystery enveloping her—if I could but have known the truth concerning that man I had found cold, stark and dead beneath the stars! How differently I would have acted.

I had thought that her love for me would induce her to tell me something of the past, yet as she stood in my embrace she was still persistent in her silence, until it seemed that she really feared lest, knowing the true facts, my affection might turn to hatred. I implored, I argued, I expressed profound regret to no avail. She would tell me nothing—absolutely nothing.

"I must suffer," was her hard reply. "I am a woman who is the sport of circumstance. Yes," she added, "I love you, Willoughby, but in a few hours will end my brief life of ecstasy. When I am dead—then will you know the reason why to-night my lips are sealed."

At that instant a rap at the door caused me to release her quickly and spring aside.

A waiter who stood upon the threshold announced—

"Mr Logan, m'lady."

Chapter Twenty Four
Introduces a Man with a History

Mention of the name of Logan placed me instantly on the alert. It was surely the man whom I had seen with her in the wood in the early hours of the morning following the tragedy—the same whom I had encountered with Mademoiselle in Chelsea—the same, I believe, who had lived in such suspicious seclusion at Hayes's Farm.

"Tell him I am engaged at present," exclaimed my love, facing the waiter without betraying the least anxiety. She was, of course, not aware that I knew the name of the man with whom I had seen her on that fateful morning. Therefore she affected a carelessness that utterly amazed me. Could it be that that bowl of flowers had been placed in the window as a signal to him, and that he had disregarded it and come to her?

The slightly pursed lips betrayed her annoyance at his presence, but beyond that she treated the man's announcement with calm indifference.

Was this broad-shouldered man her accomplice—or perhaps her lover, that she should thus communicate with him in secret? How my mind struggled to be free; how my restless reason combated with my love. I tried, but could not contradict the glaring truth which impressed itself upon my soul; and yet, though I was urged to a conviction, I could not act upon the principles which subdued me.

I could learn stoicism and be the calm philosopher in every passion, save only love; but he was my divinity, and like a defenceless babe within the giant's grasp, all struggles to evade him were but vain.

Fool that I was! poor doting fool, how had I quaffed the sweet illusions of hope only to feel the venom of despair more poignant to my soul.

"You have a caller," I said in a hard blank voice. "Perhaps I had better leave you?"

"Oh," she answered, "there really is no necessity for you to go. He may wait—he's quite an unimportant person."

"Named Logan—is he not?"

"Yes," she replied rather faintly, with a strange smile.

"A friend of yours?"

"No, not particularly," was her answer.

"Then if he is not, Lolita, why did I find you walking with him in the wood on that morning—I mean after the finding of the body of Hugh Wingfield?"

"You saw us?" she gasped, glaring at me aghast. "You followed us!"

"I saw you," I repeated. "And further, I met the man on the following night in Chelsea in company with Marie Lejeune. He was flying from the police."

"Yes, he has told me how, by your timely warning, he was saved."

"My warning also saved the Frenchwoman. She should, therefore, in return do you the service of telling the truth, and thus clearing you."

"Ah! She'll never do that, as I've told you. It would be against her own interests."

"But this man? Who is he?" I demanded, recollecting the confidential conversation between them before they had parted on the edge of the wood.

Both of us remembered how she had changed her wet, muddy dress at my house, and how I had succeeded in stealing a dress from her wardrobe and carrying it down to Sibberton. Yet no word of that curious incident had ever passed between us. With mutual accord we had regarded the circumstance as one that had never occurred, nevertheless, at the cloak-room at St. Pancras was a box filled with her boots, while locked away in an attic of my house was the muddy dinner-gown she had exchanged for her walking skirt on that memorable morning.

"You know his name?" she said, in response to my question.

"I do. But there are many circumstances connected with him which are puzzling," I said. "Among them is the reason of his concealment in the house of the farmer Hayes."

"Because he feared the police, I suppose. A watch was being kept on the house in Britten Street, you say."

"For what reason? What was the offence of the pair?"

"They were suspected—suspected of a crime," she replied. "But," she added, "their guilt or their innocence does not concern me. I alone am to be the victim," she added bitterly, pushing her hair from her brow as if its weight oppressed her.

"Then this man Logan is your enemy—eh?"

"He is not my friend."

"He is in league with the others to encompass your ruin? Tell me the truth of this, at least."

"I have not yet exactly decided whether he is my enemy or my friend," was her answer. "Once he rendered me a very great service—how great I can never sufficiently acknowledge."

"And now?" I asked, remembering that secret sign in the window.

"I am at a loss what to think," was her response. "Sometimes I believe he is working in my interests, while at others I entertain a vague suspicion that he is my enemy."

"As he is Marie Lejeune's," I added, looking her straight in the face.

"Her enemy—why, he's her best friend. Their interests are identical."

"I think not," was my calm reply. And in a few brief sentences I related to her what had transpired at the lonely Northamptonshire farm, how a murderous attack had been made upon "Miss Alice," as she was there called, and how the whole of the mysterious party had afterwards made good their escape from the neighbourhood.

"This is certainly surprising to me," she declared. "Whom do you suppose attacked her?"

"Pink's idea is that it was Logan."

"But Pink surely knows nothing about my connexion with those people?" she exclaimed apprehensively.

"Nothing. Up to the present there is no suspicion whatsoever that you were acquainted with the dead man. Indeed his name is still unknown."

I recollected how the young fellow wore her portrait in his ring, and fell to wondering again if he were actually her secret lover, and if he had been the victim of another's jealousy.

She certainly escaped from the Hall that night and met some one in the park—but whom was an utter mystery. Yet there still sounded in my ears that scream I had heard—the scream that was certainly hers and which came from the scene of the tragedy. If she were not the actual assassin, then she had of a certainty borne witness of it—and had been appalled by that terrible *dénouement*.

But when a man loves a woman as I loved Lolita, he cannot openly charge her with being a murderess. And yet how I longed and longed for strength to drive the demon suspicion from me; that fiend that sat hovering over my soul, affrighting every gleam that might afford me comfort.

"Then you have been loyal to me, Willoughby. You have kept your promise!" she exclaimed with a sad sweetness. "Would that you could rescue me from the cruel fate that must now be mine!"

I strove to speak, but utterance was denied me. She seemed so convinced of the hopelessness of the future that her very conviction seemed to carry upon it evidence of her guilt.

Could poor Hugh Wingfield, the man who had carried that secret cipher in his pocket and who had worn her portrait on his finger, have actually been struck down by that very hand that I had kissed?

Ah! no! Perish such a thought. She was my love—and my love was, I knew full well, the innocent victim of as foul and base a conspiracy as had ever been conceived by the ingenious mind of man.

I doubted her, but only on account of the character of the persons with whom she was in secret association. When I enumerated them in my mind I saw what a strange mysterious group they were—the young Frenchwoman, the man Logan, the two sallow-faced foreigners who had been diligent readers of socialistic newspapers, and, last of all, the rough-mannered hunter of big game, Smeeton, *alias* Keene—the man over whom the young Countess of Stanchester appeared to possess some secret power.

Was Marigold the evil genius of the situation? Her past had been so full of adventure, and the rumours about her—mostly untrue be it said—had been so many that I confess I felt inclined to prejudge and condemn her.

A vain, pretty married woman, fond of admiration and moving in the ultra-smart set, can seldom escape the evil tongue of gossip. Yet although I made every allowance for her social surroundings and the fact of her being one of "the giddy Gordons," there were certain facts of my own knowledge with which I could not well reconcile her position as my friend's wife. For that reason, as well as because of her open declaration of antagonism to Keene, I held her in suspicion. She had cleverly deceived me as to her real motive, and that was sufficient to cause me to regard her as an enemy.

"Why not admit this man Logan and let us consult together?" I suggested at last. "We might arrive at some way out of this deadly peril of yours."

"We might," she admitted. "But he would never meet and discuss the matter with you. Remember he is wanted by the police, and has no guarantee that you might not betray him. He told me of your meeting in Chelsea, how you raised the alarm, and how narrowly he escaped being captured. Therefore he views you with no great affection. No," she added, "for the present you must not meet. It would be unwise. He must not even know that you axe in Edinburgh."

"Why not?"

"Because—well, because if he knows you are here with me he will hesitate to act in the manner I am trying to induce him to act. Fear of you will prevent him."

"What are you inducing him to do?" I asked.

"I am trying to prevail upon him to assist me in performing a certain service—one by which I hope to gain my release from these torturing fears that hold me. It is my last resource. If my project fails, death alone remains to me."

She spoke with a deep breathless earnestness which told me plainly that her words were no idle ones. True she had spoken of self-destruction many times, but it was with the firm conviction of a woman hounded to her own destruction.

The world, curiously enough, regards a wealthy woman of title as though she were a different being to themselves, believing her to possess attributes denied to the commoner, and a mind devoid of any of the cares of the weary workaday existence. Yet if the truth be told, the woman who is dressed by Laferrier, Raudnitz or Callot often has a far uglier skeleton in her cupboard than she who is compelled to go bargain-hunting in Oxford Street at sales for her next season's gown. The smart victoria, the matched pair, the liveried servants and the emblazoned panels form the necessary background of the woman who is *chic*, but, alas! how often she hates the very sight of all that hollow show of wealth and superiority, and how she longs for the quiet of obscurity. How very true it is that wealth does not bring happiness; that there is no pleasure in this world without the gall of pain, that love finds sanctuary in the heart of the princess just as it does in that of the factory-girl. There is no peace on this side of eternity, therefore we must forever court the illusions which evade us.

What could I say? If it were to her interest to see this man alone—this man of whom the police were in such active search—then to serve her I ought not to object. I felt indignant that my well-beloved should be polluted by the presence of such an adventurer, and yet I recollected how they had walked together in the wood, and what was more—that the man must be aware of her secret, whatever it was! He had walked and spoken to her; he had seen her, her white dress of the previous night wet, mud-stained and bedraggled—he must know, or at least guess, the truth!

Did she hold him in fear on that account? Was she beneath the thrall of this adventurer?

For a long time we stood talking, until as though in fear that the man whose call had been so unwelcome and disturbing should grow tired of waiting in the hall below, she urged me gently to take leave of her.

"Go, Willoughby—for my sake—do!" she implored of me with those soft pleading blue eyes that were so resistless. "Let me see him alone. Let me do this—if—if you wish to save me," she urged.

And I saw by her pale anxious face that she was desperate.

Therefore I kissed her once again with fondness, and assuring her of my trust and love, left her, promising to return next morning.

Yes, I foolishly left her to the threats and insults of that man who knew her secret.

Ah! Had I only known the truth!

Chapter Twenty Five
Whereby Richard Keene is Surprised

In the entrance-hall of the hotel I saw the man Logan, the man who held my love's secret, seated in a chair patiently awaiting her summons. There were others, well-dressed men and women, in evening toilettes lounging there in the hour before retiring. It is curious with what studied ease women lounge at hotels. The woman who is alert and upright at home falls into the most graceful poses after dinner at a hotel, presumably to court the admiration of strangers.

The man Logan, however, still wore his light overcoat over his dinner-jacket, and his head was buried in an evening paper, whether, however, this was to conceal his features or not I was unable to determine. Still, he was wanted by the police, and was therefore taking every precaution against being recognised. From where I stood at the back of the large square hall, I saw that his features had been slightly altered by the darkening of his eyebrows, undoubtedly with that object in view.

As I stood watching unseen, a waiter approached, spoke to him, and then he followed the man upstairs to the presence of my adored.

Had I done wrong in allowing the fellow to go to her alone? That was the thought which next moment seized me. Yet when I recollected her earnest appeal I could only remain lost in wonderment at her motive. But determined on watching the man in secret, I fetched my hat and overcoat, and sat patiently in the hall to await his return.

The clock chimed eleven musically, and a party of Americans noisily left to catch the night mail to London. The staff changed, the night-porter came on duty, and the little group of idlers in the hall gradually diminished. Indeed, they grew so few that I feared in passing out he might recognise me. Therefore at half-past eleven I strode forth into the night. Princes Street with its long line of lights, looked bright and pleasant even at that hour, yet it was almost deserted save for one or two belated wayfarers.

I took up my position at the railings on the opposite side of the road, from where I could see each person emerging from the hotel. Long and anxiously I waited, wondering what was transpiring in that room the window of which was straight before me. The blind was down, but no shadow was cast upon it, so I could surmise nothing.

At last he came. For a moment he stood on the steps, evidently in hesitation. Then he descended and hurried away. I followed him closely, across the railway, up High Street, and then he plunged into an intricate labyrinth of narrow streets quite unknown to me. At the time I believed he was not aware that I was following him, but when I recollect how cleverly he evaded me I now quite recognise that he must have detected my presence from the first. At any rate, after leading me through a number of narrow thoroughfares in a low quarter of the city, he suddenly turned a corner and disappeared from my sight as completely as though he had vanished into air.

My own idea is that he disappeared into a house—probably into one of those whose doors are open always as a refuge for thieves, and there are many in every big city in the kingdom, houses where pressure on the door causes it to yield and close again noiselessly, and from which there is an exit into another thoroughfare.

I spent some little time in making an examination of the houses at the spot where he had so suddenly become lost, but finding myself baffled, turned, and after wandering for a full half-hour lost in those crooked streets of old Edinburgh, I at last found myself in a thoroughfare I recognised, and turned to the hotel more than ever convinced of the man's shrewdness.

Next morning, at ten o'clock, I found Lolita alone in her sitting-room, and on entering saw by her countenance that the night had, for her, been a sleepless one.

"Well," I said, raising her hand reverently to my lips as was my wont, "and what was the result of last night's interview?"

She drew a long breath, shook her head sadly, and replied—

"The situation is, for me, as perilous as it ever was. I am now convinced that what you have said regarding Marigold is right—she actually is my enemy, and yet I have foolishly taken her into my confidence!"

"But you are still hopeful?" I asked anxiously. "This man Logan has surely not refused to stand your friend?"

"He refuses to tell me certain facts which, if revealed, would place me in a position of safety," she responded blankly.

"But he must be compelled!" I cried. "I will compel him."

"Ah! you cannot," she cried despairingly. "If you approach him, you will upset everything. He must not know of your visit to me. If he did it would be fatal—fatal."

I held my breath, for had I not foolishly betrayed my presence to him on the previous night? And had he not cleverly tricked me? I hesitated whether to tell my love the bitter truth of my injudicious act, but at last resolved to do so, and explained the incident briefly, just as I have related it to you.

"Ah?" she exclaimed. "Then I fear that all I have arranged with him will be of no avail. He will now believe that I intend to play him false. My only hope now lies in Richard Keene."

"Then I will return to him and act as you wish," I said.

She stood thoughtfully looking out of the window for a long time. At last she said—

"I think it best, after all, to return to Sibberton. My aunt had a letter from George this morning asking her to join the house-party at once, and she seems anxious to do this and go to Lord Penarth's afterwards."

"Very well," I said eagerly; "let us all return together." I felt somehow that she would be safer at home beneath my protection than wandering about in hotels exposed to the perils which her unscrupulous enemies were placing before her.

And so it happened that on that same night we joined the party assembled in the drawing-room at Sibberton just before dinner, and there, in front of them all, the young Earl introduced Keene and Lolita, believing them to be unacquainted.

At the instant the introduction was made I chanced to glance around, and there saw Marigold standing in the doorway, her face pale as death. She had been out, and being unaware of Lolita's return was, I saw, amazed and filled with apprehension, while Keene on his part bowed over my love's hand with a distant respect as though they were perfect strangers.

Dinner was, as usual, a long function, served with that stateliness and ceremony that characterised everything in the Stanchester household. George made a point of preserving punctiliously all the ancient traditions of his noble house, even to the ceremony, and, after the port, of passing round the snuff to the men in the great old silver box that had been a present of King James the Second to the Earl of his time.

I saw that Marigold was ill at ease at Lolita's return. She had whispered something to her as they went in to dinner, but what it was I knew not. Keene, on the other hand, preserved an utter disregard of what was in progress, except that once I detected a meaning glance cast at the brilliant hostess upon whose throat scintillated the wonderful Stanchester diamonds.

Afterwards, in order to learn something more, I played billiards with him. We were alone in the room, for bridge and music were attracting the others. He was, I found, an excellent player, yet not in good practice.

"You know," he said apologetically, "I get so little billiards, living as I do mostly in the forest. I played a good deal in town a few years ago, but nowadays rarely ever touch a cue."

I complimented him upon a break of eighteen he had that moment made, whereupon he exclaimed suddenly—

"Oh, by the way! Lord Stanchester told me yesterday that it was you who discovered that mysterious affair in the park here some time ago. Tell me all about it. I'm always fond of mysteries."

He hid his dark-bearded face from me, occupying himself in chalking his cue. But his demand told me that, as I expected, he had not recognised me as Warr's visitor on the evening when, tired and dusty, he had refreshed himself at the *Stanchester Arms*.

"I suppose you read all about it in the papers?" I said, not quite understanding his motive.

"George showed me some of the accounts. Most extraordinary affair— wasn't it? They don't even know the poor fellow's name, do they?"

"The police axe in ignorance of it as far as I know," was my response.

"But explain to me the exact position in which you found him," he urged, leaving off playing, leaning with his back against the stone mantelshelf, and drawing heavily at his cigar. "I take a keen interest in such matters as this. Out after big game, we become almost like detectives so necessary it is to follow clues and footprints."

"Well," I said, "I simply heard a cry in the darkness, and got Warr, the publican from the village, to help me to search—and we found him."

"He was dead, of course—quite dead?" he asked eagerly, as though, it seemed, in fear that the victim had still been conscious and had spoken.

"Quite," I replied, still much puzzled. He had himself invited me to billiards, and it seemed for the purpose of obtaining from me the exact details of the discovery. "He had been struck a cowardly blow in the back which the doctors declared must have proved fatal at once."

"You heard his cry?" he said, looking me straight in the face. "It was that which attracted you?"

"I heard *a* cry," was my answer.

"Ah! Then you didn't recognise the voice?"

"How could I recognise the voice of a person unknown to me?" I asked.

"I mean that the cry was a man's?"

"No—a woman's."

"What?" he exclaimed, taking his cigar from his lips, and staring at me with a hardness at the corners of his mouth. "Are you quite sure of that? It isn't in the evidence I've read."

"I know it isn't," I said. "There are several things known to me that are not in the depositions."

"And what are they?"

"Matters which concern only myself," I replied. "I'm endeavouring to obtain a solution of the mystery. The police have failed, so I am making independent inquiries on my own account."

His brows again contracted slightly, and I saw that what I said was to him the reverse of welcome.

"And what have you discovered?" he asked with a dark look which struck me as curious. "You have surely good scope for your efforts in such an affair. Lord Stanchester is exceedingly anxious that the truth should be revealed. He asked me my opinion—knowing my keen interest in mysteries of all sorts."

"And what is your opinion?"

"Shall I tell you, Mr Woodhouse?" he asked with a mysterious smile, bending earnestly towards me and lowering his voice. "Well, my own opinion is that you yourself know more about it than any one."

"Me!" I cried, looking at the fellow. "You don't imply that I'm guilty of the murder, do you?"

"Oh!—not at all—not at all?" he hastened to assure me. "I intended to convey that you are in possession of certain facts unknown to the police. Do you understand me?"

"Not exactly," I replied. "If you suggest that I know the dead man's real name, then I admit it. His name was Wingfield—Hugh Wingfield."

"What!" he gasped, his sinister countenance turning pale, as he stood aghast. "You know that! Who told you?"

"I found out for myself," I answered, looking him full in the face. "I discovered it by the same means as I discovered other things—that the dead man wore on his finger the portrait of Lady Lolita, and—"

"And what else?" he asked breathlessly. "Be frank with me as I will, in a moment, be frank with you. Did you discover anything in his pockets—any letter—or anything written in numbers—a cipher?"

"I did."

"Then show it to me," he urged quickly. "Let me see it."

"I shall do nothing of the sort!" was my firm response. "What is written there is my own affair."

"Of course. But you can't read it without the key," he declared with a defiant laugh.

"I desire no assistance," I said briefly.

"But if I mistake not, Mr Woodhouse, you entertain affection towards Lady Lolita—and—well, your affection is reciprocated—at least so she tells me," he added with a slight sneer, I thought.

"And what, pray, does that concern the paper found in the dead man's pocket?" I inquired resentfully. "I know rather more of the affair than you conjecture," I added. "And as you wish me to speak plainly I may as well remark that I have certainly no confidence in the person who is guest in this house under the name of Smeeton, and whose real name is Richard Keene."

The man drew back with a start and stood glaring at me blankly, open-mouthed, his eyes starting from his head.

I smiled when I saw the effect upon him of my sudden accusation.

But next moment my smile of triumph died from my lips, and I it was who stood bewildered.

Chapter Twenty Six
Refers to Certain Ugly Facts

Richard Keene placed his cue upon the floor, and leaning upon it, looked straight at me and said—

"Yes. It is quite true that I'm in this house under false colours. But do you think it will be to your advantage, Mr Woodhouse, to quarrel with me?"

"I only know that your presence here is unwelcome to certain members of Lord Stanchester's household," I exclaimed. "And I should consider it a very wise course if you excused yourself and left."

"Why should I?" he asked triumphantly. "I'm really enjoying myself here very much. The Earl gives his guests plenty of sport."

"And you, on your part, are making sport of an innocent woman!" I said, with rising anger at the fellow's defiance.

"I suppose Lady Lolita has told you something, then?" he remarked.

"Lady Lolita has told me of your merciless attitude towards her," I said. "I am quite well aware of your secret communications with Lady Stanchester," I added. "And it is plain to me in what direction your efforts are directed."

He started again, looking at me as though uncertain how far my knowledge of his past extended. Then he slowly stroked his short-cropped beard.

"In other words then the two women have betrayed me—eh?" he observed thoughtfully in a harsh mechanical voice, as though speaking to himself.

"Not in the least," was my answer. "They dare not betray you—that you know quite well. But my affection for Lady Lolita, to which you referred just now, has caused me to make certain inquiries with somewhat curious results. Therefore, I tell you plainly, Mr Keene, that if you are not desirous of exposure you had better leave Sibberton before noon to-morrow."

"And if not?" he inquired, raising his eyebrows.

"If not, I shall go to his lordship and tell him your real name."

He laughed in my face.

"Well, that's exactly what would bring matters to a head," he declared. "Perhaps, after all, it would be best if he did know—for I could then reveal to him, and to the world, a truth that would be both ugly and startling. Tell him who I am, if you wish, but before doing so, is it not better to carefully consider all the eventualities?"

At that instant Lolita's maid Weston opened the door, apparently looking for her mistress. Her eyes met Keene's, and I saw a look of mutual recognition. But in an instant the young woman closed the door again.

Keene made no remark, but I saw surprise and apprehension written upon his sun-bronzed features.

"Then, in a word, you refuse to relieve these ladies of your presence?" I said in a firm tone.

"I refuse to obey any paid servant of Lord Stanchester," was his insulting response.

"But if you recollect the manner in which you first visited Sibberton—as a hungry tramp who drank beer at the *Stanchester Arms*—you must admit that your presence here is, to say the least, suspicious. You entrusted to Warr a letter to Lady Lolita—and village publicans will gossip, you know."

"What, has that fellow been talking—surely not?" he exclaimed quickly.

"I only speak from my own knowledge—not from hearsay."

He took a long draw at his cigar, looking me calmly in the face, as though undecided how to act. At last, after full deliberation, he said, in a much more conciliatory tone—

"Really, Mr Woodhouse, I don't know, after all, whether either of us will gain anything by being antagonists. We both have our own ends to serve. You love Lady Lolita, and wish to—well—to save her; while I, too, have an object in view—a distinct object. Why cannot we unite in a friendly manner?"

"Against whom?"

"Against those who seek to bring ruin and disgrace upon the woman you love."

"But you are her enemy," I said. "How can I join you in this affair?"

"Ah, there you are quite mistaken. She, too, is mistaken. True, I was once her enemy, but circumstances have changed, and I am now her friend."

"Is your friendship so prone then to being influenced by every adverse wind that blows?" I asked, by no means convinced of the genuineness of his proposals.

"Of course you hesitate," he remarked. "And perhaps that is only natural. Let us, however, call Lady Lolita into consultation."

This suggestion of his I readily acted upon, and ringing for a servant told him to find her ladyship at once, and ask her whether she could make it convenient to see me for a moment in the red room on business connected with next day's shooting luncheon.

Then we put down our cues and together walked through the long corridors to the old wing of the great mansion, to the red room, a small boudoir to which visitors never went, and where I knew that we might exchange confidences in secret.

I switched on the electric light, and standing together in the small old-fashioned apartment, furnished in crimson silk damask of a century ago, and red silk upon the walls, we anxiously awaited her coming.

At last we heard her light footstep in the corridor, but she halted upon the threshold, utterly taken aback at sight of my companion. She had avoided him studiously all the evening, and was of course, unaware of our present intention.

"I regret very much to call your ladyship here," Keene commenced. "But it seems to have become imperative that Mr Woodhouse and I should, in your presence, arrive at some understanding."

Though radiant in dress, her beautiful face was pale to the lips, and her thin hands trembled nervously.

She advanced slowly without a word, like a woman in a dream, and stepping up behind her I closed the door and locked it.

"I must explain, Lady Lolita," said Keene, "that had I known you were returning here I should have left before your arrival, for I have no desire to thrust upon you my presence, which I know must, having regard to the past, be most unwelcome. However, we have met, and I am a guest here in your home. Further circumstances compel me to remain here for some time longer, therefore I am anxious that we should thoroughly understand one another."

"I received the letter handed me by Warr, the innkeeper. It was sufficiently explanatory," she remarked in a hard unnatural voice, standing with her hand upon the chair back, and looking straight into his calm countenance.

"We may, for the present, disregard that letter," he said. "You will recollect what I said to you confidentially in the hall an hour ago. You admitted that you reciprocate Mr Woodhouse's affection, and you declared that he was your friend."

"And so I am," I maintained.

"Exactly. Indeed, as far as I can ascertain, it seems that he is a most devoted friend. It is for that very reason that I have asked you to come here and listen to what I have to say."

"I am all attention," she responded blankly, with that inertness born of despair. "My enemies have combined to crush me—that I know."

"Well, first let me tell you, Lady Lolita, that although I have shown myself antagonistic in the past, my convictions have now become changed, and I regret all that I may have done to cause you pain and injury. If you can really I forgive, will hold out my hand in friendship," and he stretched forth his hand to her as pledge of his sincerity.

At first she hesitated, unable to believe that the man whom she had regarded as her bitterest enemy should have become so completely, and so suddenly her friend. Like myself, she could not at first bring herself to put perfect faith in him. Yet, in a few moments, seeing his evident earnestness, she took his hand, and allowed him to wring hers in genuine friendship.

"Very well," he said in a gratified tone. "That is the first step. The second is to admit to you that while I am ready to render you assistance instead of hounding you down to destruction, as I had intended, I have also a motive—one that must remain my own secret. Mr Woodhouse, here, no doubt regards my return, my actions, and my arrival as guest in this house as suspicious. I admit that all the circumstances are exceedingly remarkable, and require an explanation—which perhaps you will give him later. But what is so immediately important is the course of action which we shall pursue, now that I am united to assist you."

"But do you really mean to act on my behalf, Mr Keene?" asked my love eagerly, as though a new future were opened out to her by the man's suggestion.

"I have given my hand as pledge," was his reply. "There is an allegation against you—a fact of which I presume Mr Woodhouse is aware. And your bitterest enemy—one who, by a word, could free you—is a woman."

"Willoughby—I mean Mr Woodhouse—has told me. It is Marigold."

"Yes. And she refuses to speak. Our efforts must be made towards compelling her," he said.

But in that moment I recollected how the Countess had defied him, and threatened him with a terrible exposure. Of what?

"And Marie Lejeune? Where is she?" inquired Lolita.

"She has disappeared, it seems. At least I don't know where she is at this moment. For the present we need not be concerned about her. We have to deal with a shrewd and clever woman, whose future depends upon your future. If you live she must die,—if you die, she will live."

He spoke the words with slow distinctness, his eyes fixed upon her, watching the effect of his utterances.

"How can I live?" she asked, in a low hoarse voice. "You know everything—you know my peril."

"True. I know everything," was the man's reply. "I know, too, how you have suffered I know how Mr Woodhouse, loving you as he does, must also suffer. Believe me, Lady Lolita, although I am but a rough man unused nowadays to the ways of good society, I am not altogether devoid of sympathy for a woman, and that sympathy will cause me to guard the secret of your affection. I wish you to consider that, in me, instead of an enemy, you have a sincere friend. I am fully aware of the exposure which Mr Woodhouse might make to George, but it would not only be against my interests, but against yours."

"Yet it would bring Marigold to her knees to beg forgiveness," my love remarked.

"Yes. But surely you know that woman well enough to be aware that her vengeance would fall heavily upon you—that you would be hurled to ruin and disgrace before she herself would give way and fall."

"I believed her to be my friend," was Lolita's remark.

"You only believed as others believe. There are many persons to whom she acts the false friend—her husband not excepted. You have only to sit in the smoking-rooms of certain London clubs in order to hear the expression of public opinion regarding her. The clubs always know more facts about a man's wife than her own husband."

"Well," I exclaimed, "what is your advice? How shall we act?"

Even now I was not altogether convinced of Keene's good-will. The horror and fear in which Lolita had formerly held him somehow clung to me, and I could not help suspecting that this man who had struck up an acquaintance with George in the wilds of the Zambesi, and had come so boldly among those whom it was his intention to unmask, was now playing us false.

Yet in word and manner he was perfectly open and straightforward.

"Have patience, Lady Lolita," he urged. "Mr Woodhouse will assist me in this very difficult piece of diplomacy that we are about to undertake.

Had it not been for the fact that our friend here unfortunately gave Marie Lejeune warning that night in Chelsea, when the police were waiting to trap her, we should have had no necessity for this present scheming. The truth would then have been revealed and the guilty would have gone to their just punishment."

"I know! I know!" I cried. "It was foolish on my part. But I believed I was acting in Lady Lolita's interests. I see, however, that I made a mistake—a fatal mistake."

"We must rectify it," he said. "Her ladyship has been frank with me concerning your mutual affection, and I will not stand by and see her hurled to her grave by the dastardly schemes of her enemies. You admitted to me that you discovered upon the body of Hugh Wingfield a certain paper in cipher. Will you not allow me sight of it?"

"A paper in cipher!" gasped my love, glancing at me. "Was that found upon him?"

"Yes," was my reply. "I discovered a paper in a woman's hand, and written in the chequer-board cipher."

"And the keyword was what?" she inquired in breathless eagerness, turning her great blue eyes to mine.

"Ah! I haven't any idea of the keyword," I admitted.

"Then you haven't been able to make it out!" she remarked, breathing more freely. "You don't know to what it refers?"

"No," I responded frankly. "I am in ignorance. But if you will remain a moment I'll go to my room and fetch it."

"You need not," was her reply. "It is quite unnecessary."

"Why?"

"Well, because I chance to know what is contained in it, and that there was nothing of importance."

Did she imply that she had written that secret message herself? I glanced at her countenance, and somehow became convinced that she was still bent upon the concealment of the truth, a conviction that was both irritating and tantalising.

Mystery had succeeded mystery, until I admit that I was now overcome by blank bewilderment.

Chapter Twenty Seven
Which Tells of a Heart's Desire

The result of our consultation did not, as far as I was concerned, enlighten me upon one single point connected with the puzzling affair.

Certain matters were arranged between the man Keene and the woman I so dearly loved, but strangely enough both were equally careful to allow me no loop-hole through which to gain knowledge of their motives or the secret they held.

I made no mention of the remarkable affair at the lonely farm a few miles distant, nor did I inquire of Keene his object in lying concealed there, or of the identity of those foreigners who were the man Logan's friends in hiding. I felt it wise to keep all this knowledge to myself.

I told Lolita, however, how I had discovered that the police had introduced a female detective as servant to the Stanchester household, and that her inquiries had been directed towards endeavouring to discover the Ownership of the Louis Quinze shoes, the print of which had been found at the spot where Wingfield had fallen.

The news fell upon her like a thunderbolt. She stood utterly unable to reply.

Keene said nothing. He merely looked at her, and then, sighing, turned away.

I did not tell them that a week ago, when passing the cottage of Jacobs, one of the gamekeepers, the man asked me to enter and see something. I had followed the man in, and producing a muddy damp-stained ermine cloak much soiled and ruined by exposure to the weather, he said —

"I found this yesterday in the Monk's Wood, sir, an' I've been wondering if it might belong to anybody up at the Hall?"

Instantly I had recognised it as Lolita's, the one she must evidently have worn on the night of the tragedy! It was torn in one part, and a small piece was missing—the piece which had been found near where the dead man lay!

In a moment I had invented an excuse.

"Why," I said, "that's the cape my sister lost when she was staying with me. She went out with her little daughter to pick wild flowers, laid it down in the wood and forgot all about it."

Then I gladly took possession of it, gave Jacobs a tip, dropping a hint at the same time that it was not necessary for him to talk about it, for if he did there would be all sorts of wild theories formed as to its connexion with the mysterious tragedy. "The police would be sure to begin worrying over nothing," I added.

"I quite understand, sir," was the gamekeeper's answer. "Mr Redway and his men are worse than useless. They've made a lot of fuss and haven't even found out yet who the poor young man was! I shall say nothing about it, for they'd only begin to question and worry me, as well as you."

And so I had taken the fur cape, and that same night had surreptitiously buried it in my garden.

When at last the stranger's consultation with Lolita had ended, I recognised how completely my love was in the man's thraldom. He held power over her inevitable and complete. Why?

Was it because he knew her guilty secret?

She had, in a moment of desperation, declared that he did, and besought him to spare her.

"I will do my best," was his rather evasive answer. "The man who loves you, Lady Lolita, will help me, and between us we may, I hope, effect your freedom."

"I am ready to do anything—to go anywhere in order to serve her ladyship," I declared, with deep earnestness. "I am only glad that we have now come to a thorough understanding."

"Your attention must be directed towards the actions of the Countess," was Keene's reply. "Watch her, and see what she does, and whom she meets. I am unable to approach her because she fears me, and also—well, to be frank—she is no friend of mine any more than she is of Lady Lolita."

"Very well," I agreed. "I will leave Lady Lolita to your protection and turn my efforts towards watching the Countess. But," I added, "I am puzzled by all this mystery and all these conflicting motives."

"No doubt," he said, as my love wished us good-night, grasping both my hands in trustful thankfulness. "It is but natural. When you know the real facts you will find it to be stranger than you have ever dreamed—more tragic—more terrible—more bewildering. The truth, Mr Woodhouse, will stagger you—as it will the world!"

And with that emphatic expression of opinion we rejoined the men in the smoking-room, had a final whisky-and-soda and cigarettes, and then parted for the night.

Next morning at five the cry of the hounds passing across the park awakened me, and I knew that the Earl was already out cubbing, leaving his party to go shooting after breakfast. Therefore I rose, and was early at work at my desk, for a quantity of the kennel accounts had come in overnight and required checking.

My mind was full of what had passed between us in the red room, and I was anxious to obtain opportunity to watch the young and brilliant mistress of the house.

The shoot that day was over at Beanfield Lawns, and after breakfast the men, including Keene, drove there in the new Mercedes car, a merry party, leaving the ladies to accompany the luncheon. Through the morning I was busy. Once I encountered Lolita in one of the corridors, and found her just a trifle more hopeful.

"Act on Mr Keene's suggestion," she urged. "Watch Marigold closely, and ascertain what she is doing. From what I've seen to-day I believe there is something curious in progress."

"Rely upon me," I answered, "to serve you dearest. I will do anything— that you know."

"Yes—I feel sure you will," she responded smiling sweetly upon me, a fresh erect figure in her clean cotton blouse. "I put my trust entirely in you."

"And I will not betray it," I declared in deep earnestness.

Then we parted. She had her hat on, and was going out, I knew, to her Saints' Garden, in order to give directions to the gardener who attended to it. The thought brought back to me a recollection of my recent conversation with the Countess at that same spot, and I returned to my room and was soon again immersed in my rather onerous duties.

About noon the ladies left in the Panhard, carrying the luncheon, and a quiet fell upon the great old mansion. I interviewed the house-steward and his wife regarding stores to be ordered, ate my luncheon in my room, and afterwards started out to walk to my house at Sibberton, for when there were guests at the Hall, and especially during the shooting-season, I was seldom able to get home, owing to my multifarious duties.

I was passing the Countess's boudoir—the door of which stood open—and having been urged to keep careful watch upon her, I searched her waste-paper basket. The torn letters, however, were of no account—

the usual correspondence a fashionable woman receives. Therefore I was disappointed. In her ladyship's every movement I now scented suspicion. Hitherto I had watched Lolita, and found mystery in all her movements, and now it was the giddy handsome woman so popular in her own gay set of banjo-playing, skirt-dancing, cake-walking and bridge-playing. I would have gone with the shooting-party over to Beanfield, but I had been prevented by pressure of work, and now I was rather sorry that I had not deferred the accounts and taken a gun.

About three o'clock the ladies returned, a gay bevy of well-dressed beauties, and as I stood chatting with them in the hall, a servant handed the hostess a telegram.

I watched how her countenance changed as she read it, then crushing it in her hand, she suddenly recovered herself and thrust it into her pocket. The message contained something that caused her anxiety — of that I was convinced. Her guests had not noticed the quick opening of her eyes, and the slight movement of the mouth betraying apprehension, as the words were revealed to her. What could they be? How I longed to discover.

Lolita, who, lounging in a chair, was chatting with a pretty young girl in tweeds, the daughter of a very up-to-date mother, looked across at me quickly, as though to place me on the alert, and then I fell to wondering how to obtain knowledge of that message.

To try and get hold of it through her maid would be a too risky proceeding, and besides if it contained anything secret she would no doubt destroy it. Therefore the difficulty seemed insurmountable. She had re-composed herself, and had at that moment declared her intention of dressing and going out again to pay an afternoon call, inviting two of her guests to go with her.

Of a sudden an idea occurred to me; therefore I went out through the servants' hall, and obtaining the bicycle belonging to Murdock, his lordship's valet, I mounted and rode down the avenue to Sibberton post-office.

"Oh, Miss Allen," I said, addressing the daughter of the village post-master, "Lady Stanchester received a telegram just now, and doesn't quite understand it. She wishes it repeated, please," and I placed sixpence on the counter, adding, "Her ladyship believes there is some mistake. I suppose it won't take long to repeat, will it?"

"Oh! not very long," replied the red-haired rustic beauty.

Whereupon I told her she need not send the copy up to the Hall, but as I was going back presently I would deliver it myself.

Warr was at the door of the inn as I passed, and he called me in. When we were in his back parlour he said to me with a mysterious air —

"Do you know, sir, that that tramp who gave me a sovereign tip has been in Sibberton again? I saw him walking through the village the day before yesterday with another gentleman—one who's staying up at the Hall."

"No, you're mistaken," I answered laughing. "It's Mr Smeeton, who's very much like him, an old friend of his lordship's. I fell into just the same error myself when I first saw him," I added, in order, if possible, to remove any suspicion from the worthy man's mind.

"Well, do you know," he said laughing, "I could have sworn it was the same man, except that his beard has been trimmed. Of course he looks different, dressed as a gentleman."

"No," I reassured him. "The man you have evidently seen is Mr Smeeton, with whom his lordship hunted big game in Africa a year or two ago." Then after a brief chat, in which he expressed surprise that the police had now relinquished all their efforts to discover the identity of the murdered man or his assassin, I went out, returning to the little low-thatched cottage in which was the village post-office.

The red-haired girl handed me a telegram addressed to the Countess of Stanchester, remarking that no error had been discovered in its transmission, and placing it in my pocket I mounted the cycle and rode away up the avenue. As soon, however, as I was alone under the trees, I took out the envelope, tore it open, and saw that the message had been handed in at Ovington in Essex. It was unsigned and read—

"To-night, Charing Cross, nine. Only bring handbag."

It showed that her ladyship was on the point of flight! Therefore I at once resolved to ascertain her destination and watch her doings.

On returning to the Hall I learnt from the servants that she had not gone out visiting as she intended, but was in her room. The men had not returned, so I took Lolita aside, showed her the telegram, and told her to go upstairs and watch if there was any sign of her intended departure. A quarter of an hour later my love came secretly to my room and told me that she had remarked casually to her that she intended to go to town to fit a dress, which she specially wanted for a garden-party, and would probably go up to town that evening.

That was sufficient for me. I kissed my love fondly, and telling her to remain under Keene's care, crammed some things into a bag and took the train at five-thirty from Kettering to St. Pancras.

I travelled by the train previous to the one she would catch, therefore I dined leisurely at the café *Royal*, and at a quarter to nine stood beneath the clock on Charing Cross platform, watching the idlers keeping their appointments and the bustle of departing passengers by the midnight mail for the Continent.

I had to exercise a good deal of caution to avoid detection; but at last, just before the hour, I saw her approach dressed in a dark-brown travelling-gown with a brown gossamer veil that gave her the appearance of an American globe-trotter, and was so thick that it would prevent recognition of her features.

She hurried across from the booking-office to the platform where the Continental express was on the point of starting, as though in fear that some one might detain her.

She was not alone, but at her side walked a man in grey felt hat and long grey overcoat. In him all my interest was centred, for he was none other than Logan.

I had, however, no time for reflection. Only just sufficient, indeed, to dash back to the booking-office, obtain a ticket for Paris, and enter the last compartment of the train before it moved off to our unknown destination.

Chapter Twenty Eight
What! Saw in the Night

The night mail for the Continent backed into Cannon Street for the postal-vans, and then rushed away into the wet stormy night for Dover Pier.

The journey, as far as there, proved uneventful, but as soon as I stepped out upon the rain-swept landing-stage, I saw that our crossing was to be a "dirty" one. Beneath the electric lamps brawny seamen passed in shining oil-skins, and amid the bustle and shouting I saw the neat figure of the Countess with her companion hurry across the gangway to the shelter of a private cabin, wherein she entered and closed the door, while Logan went below to get a drink, and change some money with the steward, an action which was that of the constant traveller.

Not wishing to appear too obtrusive, I remained on deck watching the mails being counted in, until the last bag had been flung into the hold, the cry "All out!" sounded, the hatches were closed, and then slowly the packet began to move out into the rough open Channel.

When Logan emerged on deck I stood back in the darkness, taking a good view of him. He was dressed with every appearance of a gentleman, but from the manner in which he paced the deck I saw that he was greatly agitated and concerned, whether of the Countess's safety or of his own I could, of course, not determine. Neither had I any idea why the pair were fleeing from England, unless it was to escape some exposure which her ladyship knew to be imminent.

That woman was the enemy of my love; she had deceived me. Therefore the compassion I held for her had been succeeded by a fierce and unrelenting antagonism, and I intended to watch her and discover the truth.

I sat beneath the bridge under shelter from the driving rain, and hidden by the darkness, while the man Logan walked to and fro, utterly heedless of the storm. He did not go to her ladyship's cabin to inquire after her, therefore it struck me that perhaps they might have quarrelled. In any case his anxiety was intense.

On landing at Calais he took her into the buffet, where they had hot coffee, and a few moments later were joined by a thin black-haired sallow-faced man, evidently a foreigner from the studied manner in which he bowed before her as she sat at the table of the restaurant.

Then the trio sat together in earnest consultation.

The Paris express was announced to depart, but to my surprise they took no heed. The French capital proved not to be their destination, for presently they rose and walked to the Bâle express, the *wagon-lit* of which they entered, the conductor apparently expecting them.

I was compelled therefore to return to the booking-office and obtain a ticket. As, however, there was but one sleeping-car I could not travel in it for fear of detection, and was therefore forced to enter an ordinary first-class carriage, with the prospect of a twelve hours' tedious journey.

On we travelled until the dawn spread into a grey damp day, then the sun shone, it grew warmer, and I stretched myself upon the cushions and slept. To descend to get anything to eat was to invite detection; therefore I starved upon a pull from my flask and a couple of sandwiches with which I had provided myself at the Calais buffet.

From Bâle I followed them to Lucerne, and from Lucerne by the Gothard railway to Milan, where we arrived late at night, her ladyship driving alone to the *Hotel Metropole*, opposite the *Duomo*, and the two men going off in a cab in another direction.

As soon as I had watched the Countess into the *Metropole* I went along to the *Cavour*, where I quickly turned in and was very soon asleep. Milan seemed to be their destination, for at the station they had been met by a second foreigner, an Italian evidently, a short ferret-eyed little man, smoking the stump of a cigar, and after the exchange of a few words he parted from them quickly and was lost to sight.

My own idea was that he had met Logan and his friend and had told them to what address to drive. I, however, could not follow them, being bent upon watching Marigold. Next morning I sent a telegram to Keene informing him of my whereabouts, and then set myself to keep observation on the Countess's movements.

Milan, the most noisy city of modern Italy, was parched and dusty at that season of the year, and save for a few German tourists the hotels seemed empty. There are, of course, visitors from all corners of the earth at all seasons of the year to see the wonders of the cathedral, but to the man who knows his Italy, and who loves it, there is something so incongruous, so ugly, so utterly rasping upon the nerves in Milan that it is decidedly a city to get away from. The place bears the impress of all that is bad in Italian art of to-day, combined with all the worst features of that complex life which is known as Modern Italy.

Opposite the hotel stood the great stucco arcade, the Gallery of Victor Emmanuel, one of the greatest, if not actually the greatest, in Europe, and about eleven o'clock her ladyship emerged from her hotel alone and wandered through the arcade looking into the shop windows, some of those establishments being the best and most expensive in Italy.

She little dreamed of my presence as I followed her. Previously I had bought a grey felt hat of Italian shape in order that my English "bowler" should not be conspicuous, and with my watchful eyes upon her I sauntered on, wondering why she was waiting. She returned to the hotel to lunch, and in the afternoon went for a drive around the bastions, which, planted with limes now, form the *passeggiata* of the prosperous Milanese.

It surprised me that Logan and his companion did not return to her, and I regretted that I had not ascertained whither they had gone. At seven o'clock that evening, however, she went alone to the large restaurant in the Galleria known as Biffi's, and entering found the three men seated at table expecting her. Each greeted her with deep deference, then reseated themselves, and she dined with them.

From where I sat, engrossed in my *Tribuna*—the top of my head concealed by my new grey hat—I could see that now and then the conversation was of a confidential character, and I also noticed certain strange meaning looks exchanged between the men when the woman's attention was otherwise engaged.

The three men were certainly not the kind of persons one would have expected as associates of a woman of the Countess of Stanchester's wealth and social distinction. Her beauty, however, was, I saw, everywhere remarked, even in that foreign café.

"Una bellissima donna!" remarked a man seated near to me to his companion, as he sipped his vermouth and seltzer. "English, I believe. I wonder what those thieves want with her? She evidently don't know their character, or she and the Englishman wouldn't be seen with them here, in a public restaurant!"

I was quickly on the alert. These men, probably petty officials employed in the Municipal Offices, had recognised the sallow-faced man who had met Logan at Calais, and his companion. I recollected the curious incident at Hayes's Farm, and the fact that two foreigners had been of the mysterious party who had lived in concealment there. Were they, I wondered, these self-same men. They were Italians, no doubt, for had they not read the *Avanti* and the *Secolo* and other journals, some of which they had left behind on their sudden flight?

Fortunately one of the Continental languages with which I was acquainted was Italian; therefore I turned to the two men seated close to me, and raising my hat politely explained that I had overheard their remarks, and that as the lady and gentleman were my friends I would esteem it a favour if they would give me some further information regarding the two men seated with them at table.

"Why do you wish to know?" inquired the man who had made the remark that had so attracted my attention.

"Well, because my English friends are negotiating some financial business with them," I explained.

"Oh!" he smiled. "Well then, you can tell your friends that those two men are well-known in Milan, and especially in this café, as knights of industry—persons who live by their wits. I haven't see them here for months, and believed that they'd fallen into the hands of the law. But it seems that they're flourishing still."

"What is known against them?" I asked in Italian. "Are you aware of their names?"

"Yes," was his reply. "I may as well tell you that I am a *delegato* of police myself, and I happen to know those two very interesting gentlemen. The tall man is Tito Belotto, a Roman, and the other Bernardo Ostini, a Lucchese. And the name of the beautiful Englishwoman? Who is she?"

"She is from London—a Mrs Price," I answered, pronouncing the first name that came into my head, for I was by no means anxious that this detective should know her real name.

"Well," he remarked, "you can warn her to have nothing to do with them, otherwise she must suffer, both in reputation as well as in pocket," he smiled, and then, having finished his vermouth, he rose with his companion and left.

Then the sallow-faced fellow who had met them at Calais was Tito Belotto, an adventurer! And yet as he sat there in evening dress, smoking his cigar and chatting affably with the handsome Englishwoman, his outward appearance was that of a somewhat superior man. In his shirt-front there shone a small diamond of very good water, and on his finger was another gem that caught the electric light and flashed its radiance towards me.

He had been relating some humorous anecdote to her ladyship, who was laughing heartily at it. Evidently she was in a good-humour, just as these men wished her to be. Belotto, I noticed, paid for the dinner, and then all four walked down the arcade into the Piazza where they entered a closed cab and were driven off.

My own idea is that they were going to a theatre, but as I followed them in another conveyance I quickly found that we were travelling in an opposite direction, namely up the broad Corso Venezia and out by the city gate into that suburb that lies beyond the ancient fortifications. Outside the town the streets are not well-lighted, and the quarter is not one of the most aristocratic. Most of the houses were huge blocks of flats as is usual in Italian cities, and it struck me that they were mostly occupied by labourers. Even at that hour of the night the air seemed close, and a strong odour of garlic permeated everything.

The cab in which the four were riding turned at last into a dark deserted street of high prison-like houses and pulled up, when instantly I ordered my man to stop, jumped out, paid him, and secreted myself in a neighbouring doorway before the first man who alighted could detect my presence.

From the house where they had stopped a man came forth, carrying a lantern, by the light of which he conducted them into that ponderous house of darkness.

The cab then drove off, leaving me alone in the dark dismal street. The house they had entered was a big inartistic place apparently newly-built, for it stood slightly apart from the other buildings, and behind it was a waste plot of ground. From the other tenements in the vicinity came the cries of children, the strumming of a mandoline, a woman's song, and a man's voice raised in angry altercation—that babel of noises that one hears at night in every crowded street of an Italian town, and more especially in that noisiest of European cities—Milan.

Why, I wondered, had they gone there? That Marigold was unacquainted with the place, and that she was not altogether confident in the assurances of her conductors, was shown to me by the cautious manner in which she followed the man with the lantern. Besides, I saw distinctly that the two Italians, following her, nudged each other.

Not a light showed in any single window of the place, for at most of them the wooden sun-shutters were closed, as is the Italian habit at night. In one part of the building, however, the windows were devoid of glass, from which I concluded that the place was not yet completely finished. And then it occurred to me that the man with the lantern might be its first occupant.

The minutes lengthened into hours, but I still kept my patient silent vigil. The noises in the other houses around died down, until all was hushed in sleep. I emerged from the doorway and strolled backwards and forwards in the dark and dismal roadway. The closed door of the house where the Countess had been taken was freshly painted, but beyond that I could gather nothing from its exterior.

I looked at my watch and found that it was half-past two. Then I sat down upon a heap of stones close by, waiting for the dawn, and thinking always of Lolita.

I suppose I had been there some twenty minutes or so, when of a sudden I heard a shrill whistle which, as far as I could judge, proceeded from one of the shuttered windows of the unfinished house.

Three times was the whistle blown, when a few moments later I heard the rattle of wheels, and the same cab that had conveyed them there drew up again before the door.

There were no lights on it, however, neither did any light show when the door of the house was opened.

But as I watched I saw something which caused my eyes to start out of my head in astonishment, for the dim light was just sufficient for me to discern two men emerging from the mysterious place, carrying between them to the cab the inanimate form of a woman covered with a dark cloth.

The woman's arm swung helplessly to the ground as they carried her, and I knew by their suspicious manners, and their hushed whispers, that she was dead.

Chapter Twenty Nine
Is Still More Mysterious

I held my breath. What mystery had I discovered? Marigold had been secretly done to death by these hard-faced foreigners!

There was no light save one single lamp at the far end of the road, and by its feeble rays I saw that the silhouettes of the two men who carried their burden to the carriage were those of the sallow-faced foreigner who had met the pair on Calais platform and the man who had awaited the arrival of the express at Milan.

Logan did not appear. He evidently remained in the house.

Of the identity of the victim there surely could be no doubt. It was she who had aided Marie Lejeune in the commission of some offence—that woman whose word could clear the character of my love Lolita.

What could I do? I stood in hesitation, utterly dumbfounded. I had fortunately discovered the truth how these men had ingeniously entrapped the woman towards whom Logan had shown a marked but false friendship, but alone and undefended I feared to rush forward and denounce them.

I recollected what the *delegato* of police had told me in Biffi's and stood watching, confident that ere long I should be able to give the police such information as would lead to the arrest of the whole gang.

Little ceremony was used in handling the covered body of the lifeless woman. It was simply bundled into the cab, the two men got in with it, the door closed, and the vehicle was driven off rapidly in the direction of the town.

The instant it passed me I ran after it as fast as my legs could carry me, determined to follow it to its destination. My own idea, from the fact that the horse was a weak one, was that it was not going far—in fact only just sufficiently far to place the body in some place of concealment.

The wheels rattled over the stones, awakening the echoes of the silent streets as the cab turned towards the main thoroughfare in the direction of the city.

I was panting some distance behind, and had halted for a second to catch my breath, when all of a sudden, before I was aware of what had happened, I felt a crushing blow upon my skull, and fell to earth like a felled ox.

I only recollect having seen a thousand stars at that moment when the irresistible blow fell upon me—nothing else. My soft grey felt hat did not break the blow, the full force of which came down upon the top of my head, striking me in an instant dumb and unconscious.

Of what happened to me after that I have no knowledge whatever. I had, of course, acted unwisely in my quick eagerness to ascertain the truth, for by rushing after the vehicle I had exposed myself to the detection of those of the conspirators who were evidently outside the house keeping watch. My curiosity had misled me into a distinct error of judgment, and I had no doubt been felled by those whose motive it was to keep secret the tragic affair.

My next recollection was of a terrible throbbing in my brain. My head seemed aflame! My skull seemed to be boiling with molten lead. Ah! never in all my life shall I forget the torments I suffered for about an hour, yet unable to speak, unable to complain of them. Before my blinded eyes was a dull red haze, in which stars seemed to shoot with every throb of the blood through my poor unbalanced brain.

I believe at last I spoke, but of what I said I have no idea. Merely the ravings of delirium I have since been told. I felt something strange upon my brow, like burning coal or corrosive acid, yet when I knew the truth I found to my surprise that it was ice.

My first impression was that I was demented. I could not think of anything. Strange weird visions, mostly grotesque or gruesome, floated through my mind, but without motive or coherence. I tried to recollect the past, but I found I had none. My brain had been thrown out of its usual balance, and my sufferings were excruciating.

Ah! I now know some of those tortures which are the wages of sin, and I tell you I would not endure them again—no, not for a million in hard cash. My poor brain seemed to bubble and boil, as though my skull had been emptied and re-filled with molten metal, while the sound in my ears seemed as deafening as the noise of a thousand steam-hammers.

At last I knew that I was still breathing, my sore heavy eyes seemed less clouded, and the haze grew clearer. I heard other sounds above that maddening, crashing, hammering rending that deafened me—sounds of human voices.

My hot lips were touched by something cold, and I felt a few drops of some liquid dribble into my mouth. This I swallowed, for I believed that aid was at hand.

I tried to speak, but over the articulation of my words I had absolutely no control. What I said was not what I really intended to say in the least. Never have I experienced such a strange loss of control over my tongue before. I was sane, and yet insane at the same moment.

Slowly and with very great difficulty I regained my senses, when, to my surprise, I found a face in a wide head-dress of white linen, the face of a sister of one of the religious orders.

My eyes wandered to other beds around, all of them occupied, and on the wall was a gigantic crucifix. Then I knew that I was in a hospital. My head was bandaged, and two doctors seemed to be re-adjusting the folds of linen.

I inquired in English where I was, but suddenly recollected that I was in Milan, and in the same language the elder of the two doctors replied—

"Don't trouble where you are, my dear sir. For the present remain quiet, and get better. You've taken a turn now, and will recover. Be thankful for that."

"How long have I been here?" I asked, gazing around at the unfamiliar surroundings.

"Three days," replied the sister, a calm-faced elderly woman, who wore a huge rosary and crucifix suspended from her girdle. "We thought you would not recover—until yesterday. But you will soon be better now."

Then I recollected the terrible fate of the young Countess of Stanchester.

And after pondering and wondering I lapsed again into a lethargic state, remaining so for many hours.

It was not before the following day that my senses really fully returned, and when they did there came to my bedside a short rather stout fussy little man in a soft hat and snuff-coloured suit, by whose bearing I knew him at once to be a *delegato* of the Milan police.

"I regret to disturb you, signore," he commenced, as he seated himself at my side, "but in the circumstances it is necessary. Are you aware of the conditions under which you were discovered?"

"No," I answered. "Tell me."

"Well," he said, "the affair is a mystery upon which you no doubt can throw some light, but before questioning you I have to inform you that whatever you will say will be taken down in writing, and may be used in evidence, because you are under arrest."

"What?" I said, starting up and glaring at him. "Under arrest—for what?"

"For murder."

"That's interesting, at any rate," I exclaimed, half inclined to treat the matter as a joke. "And whom have I murdered, pray?"

"A woman."

"Well," I said, "if you will tell me where and how I was found I may perhaps be able to throw some light on the affair. If not, perhaps you will send for the British Consul, and I'll make a statement to him."

At first the detective seemed disinclined to tell me anything, but finding the unconcerned manner in which I took the serious charge, he at last told me certain facts that held me utterly dumb with astonishment.

"You were found insensible by some workmen who went to do some repairs in an apartment in a house beyond the Monforte gate—you and the woman. The knife with which you struck her was lying beside you, and we also have the hatchet with which she struck you on the head in self-defence."

"What!" I gasped, amazed. "Do you allege that I killed the woman?"

"You are guilty until you prove yourself innocent," was the man's cold reply, regarding me with a keen quick glance in his dark eyes.

"Well, just tell me a little more about it," I urged. "You say that some workmen found me in the same room as the woman, and between us was a knife and a hatchet. Whose house was it?"

"Ah! you are unaware of whose place it was? You broke into it during the absence of the proprietor and took up your quarters there, of course," was the man's reply. "You are a foreigner—English?"

"I am. And I think before we go any further you'd better send for the Consul and let me put a different complexion upon your story. Your theory is, of course, the natural and only one, if, as you say, a knife and a hatchet have been found. But you have not told me to whom the apartments belonged," I said.

"They were rented by a man named Rondani, manager of the silk factory in the Via della Stella. He, however, locked up the place about a month ago, having been sent by his firm on a commission to Berlin. The other day a builder received the key by post, with orders to enter and effect certain repairs, and when the men went there they discovered you both in the dining-room and at once informed us. At first you were believed to be dead, but as the doctor declared that you were still alive you were brought here and placed under arrest."

"But I'm innocent!" I declared dismayed. "I was attacked from behind in the open street." And then I told him of my midnight vigil, and of the weird scene of which I had been witness. It seemed plain that having been recognised and struck down by the assassins they suddenly changed their plans, taking back the body of the young Countess as well as myself, ingeniously placing us in such a position as to make it appear that I was the actual murderer. No doubt they were under the belief that I had died from the effects of the blow.

I expressed anxiety to visit the scene of the assassination, to which the man replied—

"By all means. Indeed, we shall be compelled to take you there as soon as you are well enough."

"Let me go now," I urged. "I can drive there all right."

"No—to-morrow," he said.

"What have you found upon the woman?" I inquired.

"Several things—letters in English and other things. They are being translated."

"Letters in English. May I see them?"

"At the trial," he said. "Instead of gloating over your crime as you seem to be doing, would it not be better to try and establish your innocence?" he suggested.

"Why should I? I'm not guilty. Therefore I fear nothing. Only take me to the scene of the crime."

"To-morrow you shall go. I promise you," was his reply, and then he left, one of his assistants mounting guard over me, in fear, I suppose, that I might try and escape them.

The murder of Lady Stanchester was an appalling *dénouement* of the mystery, and increased it rather than threw any light upon the extraordinary circumstances. It was evident that she had been deliberately enticed there to her doom, and had I not fortunately followed her, her end would have remained a complete enigma.

The police had discovered certain letters. What, I wondered, did they contain? Would they at last throw any light upon the affair which, when it got into the papers, must startle English society.

At present her name was, of course, unknown, unless perchance any of the envelopes were with the letters. I felt sympathy for my friend George, and wondered how I could prevent her name from being known.

The hours crept slowly on; the day seemed never-ending. The presence of that scrubby-bearded little Italian sitting near me reading a newspaper idly, or gossiping with the men who lay in the neighbouring beds, was particularly irritating.

At last, however, when night came on and my guard was relieved, I slept, for the pain in my head wore me out and exhausted me.

Next day, in accordance with his word, the *delegato*, accompanied by two other police officials, arrived, and feeling sufficiently well I dressed and accompanied them downstairs, where a closed cab was in waiting. After a short drive we turned into the half-finished street so familiar to me, and pulled up before the house over the threshold of which I had seen, carried by the assassin, the lifeless body of one of the most admired women in England.

They conducted me up a flight of stairs to a landing at the back, and there entered one of the flats with a key. I noticed that the door had been sealed, for the *delegato* broke the seal before inserting the key.

Inside, the place was rather barely furnished, the home of a man with small means; but as we walked into the little dining-room the sight that met my eyes was terrible.

Upon the table were the remains of a supper—decaying fruit, half-consumed champagne and an unlit cigar lying on one of the plates. Places seemed to have been laid, for five, but the cloth had been half torn off in the struggle, and a dish lay upon the ground, smashed.

Upon the floor of painted stone, the usual floor of an Italian house, were great brown patches—pools of blood that had dried up, and into one the corner of the table-cloth had draggled, staining it with a mark of hideous ugliness.

On the ground, just as they had been found, lay a heavy hatchet with blood upon it, the instrument with which my unknown assailant had struck me down. While at a little distance lay a long very thin knife, with a finely tempered three-edged blade.

To the astonishment of my three guards I took it in my hand and felt its edge. The curious thought occurred to me that with such a weapon, thin and triangular, Hugh Wingfield had been so mysteriously done to death.

"Then this is where they enticed the woman—to an apartment that was not their own, and which they evidently entered by a false key! They invited her to supper, and then—well, they murdered her," I said reflectively. "Where is the body? May I see it?"

The confronting of a murderer with his victim is part of the procedure of the Continental police, therefore the detectives were not adverse in the least to granting my request.

"Certainly," answered the *delegato*. "It is here, in this room, awaiting the official inquiry." With that he opened the door of the small bedroom adjoining, and there, stretched upon the bed, lay the body, covered with a sheet.

I approached it, to take a last look upon the woman whose end had been so terrible, at the same time wondering what evidence the police had secured in those letters found upon her.

"God!" I cried, when one of the men with a quick movement, and watching my face the while, drew away the sheet and revealed the white dead countenance.

I stood glaring at it, as one transfixed.

"Ah!" exclaimed the *delegato* in satisfaction. "It is a test that few can withstand. You recognise her as your victim—good!"

I let the fellow condemn me. I allowed him to form what theory he liked, for I was far too surprised and amazed to protest.

The truth was absolutely incredible. At first I could not believe my own eyes.

The dead woman was not Marigold, but another—Marie Lejeune!

Chapter Thirty
A Ray of Light

Surprise held me dumb.

It seemed quite evident by the fact that five places had been laid at table that the Frenchwoman must have already been in the flat awaiting the arrival of Marigold and her companions, and, further, that Logan and her ladyship had remained behind after the unfortunate woman had been carried to the cab.

These and a thousand other thoughts flashed through my bewildered mind as I stood aghast, my eyes riveted upon the dead white face of the woman whose single word could have saved my love.

She had died, alas! with that secret locked within her heart!

I recollected her quick vivacious manner in those exciting moments when we had met on the Chelsea Embankment, and how I had made a compact with her, one which it was now impossible for her to fulfil. She had hid from the police, first at Hayes's Farm, where a dastardly attempt had been made upon her, and here, in that unoccupied flat, she had fallen the victim of her enemies. Why? What motive could Marigold and her friends have in her assassination?

That there was a motive, and a very strong one, was quite plain, but it certainly was in no way apparent to me. The mystery was maddening. I felt, indeed, that my weakened brain could not much longer stand the strain.

"You recognise her, I see!" exclaimed the *delegato*, with satisfaction. He had been watching me narrowly, and believed that the start I gave when the ghastly face was revealed was proof of my guilt.

"Yes, I recognise her," was my answer. And glancing round the room I saw that it was dirty and neglected, having been unoccupied for some time. The assassins, I supposed, had cleaned the dining-room and *salon* in order that the victim should not suspect that she was in an apartment that had been so long closed. It was certainly bold and ingenious of them to enter a stranger's house and use it for their nefarious purpose.

My captors led me back to the room in which I had been found, where one of them pointed to a dark stain upon the floor—the stain of my own blood. Beside it I saw my handkerchief cast aside. It had, no doubt, been used by my discoverers to staunch the blood. Again I took the heavy axe in my hand, and realised what a deadly weapon it was.

Then when the men had concluded making some other investigations they led me away, driving me back to the hospital in the cab, evidently entirely satisfied with their effort to fix the crime upon myself. The doctors had not yet discharged me, therefore I was put to bed again, and a detective mounted guard as before.

At my suggestion, the British Consul, Mr Martin Johnson, was informed, and visited me. He stood at my bedside, a pompous and superior person to whom I at once took an intense dislike. Happily he is now transferred, and his office is now occupied by a very courteous and pleasant-mannered member of His Majesty's Consular Service. I had, however, the misfortune to call Mr Johnson without knowing the character of the man. He was one of those precious persons of whom there are far too many in the British Consular Service; men who object to be disturbed by the Englishman in distress, whose hours are from one till three, and whose duties in an inland city like Milan are almost *nil*. Mr Martin Johnson, something of a fop, believed himself an ornament of the Service, hence his annoyance when the police called him to my bedside at the hospital. He regarded me with combined pity and contempt, at the same time drawing himself up and speaking in a ha-don't-you-know tone, supposed to be impressive.

I had heard of this superior person long ago, and as I lay in bed was amused at his attempt to impress upon me the importance of his position.

I explained to him how I had been discovered and arrested, and that I was entirely innocent of the crime alleged against me, whereupon he said snappily—

"Well, I can't help you. You'll have to prove your innocence. The police say that you've been confronted with the body of the woman, and that your attitude showed plainly that you were guilty."

"But it's monstrous!" I said. "I was attacked in the street by some ruffian, struck insensible, and carried up to the room."

"You'll have to prove that, What's your name?"

I told him, without, however, mentioning my connexion with the Stanchesters.

"And the woman? You admitted to the police that you know her?"

"She's a Frenchwoman named Lejeune—who was wanted by the police."

He sniffed suspiciously, and rearranged his cravat in the mirror upon the wall.

"Well," he remarked in Italian to the *delegato* who stood at his side. "This is a matter in which I really cannot intervene. The prisoner has to prove his innocence. How can I help him?"

"By doing your duty as Consul," I chimed in. "By having an interview with the Questore and obtaining justice for me."

"I know my duty, sir," he snapped. "And it is not to investigate the case of every unknown tourist who gets into difficulty. If you have money, you can engage some lawyer for your defence—and if you haven't, well I'm sorry for you."

"Yours is a rather poor consolation, Mr Johnson," I remarked in anger. "Am I to understand then that you refuse to help me—that you will not see the Questore on my behalf?"

"I've told you plainly, I am unable to interfere."

"Then I shall complain to the Foreign Office regarding the inutility of their Consul in Milan and his refusal to assist British subjects in distress," I said.

"Make whatever complaint you like. I have no time to discuss the matter further." And he turned rudely upon his heel and left me, while the police drew their own conclusions from his attitude.

"Very well, my dear sir," I called after him down the hospital ward, "when Sir Charles Renton asks for your explanation of your conduct to-day, you will perhaps regret that you were not a little more civil."

My words fell upon him, causing him to turn back. Mention of the name of the head of his particular department of the Foreign Office stirred the thought within him that he might, after all, be acting contrary to his own interests. He was a toady and place-seeker of the first water.

"And of what do you complain, pray?" he asked.

"Well," I said, "I chance to know Sir Charles very intimately—in fact he is a relative of mine. Therefore when I return I shall not fail to describe to him this interview." It was the truth. Sir Charles was my cousin.

"Then why didn't you tell me that before, my dear sir?" asked the pompous official, in an instant all smiles and graces, for he knew too well that direct complaint to the head of his department meant transference to some abominable and desolate hole in West or East Africa. "Of course, I'm only too ready and anxious to serve any friend of Sir Charles," he assured me.

"No doubt," I said smiling and inwardly reflecting that, happily, members of our Consular Service were not all cast in that person's mould. Previously he had put on the airs of an Ambassador—the air he assumed, I suppose, in the drawing-rooms of democratic Milan, but now he was all obsequiousness, declaring himself ready and anxious to carry out my smallest wishes in every respect.

"Well," I said, regarding him contemptuously, "I can only tell you that the tragic affair that has just occurred concerns the honour of one of the greatest houses in England. I cannot be more explicit, otherwise I should betray a confidence. I am accused of murder, but I am, of course, innocent."

"Of course," he said. "Of course! These fools of police are always trying to parade their wonderful intelligence. But," he added, "how are you going to prove yourself innocent?"

Strangely enough that very serious question had never occurred to me. I was in a country where the law regarded me as guilty, and not in England, where I should be looked upon as innocent until convicted.

I was silent, for I saw myself in a very serious predicament.

I would have asked him to telegraph to Keene or to Lolita, but I feared to give him the address lest he should institute inquiries, and I had no wish to mix up Lord Stanchester or his sister with the terrible affair.

"The only course I can suggest is the engagement of a good criminal counsel who will, without doubt, secure your acquittal at once when the case comes on for trial," remarked the Consul. "Why the police arrested you appears to be an utter enigma, but in Italy it is not extraordinary. They had to make an arrest, so they detained you."

"Shall I be detained long do you think?"

"Probably a month," he replied regretfully. "Perhaps even more."

My heart sank within me. I was to remain there a prisoner, inactive and in ignorance of the web of intrigue around my love. Too well I knew Lolita's danger, and now, with the Frenchwoman dead, she would be compelled to face the inevitable.

A month of absence and of seclusion! What might happen in that period, I dreaded to contemplate. If I were free, I might be instrumental in bringing the murderers of Marie Lejeune to justice, but detained there it was impossible.

Of a sudden, like a flash, a brilliant idea occurred to me. There was just a chance that I could secure my release by a very fortuitous circumstance—the meeting of that *delegato* of police in Biffi's café on the night of the murder!

At once I explained this incident to Mr Martin Johnson, described the appearance of the detective and his friend, and urged him to go to the Questore, place my statement before him, and if possible ascertain who was the *delegato* in question and confront me with him.

In an hour the Consul returned. He had seen the chief of police, and from my description it was believed that the detective was a brigadier named Gozi, who was that day over at Como. They had telegraphed for him to return, and he would come and see me at once.

This gave me hope, while knowledge of my statement and the interest the Consul was taking in my case aroused the interest of my guards. Even the doctor and nurses seemed to regard me differently.

The hours crept slowly by in that great house of suffering. A priest, a kindly cheery old man, came to my bedside and chatted. He was from Bologna, a city I knew well, and he had once when a young man been in London, attached to the Italian Church in Hatton Garden. The sunset that streamed through the long curtainless windows and fell upon the big crucifix before me, faded at last, the clear sky deepened into night, and the hush of silence fell upon the ward. Yet still beside me there sat the immovable figure of my guard, his arms folded as he dozed.

That night I passed in the torture of suspense. My head burned, my eyes seemed sore in the sockets, and I was apprehensive lest my hope of release might be a futile one.

In the morning, however, my friend of the café entered briskly with the doctor, who had conducted him to the scene of the tragedy on the previous day, and in a moment our recognition was mutual.

"Well," he exclaimed, standing by me and regarding me with some surprise. "What has happened to you?"

"I'm under arrest," was my reply. "Accused of murder."

"So I hear," he answered. "It seems that our meeting at Biffi's was rather fortunate for you—eh?"

"Now you recognise me, I'll tell you all that occurred," I said quickly. And then I related to them both in detail all the startling incidents, just as I have already written them down.

"Then it was not the Englishwoman who was murdered?" he said. "You told me her name was Price—if I mistake not. After I left Biffi's that night I somehow felt convinced that Ostini and Belotto were up to some mischief, and I afterwards regretted that I had not waited and watched them. They looked rather too prosperous to suit my fancy. You, of course, believed the dead woman to be your friend, the English lady?"

"Yes," I said.

"And the Englishman—what of him?"

"I did not see him after he entered the house," I answered.

Then, after I had furnished him with many other minute details of my startling adventure of that night in which I had so narrowly escaped death at the hands of the assassins, he held a brief consultation in private with his colleague, who was apparently his superior in rank.

And presently they both returned to my bedside and, to my joy, announced that it was decided to release me from custody.

Within half an hour an active search was being made for the four who had sat at table that night at Biffi's, and although I hoped that the assassin would be caught, I felt a little apprehensive lest Marigold should fall into the hands of the police and the Earl's name be dragged into the criminal court.

If she still remained at the *Metropole* the police must certainly discover her. I could only hope that she had already fled.

The mystery as to who had attacked me was still unsolved. If it were Logan, then was it not probable that she was aware of the blow that had been dealt me? The circumstances, indeed, pointed to the fact that, in the murder of Marie Lejeune, she was at least an accomplice.

That day I begged the doctors to allow me to go forth, but they were inexorable. Therefore for yet another day was I compelled to remain there in anxious uncertainty although free from the irritating presence of the guard.

Chapter Thirty One
Gives the Keyword

Still very unwell, my head gave me excruciating pain when next morning I joyfully took my discharge from the hospital. My first destination was the telegraph-office, whence I sent a message to Lolita, and afterwards I went to the *Cavour*, where I found that, in consequence of my protracted absence, my bag had been taken from my room.

However, I soon had another apartment, although the hotel people looked askance at my bandaged head, and after a wash and a change of clothes, I went forth to the Questore, as I had arranged to meet my friend the *delegato* to whom I had so fortunately spoken in Biffi's.

In his upstairs room he explained how he had circulated the description of the two men, Belotto and Ostini, to the various cities and to the frontiers, and how, owing to the pair being so well-known as bad characters, he felt certain of their arrest. That day I attended the official inquiry regarding the death of the woman Lejeune, and after giving some formal evidence, was allowed to leave.

My great fear had been that Marigold and Logan might be arrested. If so the arrest of the former must produce a terrible scandal, and if the latter the result, I feared, must reflect upon my love's good name. My only hope, therefore, was that they had already passed the frontier police at Modane, Ventimiglia or Chiasso, and had escaped from Italy.

The chief of police was very emphatic in his order that I must remain in Milan for an indefinite period, as perhaps my evidence would be wanted against the men, but after consultation with Mr Martin Johnson, now most active on my behalf, because he hoped to obtain the good-will of my cousin, his chief, I resolved to disobey the mandate of the Questore and slip away from Italy in secret. I was not under arrest, hence the police had no power to detain me.

Therefore, travelling by Turin, Modane and Paris, I arrived at Charing Cross at dawn three days later, and took train at once to Sibberton.

What had happened during my absence I feared to guess. On entering my room at the Hall at noon, I found my table piled with the accumulated correspondence. I had before my departure from London telegraphed to the Earl my intention of taking a fortnight's holiday, therefore my absence had not been remarked. Only Keene and Lolita knew the truth.

I rang the bell, and old Slater appeared.

"Is his lordship hunting this morning?" I inquired.

"No, sir," responded the aged retainer, surely a model servant. "He's across with her ladyship at the stables looking at some new horses."

"How long has her ladyship been back?"

"She returned from London yesterday, sir."

"And Lady Lolita?"

"Her ladyship has gone in the motor to luncheon at Deene, sir. Lady Maud Dallas, and one of the other visitors, a lady, are with her."

With that I dismissed the servant, and walking down the corridor went out into the wide courtyard, through the servants' quarters and round to the left wing of the house to the great stables where there were stalls for a hundred horses.

The stablemen and grooms in their jerseys of hunting red always gave a picturesque touch of colour to the huge grey old place, and I saw in a corner of the great paved yard, the Earl with a small group of his visitors watching a fine bay mare being paraded by a groom.

One of the traditions of the Stanchesters was to keep good horses, and George spared no expense to maintain the high standard of his forefathers. He had three motors, but Marigold used them more than he did because they were the fashion.

She had learnt to drive herself, and would often drive up to London, eighty-five miles, accompanied by Jacques, the French chauffeur. In town, too, she had an electric brougham in which she paid afternoon calls and did her shopping. Indeed her motor brougham with yellow wheels was a common object in Regent Street in the season.

"Hulloa, Willoughby!" cried the Earl as I approached. "Didn't know you were back?"

"I'm a day or so earlier than I expected," I laughed, at the same time saluting the woman whose adventure in Milan had undoubtedly been a strangely tragic one, as well as Keene and the other guests.

"Why, what's the matter with your head?" asked old Lord Cotterstock, noticing a bandage upon it as I raised my straw hat.

"Oh, nothing very much," I answered then. "I slipped on the kerb in the Strand, fell back, and struck it rather badly. But it's getting better. The unsightliness of the plaster is its worst part."

I dared not glance at Marigold as I uttered this excuse. I felt sure that she was aware of the attack made upon me—whether it had been by Logan or any one else.

The colour had left her cheeks when her startled eyes encountered me, and she glared at me as though I were a ghost. By that alone I knew that my re-appearance there was utterly unexpected—in truth, that she believed that I was dead!

She had turned away from the party at once, to speak with the stud-groom in order to conceal her dismay. Her face had, in an instant, assumed a death-like pallor, and I saw how anxious she was to escape me. Though she made a desperate effort to remain calm and to face me, she was unable, for her attitude in itself betrayed her guilty knowledge.

I saw in her face sufficient to convince me of the truth. She managed to move away, still giving instructions to the man, while I remained with the party watching the cantering of the horse on show. Every man or woman present there was a judge of a horse, for all were hunting people and knew what, in stable parlance in the Midlands, is known as "a good bit of stuff" when they saw it.

Presently when the decision was given, I moved away with Keene, and as soon as we were alone in the pleasure-garden I told him quickly of my startling adventure. He stood open-mouthed.

"Then the woman Lejeune is actually dead," he gasped, his brows knit thoughtfully. "The Italians must have murdered her!"

"Undoubtedly," I said, recollecting that he was acquainted with them, for had not one of them, if not both, been in concealment at Hayes's Farm.

"Well," he sighed. "This means, I'm afraid, the worst to Lolita."

"Ah! no!" I cried. "Don't say that. We must save her! We must! If I could only know the truth I feel sure I could devise some means by which she could be extricated from this perilous position."

"No," he answered sadly. "I think not. The assassination of that woman tells me that the conspiracy is a more daring and formidable one than I had even imagined."

"But what connexion could Marigold or Logan have had with the affair?" I asked. "What is your theory? Why did they travel there in secret?

If Marigold was to be their victim, then I could understand it; but she was not."

"It seems evident she was taken out to Milan by Logan in order to meet Marie in secret," he said.

"But if the murder was not pre-arranged, why should they have taken possession of a dwelling that was not their own? That fact, in itself, shows that their object was a sinister one," I argued.

"Stanchester believes that his wife has been at Bray with her sister Sibyl. He has no idea she's been abroad."

"And Logan? What of him?"

"I know nothing," he declared. "He is probably still abroad. My own idea is that he crossed the Channel in order to meet Marigold and escort her to Italy."

"Then the affair is as great a mystery as it ever was?" I remarked with dissatisfaction. I had risked my life and narrowly escaped being placed on trial for murder—all to no purpose.

"Greater," he said. "For my own part I cannot see what they've gained by sealing Marie's lips. I know," he added, "that Belotto made an attempt upon her during her stay at the farm in this vicinity, but they were prevented."

"Who prevented them?" I inquired eagerly, as this was the first time he had admitted knowledge of their concealment at the farm to which Pink had been called on that fateful night.

"Well, as a matter of fact," he answered, looking me straight in the face, "I did."

"You!" I cried.

"Yes," he responded. "Belotto, who was madly jealous of her, took her for a walk in the wood on purpose, I believe, to get rid of her. Fortunately, however, I had suspicion of his intention, and followed him. Just as she was struck, I emerged and denounced him, but too late. He then attacked me, but I defended myself. Then fearing the girl would die, the others did all they could to succour her, as they dreaded that by her death they would all be arrested for murder."

"Then the reason they left Hayes's Farm so suddenly was because they were in fear of you?"

"Exactly. Marie Lejeune was equally afraid of me, and escaped with them—abroad, it seems."

I related how the doctor, Pink, had been called to the girl, and of the investigations he and I made afterwards, whereupon he said, smiling—

"Yes, I know. I remained in the vicinity, and watched you both ride up to the house that afternoon."

"And now you have told me so much, Mr Keene," I said. "Have you no theory regarding the murder of Hugh Wingfield?"

"Ah! That's quite another matter," he said as a strange expression crossed his bearded features. "That's a question which it is best for us not to discuss."

"Why?"

"Because I can say nothing."

"But you have a theory?"

"It may not be the right one," he answered in a hard, strained voice.

"At least you know who the man was?" I said. "You have already mentioned his name."

"Can you tell me why he, a perfect stranger, wore upon his finger the portrait of Lady Lolita?" I asked.

"For the same reason, I suppose, that a woman wears in a locket a portrait of a man."

"You imply that he was Lolita's lover?"

"I imply nothing," he said vaguely. "I make no statement at all. I have indeed told you that the matter is one which it is wiser not to discuss."

"But can't you see how, in my position, that terrible affair is of greatest moment to my happiness and peace of mind?" I pointed out. "Who was he? What brought him to the park on that night?"

"I don't know."

"Lolita went forth to meet him, that I know," I said.

"Yes," he remarked. "That was proved by the marks of her heels at the spot where the body was found. She must therefore have met him."

"If so, then she must know the truth, Mr Keene," I said in a hard voice, watching his dark face. "What I want to discover is the reason he came here in secret that night."

He paused a moment his eyes fixed upon me, as though he were debating within himself whether he should betray my love's secret. Then at length he said—

"You mentioned, I think, to Lady Lolita that you had secured from the dead man's pocket a scrap of paper bearing a message in cipher—did you not?"

"Yes," I exclaimed eagerly. "It is the checker-board cipher, I know, but I am unable to read it because I am ignorant of the keyword."

"If you really desire to decipher it, and think it will help you to a knowledge of the real facts, why not try the single and very unusual word—her own name!"

"Lolita!" I gasped quickly in eagerness. "Then the keyword is Lolita!"

To which he made no response, but nodded gravely in the affirmative.

Then, without further ado, I rushed back to my room took out the folded scrap of paper that had brought Hugh Wingfield to his doom, and spread it before me together with the checker-board.

In a quarter of an hour I had reduced the numerals to letters, subtracted my love's name, and deciphered it—yes, the fatal message stood revealed.

Chapter Thirty Two
Weston Expresses Certain Fears

On reference to the checker-board which my friend had sent me, I found that the word "Lolita" read 31. 34. 31. 24. 44. 11.

These numbers I began to subtract from the first six numbers of the secret message, but the letters represented by the remaining numbers were a mere unintelligible jumble. At last, however, after considerable thought, I tried taking the numbers down the columns:—namely 63. 49. 46. 68. Subtracted by the keyword there remained 32. 15. 15. 44., which I found on reference to my checker-board was the word "meet."

At last the secret was mine! Very soon I had deciphered the numerals into this message:—

"Meet me in the avenue on Monday. Fear nothing. Marie betrayed to police.— Lol."

Lolita herself had therefore enticed the unfortunate young man to his doom.

The very signature "Lol," combined with the fact of the portrait in the ring, confirmed my suspicion that there was affection between them.

I paced the room still utterly mystified.

At four o'clock I heard the horn of the motor in the avenue, and rushed forth to meet my love. She descended in dust-cloak and veil, and took my hand in silent greeting, but Keene, who was also at the door, whispered to her, and she walked away with him. I knew that he was telling her of all that had happened to me—and of the real reason of Marigold's absence.

She went to her room, and though I waited for an hour or more, she did not descend.

I sent a message up to Weston, and the reply was—

"Her ladyship has a very bad headache after the dust."

This I told Keene, who shrugged his shoulders.

At tea in the hall, where the guests were nearly all assembled—as gay and well-dressed a crowd as could be found in all England—the Countess approached me quite calmly, and said in a loud voice—

"George has just said that you've hurt your head, Mr Woodhouse. I'm so very sorry. How did you manage it?"

The woman's imperturbable daring was simply marvellous. Her question took me utterly aback.

"I—well, I slipped in the street, and fell," I stammered. "I gave my skull a nasty knock. I suppose it would have been fractured if I had not had such a thick head," I laughed, endeavouring to turn the conversation into a joke.

"Ah! You're inviting compliments now!" exclaimed the brilliant vivacious woman, whom surely none would suspect of associating with those two men of the type of Belotto and Ostini.

"Any compliment from your ladyship is a compliment indeed," I declared, bowing with mock gravity, whereupon the party laughed, and I saw that she bit her lips in vexation. She knew that I was her enemy; and yet she dare not openly quarrel.

She feared lest I might announce to her husband and her guests her visit to Milan, and its tragic sequel.

Keene stood by, stroking his beard in wonder, half-fearing that she might burst forth in fury at my sneer and dreading the result of hot words between us.

Fortunately, however, she was discreet and laughed it off, while the Earl remarked as he passed Lady Maud her cup—

"I like to hear Willoughby and Marigold quarrel. They slang each other so very gracefully. Willoughby, you'd make a splendid ambassador. You're so very diplomatic."

"I'm a good liar, if that's any qualification," I laughed openly. "Somebody has said that the two essentials for success as an ambassador are to have a lie ever ready on the lips, and a good coloured ribbon and cross at the throat."

"Ah! and that's pretty near the mark too," observed Lord Cotterstock, who had himself been in the diplomatic service. "It is said of Lord Barmouth that when he was Ambassador at the Porte, he, for a joke, wore the Blue Ribbon, and the Turkish Court thought it the highest of British distinctions. He told the unspeakable ones that it was the Order of Saint Schweppe!"

Whereupon there was a general laugh.

Tea concluded, and the guests dispersed. I was surprised at the non-appearance of my beloved, for I longed to speak with her alone—to learn what had occurred during my enforced absence.

Keene accompanied the Earl and some others across to the kennels after tea, but by no amount of manoeuvring could I obtain an interview with the Countess alone. She walked in the garden with old Lady Cotterstock, in order that I should have no chance of speaking with her.

The house-party assembled in the white drawing-room prior to dinner, yet Lolita did not put in an appearance. I therefore sent one of the under-servants for the faithful Weston, who came to me at the top of the grand staircase.

"Her ladyship has a very bad headache, sir. She's been lying down. But she's now in her boudoir writing, and has told me that I am not to disturb her this evening."

"But isn't she going to dine?" I inquired in surprise.

"She hasn't dressed, sir. She said she, had no appetite."

"She's not well, I believe, Weston," I said.

"No, sir," replied the maid anxiously. "I've noticed this last week or two a very great change in her. She seems highly nervous, and when alone always thinking very deeply, and—and—"

"And what?" I asked, seeing the excellent servant's hesitation.

"Well, sir, I don't know whether I really ought to mention it, but one thing worries me very much. You know, sir, I've been her ladyship's maid ever since she came back from school, and I'm much attached to her."

"I know, Weston. I know quite well," I said. "You are most devoted to her. But what is this you fear?"

"I really don't know, sir," was the young woman's answer. "But of late the young mistress's mind seems constantly filled with morbid thoughts. She's always talking of her death—and only a few days ago she actually gave me some of her trinkets, saying that she would never require them again."

"That's strange," I said, sighing, for I, alas! knew the reason. "You must try and prevent her giving way to such thoughts. Go to her boudoir, and tell her that after dinner I desire to see her. I'll come up here later and see you—at nine o'clock."

"Very well, sir," was the maid's reply, and then I descended to the long meal, where the chatter was gay, and the serving of the most ceremonious character.

The brilliant women on either side of me interested me not a jot. My only thought was for my absent well-beloved.

After dinner I eagerly sought Weston, who said—"No, sir. She has not rung."

"Then take me to her," I said, "I wish to see her at once."

"But—"

"I will take the responsibility upon myself," I said. "Go and announce me."

Reluctantly the maid went along the corridor and tapped at the door. There was no response. I stood behind her as she tapped twice, then opened the door. But the room was empty. The candles were burning upon the writing-table, and in the room was a smell of burnt paper, while in the grate lay a quantity of tinder. She had been destroying some letters or papers. Weston was aghast to find that her mistress was absent.

I went to the grate and saw that every particle of paper had been consumed.

The maid went along to my love's room, but emerged quickly, saying—

"I think her ladyship must have gone out. Her cape and motor-cap have gone."

In an instant it was evident that having destroyed her private papers she had slipped out into the park unseen.

I rushed downstairs, and finding Keene in the smoking-room took him quickly out into the hall, and told him of my grave apprehensions, whereupon he was in an instant on the alert.

"She surely cannot have carried out her threat!" he gasped. "We must try to find her at once. Not an instant must be lost! The burning of her papers is sufficient proof of the fatal step she contemplated. Come, let's go in search at once."

And breathlessly, fearing the worst, we took our caps and hurried out into the chill windy night.

Chapter Thirty Three
Reveals some Secrets

For some time we rushed hither and thither in breathless anxiety, convinced that having burned all her letters, her intentions were those of self-destruction.

Some untoward event had evidently occurred of which we knew nothing, and she had been forced to the last extremity. We had explored all my love's favourite walks, but in that gusty storm that swept across the park we could hear nothing. It was not exactly dark, but the moon was overcast by heavy rain-clouds, and passing through that portion of the grounds known as "the wilderness," a wild tangle of rhododendrons and laurels, with big old trees from which the leaves fell in showers upon us, we at length approached the lake, a large sheet of water in the centre of the wild uncultivated spot, where the moorhen nested undisturbed and the lordly heron roosted high above. The spot was lonely and unfrequented—the place, no doubt, she would select if she really intended to take her own life.

We both approached it, fearing the worst. The shrill cries of the night-birds sounded above the moaning of the wind, while before us lay the broad sheet of water grey and mysterious in the clouded moon.

We had walked some distance along its edge, when Keene suddenly gripped my arm, and whispered—

"Look!—look ahead! can't you see her?—with a man!"

I strained my eyes, and there, sure enough, wearing a dark cloak, she stood erect, statuesque, with the pale light falling upon her white face, while the man had apparently gripped her arm and dragged her from the water's edge.

Next moment I was beside the pair, and to my dismay recognised that her companion was the fellow Logan, whom I had last seen entering that dark unlit house outside Milan.

"What's the meaning of this?" I cried in quick anger. "Release that lady, and tell me why I find you here with her."

"I am here to save her," was his calm reply. "I have already prevented her taking a fatal step, and if you will accompany me to the Hall I think you will find that, instead of proving myself her enemy, I shall show her that I am her friend. You think evil of me, I know—both of you. But an innocent woman's life shall not be sacrificed. I came here from London to-night, in order to meet another lady, the Countess of Stanchester, but by good fortune I met Lady Lolita, and she has told me the truth."

"Of what?" inquired Keene.

"Of what I will reveal on our return to the Hall," was the man's answer. "You know much that you have not told, but to save her ladyship here, I will now make the whole thing plain."

"But why have you not spoken before? You had plenty of opportunity," Keene remarked.

"Because something that Lady Lolita has just told me makes it plain how cleverly her enemies succeeded in closing my lips. Come, it is cold. Her ladyship is shivering."

"Come with me, Lolita," I said, and linking my arm in hers led her back along the path through the wilderness and across her Saints' Garden to the Hall.

The four of us were silent, all too occupied with own our thoughts to discuss the matter with each other. The sudden determination of the man Logan showed me that he meant at last to tell all that he knew.

"Lolita," I whispered into her ear, just as we were about to enter the house, "whatever caused you to contemplate such a terrible step to-night?"

A shudder ran through her as she answered—

"Because—because of the letter Marigold sent to me by Weston. She told me that to-night, because I refused to give you up, she would tell George the truth!"

The man Logan overheard her answer, and urged her to remain patient.

"Take us at once to Lady Stanchester, Mr Woodhouse," he urged, as we went in by a side entrance to avoid any guests who might be playing bridge in the large hall.

Thereupon I rang for Slater, and told him to make inquiries where her ladyship was, and to take us straight to her.

Ten minutes later the old butler returned saying—

"Her ladyship is with the Earl in the blue boudoir, sir." And eyeing Logan with some surprise, he added, "Will you step this way?"

We followed him upstairs, along a corridor on the first floor, until he opened a door, and bowing said—

"Mr Woodhouse desires to see you urgently, m'lady."

Next second the four of us were in the small elegantly furnished room upholstered in pale blue damask and gold, where the Earl and his wife were in consultation.

"You!" he cried in fury, when his eyes fell upon Lolita. "Leave this place at once, woman! Marigold has just told me everything—that it was you who killed your lover in the park—that it was you who—"

"Excuse me, my lord," interrupted Logan, coming forward, whereupon at sight of him the Countess fell back with a loud cry of dismay—a deathly pallor overspreading her countenance.

Her hand went to her throat convulsively and she gasped as though she were being strangled. Then, next instant, her teeth were set hard, her nails were clenched into the palms, her shoulders were elevated, and she stood rigid as a statue, and yet magnificent in her dinner-gown of pale pink and shimmering silver.

She tried to face Lolita, the woman whom she had hounded to her death, but her gaze wavered, and I saw that her effort to regain her self-composure was an utterly vain one. She trembled visibly from head to foot, while the expression in her eyes was sufficient to show the terror now consuming her.

The Earl noticing the change in her, and how she shrank from us, looked from Keene to the stranger, and asked—

"Well, sir? I have not the pleasure of knowing you. Who are you?"

"My name is Alfred Logan, architect by profession and—well, adventurer by inclination," he replied. "I presume from your words that your wife has denounced your sister, Lady Lolita, as the murderess of young Hugh Wingfield in your park, and has also laid certain other charges against that lady? Fortunately, however, I am in a position to reveal to you the other side of the question, and reveal facts which I believe you will find both startling and remarkable."

"Tell me?" exclaimed George hoarsely. "I suppose you intend to retaliate by making charges against my wife—eh?"

"Yes!" cried the unhappy woman, clinging to her husband. "That man is my worst enemy, George—save me from him—save me if you love me!"

"Your husband has no power to save you, madam," exclaimed Logan in a cold distinct voice, while we all stood rooted to the spot. "It is my duty, knowing the truth as I do, to tell it, and to leave your husband to form his own conclusions. To-night, knowing that Lady Lolita, driven to desperation by you, had threatened to commit suicide, rather than a scandal should rest upon her noble house, you have written to her, telling her of your intention of making these charges, with the sole object of causing her death by her own hand, and thus placing yourself in a position of safety. Heaven, however, is just, and I am here to reveal those things that you have hidden from your husband—to tell the world what I know regarding your past."

"Ah! no!" she cried, covering her face with her hands. "No! Enough! Spare me!"

"You have not spared Lady Lolita, therefore you must hear the hard and bitter truth." Then, disregarding the terrible effect his words had upon her, he faced the Earl, and said, "What I am about to say will be borne out partially by our friend here, Mr Richard Keene—whom you know by the name of Smeeton—partly by Mr Woodhouse, and partly by your sister herself."

"Go on," said the Earl in a low voice. "I am all attention."

"Then, in order to understand events in their true sequence, I must begin at the very beginning," he said. "You will recollect that two years before your marriage you, with Lady Lolita, spent the spring at the Villa Aurora at San Remo, while Lady Marigold was staying with her mother at the *Hotel Royal*, close by. At the same hotel was staying Richard Keene, the man you afterwards met out in Africa under the name of Smeeton, together with his valet, a good-looking young fellow named Hugh Wingfield. The latter had very foolishly given a promise of marriage to a rather pretty young French lady's maid named Marie Lejeune, but on sight of Lady Lolita, he forsook the young woman and fell madly in love with her ladyship. The latter, of course, had no idea at the time that he was a valet. They first met casually when walking in one of the olive woods behind the town, and he rendered her some little service in arranging the easel upon which she was sketching. He spoke well, dressed well, and as he mentioned he was staying at the *Royal*, the best hotel, she naturally concluded that he was a gentleman. She had, of course, no suspicion of the passion for her which had been aroused within his heart. The young Frenchwoman, however, quickly discovered the truth, and her intense jealousy was at once aroused. She was a woman of rather questionable character, being in association with two Italian adventurers named Belotto and Ostini, who lived over at Mentone, and at once set to work to intrigue against Lady Lolita and Lady Marigold Gordon. The two being great friends, in consequence of your engagement to Lady Marigold, revenge did not present any very great difficulty to that interesting trio who lived by their wits. I admit that I, myself, was living upon what I could win at the tables, and being at that time very hard-up had been induced to join them in various nefarious schemes which, although they brought us the wherewithal to live, caused us to be wanted by the police for helping ourselves to other people's property."

"To put it plainly," remarked the Earl, "you were thieves."

"Exactly," Logan replied. "But our recent schemes had met with little success and we were at our wits' end for money, when Marie Lejeune, who was a born adventuress, suggested a scheme whereby, in addition to revenging herself upon the woman who had robbed her of her lover, we could blackmail both Lady Marigold and Lady Lolita. Therefore, after considerable forethought and much ingenious intrigue, the scheme was put into practice. A watch was placed upon Lady Marigold, and it was found that she was in the habit of meeting clandestinely on the sea-road towards Bordighera an old friend, a certain Major Atherton, and that she one day went over to Monte Carlo with him in secret, where she was seen by the valet Wingfield, who told his master. It was found that Atherton was an old lover of her ladyship's, and a letter of hers was secured in which Lady Marigold wrote, 'I am only accepting George for his money. You know my heart is yours alone.' Having secured that, the intriguers turned their attention to young Wingfield and Lady Lolita. Marie, with the Frenchwoman's keen jealousy, discovered that she had met the young man once or twice, and that he had copied his master's checker-board cipher, and with her own name as the keyword, corresponded with her by its means. Lady Lolita had already discovered, to her great surprise, that the prepossessing young man was desperately in love with her, and his affection rather amused her than otherwise, for every woman is flattered by attention. At last, however, the adventurers, of whom I myself was one, contrived to effect a coup that was about as ingenious as any devised by a gang of evildoers. The love-sick valet—still concealing his real avocation—had arranged to meet her ladyship after dinner one evening in the olive wood at the back of your villa, but his master gaining possession of a cipher message which Lady Lolita had sent him, was, of course, able to read it and resolved upon watching the pair. What he saw he will, perhaps, relate with his own lips." And then the speaker paused and turned to Richard Keene.

"Yes," he said, "as far as I know, all that Mr Logan says is absolutely correct. Young Wingfield was my valet. He copied my checker-board cipher, and by its means had the audacity to correspond with her ladyship. When I realised what was going on I felt impelled to go to her and tell her. Yet she being a perfect stranger to me, it was really no affair of mine, so I hesitated until the evening in question, when I watched my valet meet her and walk with her in the olive grove about half a mile from the villa. It was one of those brilliant moonlight nights of early spring on the Mediterranean, and it seemed to me that her ladyship was in no way averse to the young fellow's attention. They walked together for half an hour or so, in earnest conversation, when he at length took leave of her and, apparently at her desire, left her to return home alone. I followed her in secret, but she had not, however, gone far before I heard her utter a cry of surprise and dismay. 'Help! help!' she cried, and in the darkness I saw black figures scuffling, the report of a revolver, followed by a man's loud groan. I rushed forward, but ere I reached the spot the men's figures I had seen distinctly had disappeared, but in their place stood the woman Marie Lejeune. Upon the ground lay a man dying, and just as Wingfield, attracted by the shot returned, the woman, who had bent tenderly over the prostrate man rose, and in her voluble French accused Lady Lolita of murder. At first her ladyship was too startled and too utterly dumbfounded to deny this astounding allegation, but when she did the Frenchwoman declared to Wingfield that she had been witness of the crime, and taking up the revolver lying at the poor fellow's side pointed out that the weapon belonged to Lady Lolita's brother, the young Earl of Stanchester—that his name was engraved upon it. Denials were useless, but the crafty Marie, determined to await her opportunity to levy blackmail, urged her ladyship to take back the revolver, and return to the villa at once, which she did. But as she turned away I addressed her, offering to walk home with her, told her my name and escorted her to her own gate. My own opinion was that she had met the man there and deliberately shot him, an opinion which I have held till quite recently, for it was strengthened by the fact that the dead man, when discovered next day by the police, was found to be one of her most intimate friends and admirers, Lieutenant Randolph Glover, a wealthy young man who had, after distinguishing himself at Ladysmith, been invalided to the Riviera."

"I recollect the tragedy quite well," declared the Earl. "And also what a great sensation it caused. The police theory was that he had fallen into the hands of sharpers, who had robbed him at *roulette* and afterwards made away with him, fearing his revelations."

"Exactly. And the police theory was right," Keene said. "Marie, who had fascinated him, while her accomplices had extracted from him almost his last penny, shot him herself, without a doubt. But this did not prevent her levying blackmail upon poor Lady Lolita by threatening to denounce her as the actual assassin. She had also convinced Wingfield of her ladyship's guilt, pointing out their intimate friendship previously, and insinuating that the tragedy was owing to jealousy. I must admit that I believed her ladyship guilty, even though, when we met on the following day and she spoke to me on the promenade, asking me to preserve silence, she again denied her guilt. I promised her to remain silent, hence the police of San Remo were in ignorance of her alleged connexion with the crime, and believed it, as it really was, a case of robbery and murder. Yet Lady Lolita was held in bondage by that woman."

Then Keene paused, and a dead silence again fell among us.

"Well," remarked Logan at last. "You have heard the truth regarding that incident by one who was its eye-witness. Therefore, I will go further and tell you what happened afterwards."

I looked at the proud woman who had sneered at my love for Lolita, and who was now swaying pale and unsteadily before us, but even then, after these startling revelations, I did not discern with what marvellous cleverness and daring she had schemed to shield herself at the price of the life of my well-beloved.

Chapter Thirty Four
The Affair in Sibberton Park

"The woman Marie Lejeune quickly developed from the smart ladies' maid of the Comtesse de Martigny, a gay Parisienne, into the shrewdest and cleverest of adventuresses, and aided by the two Italians, made several large and successful coups at Vichy, Aix-les-Bains, and elsewhere," continued the man Logan, speaking in the same clear, decisive tones, addressing the Earl. "I, however, had parted from them, and was conducting an honest business in London, while Mr Keene had left on a shooting expedition in Africa, where he afterwards met you, and I presume gave his name as Smeeton in order that you should not connect him with the person who had been at San Remo that season.

"Until your marriage, the Frenchwoman did not trouble your wife nor Lolita in the least. She waited her time until Lady Marigold had married and was wealthy and you returned to London from your honeymoon in Cairo, when one day she called at Stanchester House, saw the Countess, and by showing her the letter she had written to Atherton succeeded in extracting blackmail from her, a course which she has continued until quite recently. And not only this," he added, "but she approached Lolita secretly and made large requests, threatening that if they were not complied with she would denounce her as the murderess of poor Randolph Glover at San Remo! Her ladyship, helpless and terrified, was forced to comply with these demands although entirely innocent of the crime. On the other hand, however, there was some truth in the woman's allegation against Lady Stanchester—who, by the way, believed that Richard Keene was dead—and these facts were confirmed by Wingfield who, previous to being in the employment of Mr Keene, was valet to Major Atherton.

"One day, it appeared that the woman Lejeune, in an interview in which she repeated her usual demands for money, told her of Wingfield's allegations against her and how she could ruin her in your eyes by bringing forward the young valet. The Countess thereupon paid the sum demanded, but from that moment entered into a conspiracy against Wingfield, fearing the revelation he might make concerning her. Her friendship with Atherton had long ago given rise to rumour, and these, she knew, had reached your ears before your marriage. Therefore she was now in fear of both the Frenchwoman and the valet. She knew where Marie Lejeune, Belotto and Ostini were living in London, and in order to free herself gave information to Scotland Yard, who held a warrant from the French police for their arrest. The trio were, however, wary, and fearing arrest rapidly changed their place of abode, with the result that the police were baffled."

"And all this time Lolita was being blackmailed?" asked the Earl.

"Yes," answered my love faintly. "It is true, George, all this—every word of it."

"Matters continued thus for two years, until last August, when a tragedy occurred," Logan went on. "The young valet, Wingfield, whose love for Lady Lolita had now cooled and who had told her ladyship of his lowly station and of how he had been in the service of Major Atherton, had some time before got into low water, and Lady Lolita, in order to assist him, had first given him money and then, when her private resources were drained by the woman Lejeune's demands, had given him articles of jewellery, which he sold or pawned. The young man's opinion regarding the death of Randolph Glover had changed, for he explained to her ladyship how he had discovered in San Remo that the unfortunate young officer had fallen a prey to those harpies, and that the manoeuvre had been carried out and the charge laid against her ladyship in order to extract blackmail. Lady Lolita had then entered into negotiations with young Wingfield to effect her release from the bondage in which the Frenchwoman held her, and these continued for some months, until that fateful night in August. Of what occurred then her ladyship herself can best explain to us."

And, pausing, he turned to my love to allow her to tell us with her own lips.

For a few moments she remained pale and silent. Her great blue eyes met mine, and then looking me straight in the face she said—

"What Mr Logan has told you is perfectly correct. The poor young man was working in my interests, and I had written him a cipher letter making an appointment to meet me in the park at a spot where we had met several times previously, as I knew, secretly watching the Frenchwoman and her accomplices in London as he was, he had something to report to me. That afternoon, however, as I drove through the village I saw at the window of the Stanchester Arms the one man whom I feared would denounce me—the man who had been witness of the affair at San Remo, and who had openly expressed belief in my guilt—Richard Keene. He had come to Sibberton evidently to make inquiries about me. By his presence there, I knew he meant mischief.

"That same evening I also received a secret visit from Marie Lejeune. Still I kept the appointment and walked across the park by a circuitous route, in order that none of the servants should recognise me. I knew I had plenty of time by the chiming of the stable clock, therefore I did not hurry. But when I reached the hollow I found he was not there, and had waited for a moment in expectation, when of a sudden I saw something in the darkness lying close to me. I bent and to my horror discovered that it was the young man Wingfield—dead! I screamed and rushed away, not knowing whither I went, but scarcely had I gone a few yards when I ran right into the arms of Mr Logan. I had, in my horror, picked up the knife lying at the dead man's side, a long, thin Italian dagger, and when he met me I still held it in my hand. That very fact, of which I was unconscious at the moment, convinced him of my guilt. Thus on a second occasion was I suspected of a crime of which I was innocent. Of what occurred afterwards I have little recollection. I only know that Mr Logan took the knife from my hand, and that for hours we wandered, he trying to obtain from me the true facts against Marigold which the dead man had alleged. Then at dawn we parted, and I was met by Mr Woodhouse, who set about swiftly to remove every piece of evidence that might convict me of the mysterious crime. Ah!" she cried, "God alone knows how much I have suffered—how Marie Lejeune and her accomplices have tortured me."

"I admit," declared Logan frankly, "that I believed Lady Lolita to be guilty. The horror at finding the dead man and the knowledge that the great intrigue was still in progress produced upon her an effect which I unfortunately mistook for guilt. You must first know that on the night in question, being again associated with Marie Lejeune, I had accompanied her to Sibberton, whither she went at Lady Lolita's request. Her ladyship saw her privately, while I awaited her in the 'Mermaid' over at Geddington. Marie had, by secret means, learnt of Lolita's intention to meet Hugh Wingfield in the park that night, therefore on leaving the Hall she awaited in order to watch and obtain knowledge of the negotiations against her which she knew were in progress between the valet and her ladyship, while I, surprised at her long absence, strolled across to the park in order to meet her on her return, as the way was dark and lonely.

"According to the statement she afterwards made to me, it appears that she watched the young valet's arrival. He stood listening for about five minutes, when suddenly a woman, whom by her ermine cloak she knew was Lady Lolita, approached in the gloom, but as the young man uttered her name and put his hand out to welcome her, she stepped nimbly past him and struck him full in the back—a fatal blow. It was but the work of a single instant. 'Ah! my lady!' he gasped, clutching at her cloak. 'You—

you've killed me!' And he sank upon the ground and expired. At that instant Marie Lejeune stepped from her hiding-place and the two women met face to face. Then Marie was staggered to discover that the woman who wore Lady Lolita's cloak was not Lady Lolita herself—but that woman standing there!" he exclaimed, pointing to the Countess, "Lady Stanchester!"

"Lady Stanchester!" we all gasped in one breath, while the wretched woman thus denounced stood before us, swaying and shrinking from our gaze.

"But surely she was still at Aix-les-Bains!" I cried.

"No," he declared. "She had returned to London on the previous day, and was living at Burton's boarding-house, in Hereford Road, Bayswater, under the name of Mrs Frith. That very morning she had seen the young valet in Westbourne Grove, and had followed him down to Sibberton. As soon as she saw him take a ticket for Kettering she knew of his intention to meet Lady Lolita clandestinely, therefore she saw in that her opportunity to deal him a fatal blow, and thus prevent any ugly revelation regarding her past."

"But the cloak?" I asked.

"Lady Lolita had lent it to her just before her departure for Aix, and she wore it on that night." Then I saw how, by my neglecting to tell Lolita of the finding of the cloak by the gamekeeper Jacobs, I had myself withheld the truth from her! Had she known that the cloak she had lent Marigold had been found torn and cast aside, she would of course have suspected the identity of the assassin.

"The young man's acquaintance with Lolita and Marigold accounts, I suppose, for his having watched my movements in London!" remarked the Earl.

Chapter Thirty Five
The Truth

"You see," Logan went on, "Lady Stanchester feared the revelation which the young valet could make concerning her, therefore, knowing that Lady Lolita was in the habit of writing to him in cipher and that they had arranged to meet that night in the park, she saw that if she killed him suspicion must be thrown upon her husband's sister. Besides, she was believed to be still at Aix, the only person having knowledge of her secret presence in London being Marie, with whom she had an interview that very day. Judge her dismay, therefore, when at the moment of the committal of the crime she came face to face with Marie herself, her bitterest enemy! Only a gasp of surprise escaped the mouths of both women. They glared into each other's faces, and while the Countess knew that her terrible secret was not her own, Marie Lejeune saw gloatingly that her power over the wealthy woman was now that of life or death. It was not to the Frenchwoman's interest to tell the truth to the police while Lady Stanchester submitted to blackmail, therefore in this second case, as in the first, the facts against Lady Lolita were sufficiently circumstantial to secure her conviction, and more especially that she held the knife in her hand when I had encountered her at the scene of the crime."

"But surely you told Lady Lolita that you were satisfied that the charge against her was a false one?" I asked.

"Certainly I did—after Marie Lejeune had told me the truth. I did not, however, tell her who was the actual assassin, as Marie would not allow me. Nevertheless in neither case could her actual innocence be proved unless Marie Lejeune spoke the truth—and this she refused to do, first because she must by so doing implicate herself; and secondly that she would then lose the power for blackmail which she had established with such devilish ingenuity. It was true, as Lady Lolita declared to me, she was their victim—and to drive her to self-destruction was equally their object—in order to save themselves."

The Earl stood listening to the terrible allegations against his wife, scarcely moving a muscle of his features.

"From the moment of Wingfield's death Lady Stanchester, against whom the French police held a warrant for her implication in certain frauds of the gang, was entirely in the Frenchwoman's unscrupulous hands," Logan continued, "but knowing Lady Lolita's peril, and sympathising with her—the unconscious victim of the evil deeds of both these women—I took her side against them and joined myself in secret with Mr Keene, although at the time I was still allied with them.

"Keene also joined us, but with a view to freeing Lady Lolita from the false charges against her. He knew the truth regarding Lady Stanchester, and with us sought concealment in a farm in the vicinity, our object being to keep observation upon the movements of the Countess. We should have remained longer, had it not been for the jealousy of Belotto, who one night attacked Marie Lejeune and we were compelled to call in a doctor. Moreover we were compelled, owing to that, to escape abroad again. After a short time, however, the Countess—still compelled to submit to blackmail heavily and even to give some of her jewellery in lieu of money, and living in daily terror that the Frenchwoman should give secret information to the police regarding the assassination of Wingfield—wrote to me in Lucerne expressing a desire to meet Marie again, and come to some amicable arrangement with her. I arranged the meeting, came to London, and escorted Lady Stanchester to Milan. By some means Mr Woodhouse obtained knowledge of her intention and follow us. Perhaps he will tell you what occurred."

"Certainly," I said. And then I related the result of my vigilance, and the adventure which subsequently happened to me.

"You were struck down by a man whom Marie had on watch outside the house and carried into the place afterwards," explained Logan, when I had concluded my narrative.

"Why Marie received us in the apartment that was not her own," he continued, "was in order that the Countess should not afterwards be able to inform the police of her whereabouts. She invited Lady Stanchester and ourselves to supper, when a fresh and very ingenious scheme of fraud upon jewellers in Paris, in which she intended to compel her ladyship to take part, was discussed. Presently the two women quarrelled, mutual recriminations followed, whereupon Marie openly accused her visitor of Wingfield's murder and threatened that if she refused her assistance in this new scheme she intended to denounce her. Scarcely, however, had the Frenchwoman uttered these words when Lady Stanchester rose suddenly, drew a knife, and stabbed her to the heart while she sat at table. For a moment we all sat dumbfounded and horrified. Then the question arose how best to dispose of the body. The man who had driven us there was one of our accomplices, therefore it was resolved to drive out about two miles, and place it in the canal.

"While they carried it out I was to remain behind, to remove all trace of the crime. The murderess sat motionless in the corner of the room, appalled by her own deed. Judge my surprise, however, when, a few minutes later, the body of Marie was brought back again, and then Mr Woodhouse, whom we all believed to be here, at Sibberton, was carried in! He was placed in such a position that whoever discovered the tragedy would believe that he was the murderer. The guilty woman screamed aloud when her eyes fell upon her husband's secretary, saying, 'Strike him again! Make certain he's dead, or he will tell the truth—he will expose me!' But we dragged her away, and two hours afterwards I sat with her in the Bâle express, travelling towards London.

"To-night I came down here to see her in secret, in order to plead with her to release Lady Lolita from the terrible thraldom of suspicion—yet it seems that in order to save herself she had actually uttered the false charges to her husband. Had I not met Lady Lolita in the pleasure-grounds to-night, she would, ere this, have been driven to the last extremity."

"Ah!" I cried, standing aghast at the extraordinary story, "it is, indeed, the hand of Providence that has directed your presence here to-night, Mr Logan. You have, if nothing else, made atonement for the part you yourself played in the affair, by coming forward and exposing a guilty woman and saving from death one who is pure, innocent and long-suffering—the woman I love."

Lady Lolita grasped my hand tightly, but no word passed her quivering lips.

Keene, however, said—

"Although Lady Lolita looked upon me as her enemy from the first, I was, in reality, her friend. I allied myself with Mr Logan and the two Italians in order to discover their intrigue and to save her ladyship."

"And you have done so," Lolita declared. "I can never sufficiently thank either you or Mr Logan. You have, moreover, saved me from the sin of self-destruction," she faltered, and then she burst into tears.

"And you?" cried the Earl, in anger and loathing, turning upon his statuesque wife who stood there, erect, immovable, as though turned to stone. "And you, woman!—What have you to reply to all this?"

Her white lips moved, but no sound escaped them. She tried to speak—to deny the truth, perhaps, but words failed her. She raised her hand, moved slightly, then, staggering, fell forward heavily without a hand to save her.

So painful, so terrible, so dramatic was that scene between husband and wife that we all of us withdrew and have ever since been trying to efface it from our recollections.

Thus was the awful truth revealed that the woman whom half London envied had committed a second murder in order to conceal the first, and that she had actually gone out to Milan with the distinct and premeditated object of taking the Frenchwoman's life.

Never till my dying day shall I forget those terrible moments when before our eyes the love of the Earl of Stanchester turned to hatred, and when he spurned her senseless body with his foot as he turned from her in disgust and left the Hall. I will not attempt to describe it—it was far too painful, too terrible, too awful to be placed upon record.

Would that it could for ever be wiped from the tablets of my memory.

And what occurred afterwards? Patience, and I will tell you.

Chapter Thirty Six
Containing the Conclusion

The tragic and untimely end of the smart, pretty, wonderfully-dressed Countess of Stanchester will still be fresh within the memory of newspaper readers.

It will be recollected how, with her maid, she left Sibberton Hall for Paris, and how in her room at the *Hotel Continental* she was found dead, having unfortunately taken an overdose of morphia.

At least such was the newspaper story, and happily so, for it spared scandal and disgrace to one of England's noblest houses. To the public the truth never leaked out, and as a consequence the society papers were full of regrets that a woman so young, so popular and so full of life and energy should have been cut off by accident in such a manner, while everywhere the deepest sympathy was expressed towards her husband.

Keene and I accompanied him to Paris, and we three were the only mourners at those terribly tragic last rites at Père Lachaise. He stood motionless with uncovered head until the final act, and then with a great bursting sob he turned away, and for a week I saw nothing of him.

I returned to London on the following day, and in the great drawing-room of Stanchester House, overlooking the Park, I stood and grasped the hands of my well-beloved. In her plain black, she presented a wan and fragile figure, yet upon her cheeks showed the flush of hope and pleasure, and as our lips met in a soft sweet caress I knew that she was mine—mine for ever.

We sat together at one of the long windows of that magnificent room until the golden haze over the Park faded into dull crimson and the London day drew to a close, talking of the future and of what it meant to us, for she held in her hand a brief letter from her heart-broken brother, posted in Brussels, in which he wrote:—

"I know that you love Willoughby and I have no objection whatever to your marriage. I welcome it. He has saved your life, and he has saved our house from dishonour. In such circumstances, my dear Lol, nothing will please me better than a union between you. He is poor, but tell him not to worry on that account. You have sufficient for yourself, but I shall make over Chelmorton to you for your lifetime, which will provide you both with income sufficient."

"Ah!" I cried joyfully when I read that letter. "Then, after all, George does not object to my birth and station! He is indeed generous!"

"No, dearest," was her kindly answer as she placed her hand tenderly upon my shoulder and bent of her own accord to kiss my lips. "He does not object because he knows that we really love each other, and that no man has greater claim to me than yourself."

The words spoken between us are surely of little import to you, my reader, save to know that we mutually resolved that the name of Marigold should never in all our lives again pass our lips. This and other firm resolves we made, until the autumn dusk darkened into night and the footman entering to switch on the lights and draw the curtains, recalled us to the realities of the life about us.

Since that glad reunion when I held my love in my arms, and she promised to be my wife, nearly two years have passed happily, blissful years that have slipped by like mere weeks so unheeded has been Time.

And to-day? Well, there is little to record, save that this season the famous Stanchester hounds are hunted by Frank Blew, the huntsman, for the Earl has been, ever since our marriage, out in Mashonaland hunting with his most intimate friend, the honest, big-handed, weather-beaten sportsman, Richard Keene. Of Alfred Logan we see something on rare occasions, for having been "set upon his legs" by George, he has now an increasing architect's practice in Great George Street, Westminster, enjoying the great advantage of being the architect to the Stanchester estates.

And ourselves?

After the terrible anxiety and awful suspicion of those dark, never-to-be-forgotten days all is now happiness. The barrier 'twixt me and the rapturous peace I so long panted for is removed, and we have both emerged at last from that fatal region of mystery and doubt. At Chelmorton Towers, the beautiful old ivy-covered place in Sussex which George so generously gave to his sister for our use during her lifetime, I live in the sunshine of Lolita's matchless beauty, charmed by the secret tenderness of her voice and thrilled by her soft caresses. Nought else I desire. We have, both of us, found happiness in each other's pure affection.

And as day succeeds day, and every rising sun blesses me with sight of my sweet beloved and ushers in fresh ecstasy, I feel myself in full possession of the world of joy. In vain have I re-dipped my pen to trace the raptures that enchant me; but the thread is broken, and to give to language what my soul conceals is not in me, nor in the brain of human nature to impart.

Life and love are ours, and to us they are all-sufficient.